HE WAS ALL SHE DESIRED...

"Genna," he said, "when you press yourself against me, all I can think of is making love to you."

Jason's words sent sparks coursing through her body, turning her legs weak and her skin hot. She wanted him to make love to her; this instant, on the floor, if that's what he desired. She wanted him to take her.

Her stomach clenched in pleasurable ripples as his mouth moved gently across hers, and his tongue slipped along the heated contours of her lips.

Lifting his mouth a fraction from hers, Jason breathed, "You fit perfectly to me."

His words were fuel to the fire he had ignited. Genna raised her arms to run her fingers through the cool thickness of his blond hair, smoothing back the lock on his forehead before plunging again into the tactile silkiness. Then, lips parted, unable to resist the desire he kindled in her, she pulled him to her, completely surrendering to her longing for him.

This man was all she wanted, all she needed....

DANA RANSOM'S RED-HOT HEARTFIRES!

ALEXANDRA'S ECSTASY (2773, $3.75)
Alexandra had known Tucker for all her seventeen years, but all at once she realized her childhood friend was the man capable of tempting her to leave innocence behind!

LIAR'S PROMISE (2881, $4.25)
Kathryn Mallory's sincere questions about her father's ship to the disreputable Captain Brady Rogan were met with mocking indifference. Then he noticed her trim waist, angelic face and Kathryn won the wrong kind of attention!

LOVE'S GLORIOUS GAMBLE (2497, $3.75)
Nothing could match the true thrill that coursed through Gloria Daniels when she first spotted the gambler, Sterling Caulder. Experiencing his embrace, feeling his lips against hers would be a risk, but she was willing to chance it all!

WILD, SAVAGE LOVE (3055, $4.25)
Evangeline, set free from Indians, discovered liberty had its price to pay when her uncle sold her into marriage to Royce Tanner. Dreaming of her return to the people she loved, she vowed never to submit to her husband's caress.

WILD WYOMING LOVE (3427, $4.25)
Lucille Blessing had no time for the new marshal Sam Zachary. His mocking and arrogant manner grated her nerves, yet she longed to ease the tension she knew he held inside. She knew that if he wanted her, she could never say no!

Available wherever paperbacks are sold, or order direct from the Publisher. Send cover price plus 50¢ per copy for mailing and handling to Zebra Books, Dept. 3918, 475 Park Avenue South, New York, N.Y. 10016. Residents of New York and Tennessee must include sales tax. DO NOT SEND CASH. For a free Zebra/Pinnacle catalog please write to the above address.

AMBER KAYE

ENDLESS SURRENDER

**ZEBRA BOOKS
KENSINGTON PUBLISHING CORP.**

ZEBRA BOOKS

are published by

Kensington Publishing Corp.
475 Park Avenue South
New York, NY 10016

Copyright © 1992 by Alison J. Hentges

All rights reserved. No part of this book may be reproduced in any form or by any means without the prior written consent of the Publisher, excepting brief quotes used in reviews.

If you purchased this book without a cover you should be aware that this book is stolen property. It was reported as "unsold and destroyed" to the Publisher and neither the Author nor the Publisher has received any payment for this "stripped book."

First printing: September, 1992

Printed in the United States of America

Chapter One

Paris, January 1812

Alighting from her barouche, Genna, Contessa di Ponti, smiled her thanks as Alphonse, the lackey, helped her down. The January wind bit into her skin and she shivered, pulling her fur lined cream satin cape tighter. Overhead, clouds scuttled across the sky, alternately hiding and revealing the full moon. It was a night full of mystery and superstitious dangers . . . if one believed in such. She did not.

Behind her came Aunt Hester, a short, rotund woman with gray hair pulled up in back and frizzed on the sides in the current mode. Hester's normally round, blue eyes narrowed in irritation as she muttered, "'Tis a pity that there is no better light, even here in the best part of Paris. A ruffian could be lurking in the shadows, and we would never see him until it was too late."

"Aunt, you're exaggerating the danger," Genna

said lightly, trying to keep the older woman from letting her fears run away with her.

But Hester was right. They should have never come to Paris. The poor lighting was immaterial; it was the French who were dangerous. They didn't take kindly to defeat, talking constantly of Napoleon escaping his incarceration and taking every opportunity to prove themselves better than the British flocking to their country. Being that Hester was Scottish and Genna half Scottish, only made the French antagonism that much more hazardous.

The sound of shoes scraping on the cobblestones made the abstract thought of French imposed danger flee from Genna's mind. From the corner of her eye, she saw movement.

She froze. The breath caught in her throat. Her tongue refused to move. Footpads were so common, even here. Was Hester to be proven right?

A shadow detached itself from the edge of their rented house. It lurched toward them, feet shuffling along the cobbles, arms out to balance it. In that instant, the moon broke free of the clouds, and its harsh light emphasized the gaunt, scarecrow angles of bent elbows and the elongated expanse of legs that stumbled with each movement.

"Mademoiselle," a hoarse voice came from the dark apparition. *"Secours."*

Genna almost missed the plea for help, so weakly was it spoken, yet chills ran the length of her spine at the velvet richness of the tone. Then he was upon her.

"Alphonse!" she called for the lackey as the

strange man bore her down. She folded under his weight, her arms going around him automatically as she hit the ground with her knees, the man sprawled on top of her. Seconds later Alphonse was by her. She held the unconscious man's head in her lap as the lackey ran an expert hand over him.

"Is he hurt?" Genna asked. Even though she tried to breathe slowly to calm her rapidly beating heart, her voice trembled.

"I cannot tell, ma'am. We must get him inside."

"Gracious, Genna," Hester said, coming up to them with the butler behind her. "Here, Michaels, hold the candle aloft so we can see what this ragamuffin looks like."

"Later," Genna said, her hand making a small chopping gesture of impatience. "Michaels, you take his shoulders. Alphonse take his legs. Carry him to the Gold Room. I'll bring the candle." She spared a smile of apology for her aunt, before easing the man's head from her thighs and laying him gently down for the servants to pick up.

"Genna!" Hester said, gripping the younger woman's arm with pudgy fingers, "you cannot take him into our house. The man is not one of your animals. You cannot take him and put him on a bed of old blankets and tend his wounds with no other thought than that of making him better. He's a *man* and obviously a scoundrel and will very likely rob us before doing . . ." she shuddered visibly, "worse."

Genna's lips twitched in humor at the melodramatic horror in Hester's voice, even though it irritated her to have Hester always carrying on about leaving the weaker to fend for themselves. She knew her aunt was not a cruel person: Ladies just did not concern themselves with the unpleasant. It would be simpler for them both if she agreed with her aunt, but she couldn't.

Taking the candle from Michaels, Genna paused long enough to say, "Dearest Aunt, you know I can't leave a sick or hurt man to die on these filthy streets. Why, if we don't take him in, someone else is sure to come along and take the clothes off his back. Even murder him." Not waiting for a response, she rushed to open the door and to warn her housekeeper of the added burden.

"Humph!" Hester knew further argument was futile, but followed them up the stairs. "Genna, he is a scoundrel. 'Tis bad enough that you bring home every stray animal. I remember that weasel you had to keep until its broken leg mended." She shuddered so her shoulders shook like pudding.

Genna looked back at Hester, who stood half the stairs below, and smiled gently. "I must do this, Hester. I would never be able to forgive myself if I left a person to die because I was afraid."

Hester snorted. "You can't forgive yourself if you leave *anything* to die."

Anger flared in Genna, but quickly subsided. The dim light of the candles in wall sconces showed the tight grip her aunt had on the banister. Hester was genuinely scared.

"I'm sorry," Genna said, knowing it was inadequate, but also knowing that the man's wounds must take precedence. "I'll come to you after we've taken care of him."

Turning, Genna caught up with the housekeeper, passed her and flung open the door. Without pausing, she began lighting the room's candles. Mrs. Michaels motioned a trailing footman to start a fire while Genna ripped the heavy gold threaded coverlet from the massive rosewood bed.

"Mrs. Michaels," Genna said, "I'll stay here while you get bandages and hot water." She looked at the blood on her hands. "This isn't mine. You had better bring the basilicum powder, too." She chewed her lower lip as she watched the housekeeper exit and the patient enter.

Anticipation pumped through her veins. How badly hurt was he? Could they help him? It wouldn't be like nursing, Luigi, an old man dying of age. This man was young and would fight for life. She need not dread the sorrow of losing someone she had cared for long and hard.

"You had best leave, milady," Michaels said, laying the unconscious man's shoulders on the bed.

Alphonse nodded his agreement. "We are going to have to strip him to see how badly he is hurt. This will be no place for a lady." He laid his half of the burden down.

Their words, so typical of men, made her smile. Their expressions were so grim she couldn't resist teasing them, although they all knew she was serious. "You might as well undress him. I am a widow and I wager he has not got anything I haven't seen before. However," her eyes sparkled,

"I *will* turn my back until you have him under the covers."

The men's faces were momentarily stunned, until they exchanged a glance of mutual resignation before going about their business.

Genna turned her back. They might not like what she intended, but they were loyal servants and knew she was stubborn. They also knew she had much practice in a sickroom. She had learned while nursing her dying husband that practicality was more important than propriety when nursing. During the last year of his life, Luigi had wasted away, the vitality that had animated him shrinking with his body. He had been a difficult patient, but she had persevered, knowing when to force and when it didn't matter whether he did as the doctor directed.

That had been a year ago, and this was now. This man needed tending, and she had the skills.

Alphonse's grunt stopped her reverie. The mutters and sounds of rustling sheets, followed by the thud of shoes hitting the floor, told her they were stripping the man as quickly as possible.

"Are you finished?" she asked.

"Yes," said Michaels, his clipped British accent heavy with disapproval.

She pivoted on the ball of her satin clad foot. "I know I'm a sore trial to you, Michaels, and have been since you were a footman in my father's house." She approached the bed, then shook her head. "How do you expect me to tend his wounds when he's swaddled like a newborn babe?"

Not waiting for an answer, she carefully pulled

the sheet down, following the dried blood and slow oozing of a knife slash running diagonally from his left shoulder to his right hip. She sucked in her breath, not sure whether she was taken aback by the severity of his wound or the breadth of his shoulders. Luigi had been narrow where this man was well muscled.

She pushed the thought aside, concentrating on the present. "At least the bleeding is almost done." She glanced at the pile of discarded clothes. "Although it seems he bled enough to soak his shirt and coat."

"He had an extra cloth pressed to it. That probably kept him from leaving a trail," Alphonse said.

Genna looked at her lackey. "What do you mean?"

"To have a wound like this, he was probably attacked."

"Obviously not for his money," Genna murmured, nudging the ragged clothes with her foot. But if not for money, why try to kill him? Her hands trembled slightly as she tucked the sheet around the man's hips, careful to avoid the wide expanse of exposed chest and the narrowing vee of curly hair that snaked the length of him.

"Perhaps it was over a woman," the housekeeper said, disapproval wrinkling her forehead as she entered and closed the door behind herself.

Genna's eyes narrowed as she considered Mrs. Michaels's words. The stranger had sun bleached hair, thick dark eyebrows, and lashes as full and brown as beaver fur. His forehead was high and his cheeks were well-defined, almost gaunt, shading into a strong jaw.

Genna spoke thoughtfully. "Hmmm . . . he's definitely attractive enough to have his pick of the tavern wenches." Or highborn ladies, she added to herself.

"Humph!" Mrs. Michaels snorted and gave Mr. Michaels a very penetrating look. The butler just smiled. Without another word, the housekeeper put the tray of bandages and water on the heavily carved rosewood bed stand, then dipped a cloth in the water and wrung it out.

"I'll do that," Genna said, reaching for the cloth. She would not meet the other woman's eyes as she took it, knowing that Mrs. Michaels fully expected to be the one saddled with the burden of nursing this man and unsure herself of why she wouldn't let the other woman do so. "I cared for my husband," she added as justification, beginning to feel defensive because of all the censure the servants were not trying to hide.

"Yes, milady," Mrs. Michaels said, turning to say something to Mr. Michaels.

But Genna saw the question in the housekeeper's eyes. It was a question she could not answer. For some reason, she found herself drawn to the man; concerned about him. At first, it had been the action of the moment, of helping someone obviously in need. Now . . . what was it that kept her from leaving him to Mrs. Michaels and Alphonse who were both as capable as she? Curiosity, she was sure . . . and worry. Someone had tried to kill him.

Was there possible danger to those who took him in? She must find out. Too many people depended on her, and she had no right to endanger them if this man had done something that put him on the wrong side of the law. Or worse, what if another criminal bent on revenge followed him here.

But right now, she must help him. She started to gently wipe away the blood. She hoped he wouldn't gain consciousness until they were done. The knife had left a deep gash, and it looked like it would have to be stitched closed in places.

Genna was cutting the end of her best silk thread, the last neat stitch taken, when she felt his gaze upon her. How long had he been awake? He hadn't said a word or flinched, so hopefully he had just wakened.

His face was beaded with perspiration, and his eyes were long and moss green and the pain in them hurt her. She wanted to stroke the lines from between his eyebrows. Instead she laid the needle and thread on the tray and reached for the cloth to wipe his forehead.

"Alphonse," she said in a low voice, "please bring the brandy. Our patient is awake."

"Are you a redheaded devil or a fiery angel?" the stranger asked hoarsely, his French faultless, but with a patois not common in Paris.

"Neither," she answered in the same language, taking the glass from Alphonse. "This will help with the pain." It had always eased the worst of Luigi's discomfort. She put her left arm under his shoulders and put the glass to his lips.

He gulped the stuff without a cough. "A tyrant in satin skirts," he said when he was able. "And a redhead without freckles."

She smiled at him, admiring his banter when she knew he must be in agony. "Alphonse, we must bind up my handiwork." Leaving the servant to get the strips of clean linen, she removed her arm from behind the man's shoulders. "Now lie back while I give you a good dusting with this basilicum powder."

His eyes never left her face as she sprinkled him with the infection-fighting powder. It made her uncomfortable to be watched so closely. Her hand shook.

Righting the container, she took a deep breath before saying, "There! Now if we can get you propped up against these pillows, 'twill be easier to bandage you."

He rose on his elbows and with her arm under his shoulders began to lever himself upward. Sweat broke out on his upper lip, but he said nothing.

His discomfort was more than she could tolerate. "Stop. Wait until Alphonse gets back. This is too much for you, injured as you are." He collapsed back, his eyes tightly shut, pain creasing their corners. "You've a nasty cut. . . ." She trailed off, inviting him to explain his wound.

He opened his eyes to stare at her. "Yes, 'tis painful, too. Thank you for taking me in."

He was so grave, as though she had done something of extreme importance, that she didn't press him to answer her unasked question. Instead she responded to his gratitude. "Anyone would have done the same."

His jaw tightened from the strain of talking. "No, they would not have. Most would have left me to die or at the very most left me to their servant's care."

Now it was her turn to ignore the inquiry in his eyes. She didn't know why she had personally tended him, other than that she had been compelled to see to him. It was an uncomfortable situation. Alphonse entered the room with bustle and noise, preventing her from having to continue the conversation.

"Had to get more," Alphonse grumbled, coming toward the bed, his hands laden with sheets. "Mrs. Michaels fussed about the waste of her new linens, but I have enough to do the job."

There were several tense minutes positioning the patient and wrapping his wound tightly. Genna could feel the tautness in the man's shoulders as he strained to keep erect enough for them to bandage him. Under her fingers his muscles bunched and hardened. He would have put up a good fight, and she wondered if his assailant had surprised him. She couldn't imagine him being overpowered otherwise.

She glanced at his face. It was closed, but she could see the exhaustion. Perhaps in his weakness she could get him to tell her what had happened. Instinctively, she knew that if she waited until he was well to question him, she would learn nothing. And she had to know. She had the safety of her servants and her aunt to consider. However, she would have to get rid of Alphonse because this man would never talk in front of more than one person. Of that, she was certain.

"Alphonse," she began after they laid the man down, "we'll be fine now. I just want to finish settling our patient. In the meantime, you need to go to bed."

"Milady, I cannot leave you here alone with him." He looked askance at her, then menacingly at the man. "I will leave when you do."

Her laughter was soft and melodic. She could not be cruel to Alphonse. Alphonse had been Luigi's valet, and they had grown close nursing her husband. Alphonse had stayed on after his master's death to care for her, the young widow.

"Alphonse, I am a strong woman and he," she waved her arm at the man, "is a weak man. He has lost too much blood to even get out of bed, let alone attack me."

"He's right," the stranger spoke, making her jump with the force of his statement. "A lady does not stay alone with a man... especially in a bedroom. No matter how weak the man or how strong the lady."

"So that rankled." She couldn't be sure that the flush on his face was caused by her words or by his wounds, but he *was* grinning. It gave her hope that he would trust her if she could get Alphonse to leave them alone. "But I don't need you taking Alphonse's side, or I'll never get him to leave and go to sleep as he needs to."

The man shook his head in disapproval, but said no more. Behind her, Alphonse made a noise meant to show his approval of the man in the bed. She smiled in spite of herself. Men were forever thinking of a woman's reputation, either for good or bad.

"Alphonse, 'tis fine. You must get up early while I may sleep late." She smiled at him to soften her next words. "I don't want to order you, we go back too far and have gone through too much together for that."

The old man scowled, and she could see that he longed to argue, but he left, his mouth pressed into a white line. As the door closed with a definite click, Genna shook her head in exasperation and humor at her loyal retainer. But right now she had more important matters to worry about than Alphonse's offended sense of propriety.

Turning back to her patient, she asked, "How long were you conscious while I stitched?"

He sighed deeply, making the sheet covering him rise and fall. "Long enough to know you're a good seamstress."

"I'm sorry it had to hurt you, but there was nothing else I could do. You must have angered someone greatly. Will you tell me about it?" When he did not answer, she added, "Tomorrow I'll send for a doctor."

"No!"

It was only what she'd expected. What had this man done that he wouldn't even allow himself to be seen by a doctor? For all she knew, he could have killed someone. Perhaps she had been too hasty in taking him into her household.

"You are seriously wounded," she began, licking her lips as she chose her words carefully. "I don't know if you will become infected. And if you should, I don't have the skills to help you. You must have strong reasons to risk your life by refusing a doctor."

He opened his eyes and met her look squarely. "I do. I'm no fool. I know how serious this gash is, but I have no other choice."

Just the effort to speak told in his voice. Where it had started strong, it had weakened until she barely heard the last words.

"No other choice? Surely, that is an exaggeration."

He jerked up in bed and grabbed her wrist. She flinched at the grip, but twisting didn't loosen his hold.

"Do *not* call a physician," he gritted between clenched teeth.

Her insincts warned her that he was a dangerous man, but her eyes told her he was at the end of his endurance. The effort to grab her and to continue holding her prisoner by the bed had caused sweat to pop out over his torso and shoulders, glistening his body to a golden glow in the flickering candlelight. This was important to him. She relented.

"I'll wait until I see how you're doing tomorrow. That is all I can promise, for I don't intend to have your life on my conscience." He released her wrist and fell back onto the pillows. "However, I must know if you're in the kind of trouble that will endanger the people of my household." She spoke calmly, but her pulse pounded in her throat.

Would he answer her? Would it be the truth? To ease the tightness in her chest and to give him time to consider what he would say, she turned to the washbowl and wrung out the cloth to wipe away the moisture his exertion had caused.

His eyes were narrowed when she turned back toward him, but there was no emotion in his face. He would make a good card player. Perhaps that's what had happened: He had played well and one of the losers had sought to get his losses back.

Would he never answer?

Finally, he spoke, considering each word. "I don't think there is any danger, but you're wise to worry. I'll leave now. 'Tis the least I can do to repay you for my life." He pushed up with his elbows, groaned and bit his bottom lip until blood beaded on it.

At the pain contorting his features, all thought of danger to her household fled. Dropping the cloth, she swiftly pushed him back onto the bed, and blurted, "You stupid man! You are in no condition to go tonight."

He collapsed with a heavy sigh. "You're right. I'm too weak. Tomorrow I will leave."

Consternation sharpened her tongue. "Tell me why you were attacked. If it was over cards or a woman, then there is no reason for you to leave until you're well." The thought that he might have fought over a woman caused her a pang of regret, but both women and cards were common among men.

"Neither."

She could barely hear the word, but it brought

relief, only to have worry nip at its heels.

"Was it illegal?"

"*I* do not think so."

She met his look. His pupils were dilated and his brows were drawn together in discomfort, but he didn't flinch under her perusal or try to avoid her eyes. Whatever he had done, he believed himself to be right. Somehow she didn't doubt his integrity.

"Then I must take your word for the present." There was nothing else she could do, short of throwing him out into the street from which she had rescued him. It was checkmate.

She turned back to the basin to get the cloth and realized she was using his need to be sponged as a way to defuse the tense situation between them. Her usual sangfroid eluded her with this man.

"Right now, I'm going to dampen this and sponge you off before giving you some more brandy laced with laudanum. We'll continue this discussion in the morning." The return to practical problems eased the tightness in her throat.

His eyes closed when she ran the cloth over his temples and cheeks and then his neck. Glancing at his impassive face, she dared to wipe his shoulders, moving over the broad expanse that was rangy even as it was well muscled. Her fingers trailed surreptitiously behind the cloth, experiencing the smooth finish of skin that contrasted with the crisp curls of honey blond hair.

She wiped around the top of the bandage, noting that there was no fresh blood. Next she sponged down his arms to his large, well-shaped hands. The fingers were long and tapering, an artist's hands, but they were strong enough to hold her prisoner. Her wrist still tingled where he had gripped her.

The cloth was warm now, so Genna dipped it again before lowering the sheet that covered him until it rode his hips. He was so hot. If they weren't careful, he would run a fever. She had no experience with fevers; Luigi's skin had been dry and cool like leather. Luigi's emotions had been dry and cool, too.

She knew this man, with his furnace-hot body, would not be reserved like her dead husband had been. This man would have feelings that ran as deeply and as intensely as his belief that whatever he did to be knifed was necessary.

She returned the cloth to the basin and turned back to him. It was a jolt to realize that his heavy-lidded eyes were watching her, their moss green color dulling into a murky brown. Had they not been glazed with pain, she would have said he was studying her, weighing her against the situation in which he found himself. She doubted he could concentrate enough to do it properly at the moment.

His eyes closed. He had finally succumbed to the laudanum and brandy.

She slumped into the chair near the bed. Her shoulders drooped, her temples ached from tension, she was exhausted. Eyelids heavy with sleep, she glimpsed a stain on her skirt. Looking closer she saw it was blood. Her head began to pound.

What had she done? This was not the same as

caring for a wounded dog or horse that had been mistreated. This was a man who had been attacked and left for dead, and she didn't even know why. Still, she had let him stay, she belonged in Bedlam.

She forced herself to breathe deeply. There was nothing she could do at this moment. She could no more throw him out into the cold night, her only alternative, than she could stop the approaching headache.

Genna muffled a groan, admitting to herself that the man would stay and she would have to lie down. Surely nothing would happen in the next couple hours, he would be all right and no one would come looking for him.

Her decision reached, she rose and went to the fireplace where she laid extra logs, jostling the old ones so that the new would catch.

"A servant should do that."

His deep voice made her jerk around, trying to ignore the frisson running down her spine. Taking a step toward the shadows of the bed, she lifted her candle and looked hard at him. When she searched for it, she could see the determination that held him awake against the laudanum he had ingested.

The planes of his face were sharp in the sputtering light of the candle, almost sinister in their angularity. She pushed the hint of fear aside, but wondered nonetheless what kind of man resisted drugged sleep as he did. She had no experience with his type, only the self-indulgence of Ricci, her betrothed, or the stubbornness of an old man.

"You should be asleep," she said, keeping her uncertainty about him from showing in her voice.

"I will be soon. Why don't you call a servant?" he persisted.

"Because they are abed. Morning comes early when you aren't the master or mistress." She let her eyes slip away from his, not wanting to give him the edge of knowing she would protect his secret, yet unwilling to do otherwise. "Besides I know you need privacy. Whatever you did to be knifed probably isn't something that needs to be bandied about. And servants talk. Even the best."

His eyes met hers squarely. "I would tell you if I could."

Against her better judgment, she believed him, just as she knew she would let him stay. But right now, she had to leave. He needed sleep and she needed time to think without his disturbing presence.

Closing the door behind herself, Genna turned and bumped into someone. "Alphonse!" she gasped, a hand going to her throat. "You scared me."

"You should be scared," the lackey said, "leaving a strange man alone in this house and under the circumstances."

She scowled at him. He'd changed from the turquoise and silver livery of the House of Ponti to dark clothes. Not bedclothes. "Alphonse, why aren't you in bed?"

He scowled back at her, refusing to be intimidated. "Someone has got to watch that man, even if he did agree with me about your staying in the room alone with him. And I know why you wanted me out, milady."

Genna giggled at the affronted look on his face. She couldn't help it. This whole situation would be hilarious, if it weren't so nerve-racking. "I know you aren't afraid of me, Alphonse, so you've no need to glare so. And of course you know why I wanted you gone, I told you so. You need some sleep."

"*You* wanted to question the man, milady, and you thought he would not tell you anything with a servant in the room," he finished smugly.

Genna shook her head slightly. Was she that transparent? Well, she needed to talk to someone about it and Alphonse was the best person. She trusted him implicitly.

"You're right, old friend, as usual," she said, leaning back against the wall. The flickering candle Alphonse held gave them a small pool of light, the hall candles having been doused hours earlier. "But he wouldn't tell me anything, except that what he did wasn't illegal and that it was something he felt he had to do. And as prudent as it might be to do so, I can't throw him out, even as I worry about any danger he might bring with him."

"Hmmm. . . ." Alphonse rocked back on his heels. "I feel that we can trust him in what he said, but trusting the person who may still be hunting him is another question. He was afraid of being followed or he would not have padded the wound. He did a good job, too. Before coming back, I checked outside to make sure there was no betraying blood on the cobbles. None."

She was so tired, and all this blood and betrayal was so complicated. She winced as pain shot through her temples. A little rest would take care of this headache, but that man seemed likely to keep her from it. She *had* to think.

"I will stay the rest of the night with him," Alphonse said. It was a flat statement that brooked no argument.

Genna knew when to concede defeat. "It will be hard on you. Tomorrow you must sleep. In the morning, I'll position extra footmen with the excuse that I am uneasy in Paris right now." She sighed and rubbed at her temples. "That's a good reason and probably would be wise even if we didn't have our strange guest."

Alphonse nodded, then entered the sickroom, closing the door quietly behind himself.

Genna stood staring at the heavy wooden door. Coherent thought was beyond her, and she still had to check on Hester. Suppressing a sigh, she moved down the hall to stop at the room opposite her own. Genna had promised her aunt that she would check on her and she always kept her word. A soft knock brought no answer. She tried again, and again nothing. It appeared that Hester had managed to sleep in spite of her fears.

Hopefully, sleep would not elude her either, Genna thought, as she entered her own room.

Jason watched her leave the room. The warm glow that had sustained him went with her. He smiled ruefully. Only he would be wounded nearly to death and then find a woman he wanted to impress. If only he could trust her, but he didn't even know her name let alone where her sympathies lay. Her French was good, but it had undertones of other accents. And Alphonse was a French name.

No, he couldn't risk everything he had worked to accomplish the last two years by taking her into his confidence until he had to, or until he knew who and what she was.

Damn! He wanted to trust her. Her large, brown eyes and wide coral mouth were too soft to belong to a woman who couldn't be trusted. And the cleft in her chin had begged him to kiss it. He grimaced, reminding himself of the hurt he had inflicted on his own lips. He was in no shape to do more than be thankful to her.

Tomorrow he would learn more about her and then he would have to leave. He couldn't take the chance that the person who had knifed him would trace him here and possibly hurt her or the people who worked for her. He owed her more than that. If not for her, he would probably be dead by now.

He had to put her from his mind . . . and his body. He grinned ruefully to himself. He needed rest. This was the first time in months that he had the leisure to sleep without keeping one hand on a knife. He must take advantage of it. Morning would be time enough to decide how to leave Paris.

Chapter Two

Genna woke with a start. What had roused her? Then she heard it, carriage wheels on cobblestones. She still wasn't used to the sound. In Venice people traveled by water, but this was Paris and she had been here for several months.

If the outside noises weren't enough to remind her of that, the interior of this rented house should be. Instead of floor to ceiling windows letting in the bright sunshine of Italy, she was confronted with heavy velvet draperies, covering minimal windows that kept out the unwanted intrusions of downtown Paris. Instead of polished marble floors with marigold yellow area rugs, she stepped onto thick brown carpeting that made her massive bedroom seem dark and sepulchral. Even the furniture was overpowering, massive and ornate relics of another era.

She wouldn't have picked this house, with its dark atmosphere and proximity to the center of Paris. Ricci had chosen it, saying that with everyone flocking here to celebrate Napoleon's incarceration on Elba there were no better accommodations to be had.

She sighed in resignation at the thought of Ricci, her future husband and the last surviving male in the House of Ponti. She had been coerced into accepting Ricci. It was a memory she would prefer to forget, but. . . .

"Genna," Luigi said.

Her husband's voice came soft and raspy from the mountain of blankets that covered his wasted frame. Looking up from her book by Jane Austen, Genna saw his hand held out to her. Immediately, she set aside what she was doing and rose. His fingers were cold and they clung to her warm flesh, as though trying to draw life from her. With all her will, she wished she could give him what he needed since the doctor had said his time was short.

"Yes, Luigi?" she asked quietly, her heart aching for him in this last lingering indignity.

"Genna, we both know I am dying." A fit of coughing stopped him.

She held his shoulders through the racking movements, wanting more than anything to ease the pain that held him. A tear formed, but she refused to let it fall. He would not appreciate it. When he was at last finished coughing, she laid him back against the pillows and tenderly smoothed the lank gray hair from his brow, dry in spite of his exertions.

He sucked in breath, as a drowning man surfacing momentarily. "You have been my support and my right hand through the five years we have been married. I need you to be my partner after my death also."

"Shhh," she coaxed. "You need your rest."

His gray eyes hardened, and a sense of impending doom slithered down her spine. She knew what he would say. They had had this conversation every day since his infirmity confined him to his bed. So far, she had managed to divert him, but she sensed he was getting desperate and would not be denied again. She didn't want to do what he demanded, but how could she refuse? How could she measure her debt to him? She didn't know, but, surely, the rest of her life was too much for him to ask of her. She knew he did not agree.

"I will not be hushed again," he said, his voice gaining false strength. "I will not live out the night. Before I go I want your word on this."

And he would have it, she knew with a certainty, her spirit sinking. Where the House of Ponti was involved, Luigi was like a juggernaut.

"You must marry Ricci. The fortune must stay with the title." He paused to gasp air.

"Leave the money to Ricci," she pleaded. "I don't want it."

His hand bit into her fingers where he still held her. "You forget about your mother."

The statement chilled her, but she knew he didn't intend it cruelly. Her mother was in a Swiss sanatorium with consumption, and had been there for years. Her mother's health was the reason

Genna had married Luigi. It likewise would be the reason Genna would marry Ricci, unless she could convince Luigi differently. She had to try.

"Then leave me enough for her care," Genna pleaded. "The rest can go to Ricci."

"Ricci would squander it in a fortnight on his women and his cards. We both know that."

The ferocity of his emotions lent animation to his face, making it glow as though health were his once again. Seeing it, Genna knew she was lost.

"You would condemn me to life with a man like Ricci?" she asked softly, using it as her last defense. Even as she spoke these words, she knew it would not suffice to change Luigi's mind.

"I will do whatever is necessary to see that my house does not suffer. You know how to manage the money, you have done it for me the last two years. And who knows, married to a good woman might be the making of Ricci. Heaven knows, many a rake has been reformed by love."

"Love!" Her laugh was soft and bitter. "Ricci doesn't love me, nor I him."

"That may come. I hope so for your sake, because I must insist. Without your promise to me, I will leave all of it to Ricci. None for the care of your mother. My lawyer awaits my word."

She tried to pull her hand from his grasp, but he held her like a vise, his look boring into her. In a daze, she watched him reach with his free hand for the gold bell on his night table. It had barely rung when the door opened and his man of business entered. Where was the tender man she had married? Lost behind the will to continue his dynasty. They had not had children, so Ricci was his last hope to carry the Ponti name, but Ricci had to have funds. She was to see that he did....

Now she was betrothed to Ricci, a circumstance her honor wouldn't let her end even though Luigi was dead and could not rise from his grave to stop her. No, she was tied to a future marriage of Luigi's planning.

Sighing at the unfairness of it all, Genna raised her arms above her head and stretched. Her life and happiness were sacrificed for the future of a line of dissolute Italian counts. There was nothing she could do about her betrothal to Ricci, but she could check on her latest patient and decide what to do with him.

She got out of bed, noticing for the first time that she was still in last night's gown. Her head had hurt so much, and she had been so tired, that she had not bothered to change.

Peeling out of the soiled gown, she washed in the cold water, gooseflesh rising on her skin. Then she opened the massive mahogany wardrobe and rifled several times through her clothes before settling on a pansy purple morning dress with simple lines. She donned it quickly.

In a nearby full-length beveled mirror, she surveyed herself critically. Dressed properly, she could be considered attractive, but she was no beauty. Her eyes were too determined and her chin was too strong. Even her figure was out of fashion:

too full bosomed, too Junoesque. Luigi had admired her ample curves, for his youth had been lived during the time when women were expected to be well-endowed and admired for it.

She smoothed the material of her dress, frowning at the way the high waist accented the flare of her hips when the style should have made her look willowy. Unbidden, an image of the strange man in the Gold Room entered her ruminations. Would he appreciate a figure such as hers? She doubted it.

Twisting away from her reflection, Genna squeezed her eyes shut. Why did it matter? Never before had she cared about being desirable to a man. Not even Luigi.

And why were her memories of Luigi coming back? It had been a year since his death. Yes, she had cared for him, but it had been as a daughter for a father. He had not been her grand passion—such as her parents had shared. She had long ago decided that love such as her mother and father had experienced was not to be hers.

A bitter laugh escaped her before she could stop it. It was a good thing, too, for she was bound for another loveless match.

It did no good dwelling on what could not be changed. Her word was her honor and she wouldn't besmirch it by reneging on her commitment to Ricci.

But there were things to accomplish this morning before her betrothed's visit, and she wasn't even finished with her toilet. She picked up her gold backed brush, one of the few personal items she had brought with her from Venice, and pulled it viciously through her hair. A quick twist, and her hair was secured with a purple ribbon to the top of her head, the thick, copper waves falling loosely down her back.

Minutes later, she strode down the hallway to the room where her uninvited guest lay. She stopped short at the entrance and knocked softly. Seconds later, Alphonse came out, closing the door behind him.

Jerking his head at the door, Alphonse said, "You must have dosed him like a horse, milady, because he has slept through the night without a murmur. He is just now starting to stir. I am going to get my shaving gear. No matter who he is, he will feel better for being clean."

"Yes," Genna murmured, "having a face without whiskers always improved Luigi's disposition. In the meantime, I'll check on our guest. Also, talk with Michaels about hiring more footmen." She nodded at Alphonse's grim look.

She didn't watch Alphonse leave, but entered the room. The curtains hadn't been opened, and shadows hung heavily, causing her to pause and allow her eyes to adjust. There was a small fire going, and a large armchair was pulled close to the bed. Genna moved toward it.

The man was sprawled diagonally across the mattress, the covers wrapped cocoon-like around his middle, leaving the rest of the bed stripped. One bare leg, liberally dusted with golden-brown hair, dangled over the side. Even at this angle, she could see that his calves were well-formed and his foot was long and narrow with a high arch. A nobleman's limb.

She smiled, thinking how uncomfortable he would be to sleep with. Probably, whoever shared his nights would find herself on the floor regularly. By habit, she moved to tuck him back in. Before she could, he twitched. She darted a look at his face. His eyes were openly appraising her.

"Oh," she said, stepping backward. "I didn't realize you were awake. Alphonse has gone to get water and a razor. How are you feeling? Alphonse said you slept like the dead." She was blathering, something she never did. This man affected her equilibrium. It was because he was a mystery, she told herself.

His grin showed strong, even, white teeth. "You jumped like the devil himself had appeared in front of you. I'm sorry I startled you. I heard the swishing of skirts and thought it might be you, since your lackey doesn't favor petticoats."

"It might have been the housekeeper," she retorted, enjoying his levity. It wasn't often she found someone with a sense of the ridiculous.

"Possibly, but her tread is heavier than yours."

Her eyes narrowed. He was very discerning. "'Tis interesting that you notice something as small as that. Your line of work must require you to pay attention to such details."

His smile faded. "Yes, it does."

"You're still unwilling to tell me anything," she said, not trying to keep the exasperation from her voice. "Then at least tell me your name so I may call you something besides 'the stranger' or 'the man'."

"Jason."

She was so irritated, she snapped back, "Jason what?"

"Jason is all I can tell you, unless you want a lie. I would rather not lie to you."

His eyes met hers squarely. They were beautiful eyes, heavy-lidded and long, the thick eyelashes framing them drawing attention to the green irises that danced with golden flecks. His eyes spoke to her of trust and promises fulfilled, frightening her more than his unexpected arrival on her doorstep, because they gave the hope of . . . of what?

This was madness. She was demented to read more into a look than could possibly be there. He was not interested in her beyond her willingness to care for him while he healed. She was not interested in him beyond healing him. Whatever she thought his eyes said to her, she was imagining it.

Frustration ebbed from her to be replaced with resignation that she could never find love with this man or anyone else. She had committed herself to the House of Ponti.

To break their unspoken communication, she turned her head. "Well," she sighed, "I don't want lies, so Jason will do. Although, I must tell you that even though your French is flawless, your name is English. And even I, as dumb as you must think me, realize that you aren't French." She was behaving churlishly, and she knew it. But he was leaving large gaps in the little bits he told her about himself.

"You're very astute," he said. "Or I'm very lax. Either way, it would be best if I left. If your man will get my clothes, I'll be gone immediately."

"No!" The word shot from her. He was too weak to leave.

He grinned.

Seeing his reaction, she remembered his vehemence the night before when she had suggested sending for the doctor. It seemed the two of them were similar in some aspects.

"I won't see a doctor, and you won't let me leave," he said. "We are at a deadlock."

Puzzled by his easy acceptance, she asked, "Who are you really? You must be British."

The door opening kept him from having to answer.

"Milady," Alphonse said, "I insist that you leave now. No man wants a woman around while his face is being scraped. And besides, the Conte di Ponti is waiting for you."

Unable to resist the last word, she said, "I've seen a man have his face scraped, as you put it. I've even done it."

She heard Jason chuckle, but she exited with such alacrity that she lost the chance to see his grin. She regretted that, remembering the way his features lightened when he smiled. Still, it would almost be a relief to see Ricci. She understood him, and she was not confused around him as she was around *this man*.

Jason, she reminded herself, sounding the word silently. It was a nice name, giving a sense of courage and dependability even though it opened another Pandora's box regarding why he was pretending to be French.

"Genna!"

Ricci's petulant demand interrupted her thoughts. He was standing on the stair landing, one leg forward to best show his thigh encased in closely fitted buff breeches. His coat was slender-waisted and under it he wore an intricately embroidered vest. Ricci, Conte di Ponti, was a man of fashion right down to his meticulously curled black locks. He boasted snapping black eyes that he used to advantage with the women, and a full, curving mouth that was in a pout at the moment.

To Genna, he was nothing more than a grown-up child, even though at twenty-six he was one year her senior. How had she let herself be talked into marriage with him? Her promise to a dying man. She sighed and moved to meet Ricci.

"Well, do not just stand there, Genna. I expect to be welcomed as befits the man you will marry in twelve months."

Ricci's demand hung in the air between them. On leaden feet, she walked the distance separating them until she was on the landing with him. She presented her cheek for a kiss, unable to give him her lips. Resignation to the match was something she had reached long ago, but it didn't carry with it a willingness to go beyond what was necessary. Normally, Ricci appeared to agree.

"Come, come," he said in his light voice, "what sort of greeting is this? I intend more than a brotherly peck."

His arms circled her, drawing her close until they were face-to-face. He was barely an inch taller than she and his build was slight. She knew that if she wished to cause a scene, she could escape his embrace. But she had given her word, and a kiss was, after all, just a kiss.

His lips were wet, as he forced her mouth open for his tongue. She shuddered with distaste. The marriage bed would not be pleasant.

He smelled of expensive cologne, such as a woman would wear. He had come to her from his latest paramour. She had thought she was reconciled to this, for it wasn't the first time. It had never mattered before because she didn't love him, so why now?

Because you are being stupid, she told herself. You look into a strange man's eyes and see dreams of things you never thought could be yours. They are still not yours. Ricci was her betrothed, and his infidelity was something she would be living with for the rest of her life. She would not let it embitter her.

After an eternity, he moved away. She stepped back and said calmly, "Shall we go to the breakfast room? I haven't eaten yet."

Not waiting for an answer, she moved past him with her head high and her carriage regal.

"You are a cold bitch," he said just loudly enough for her to hear.

She didn't answer him. If she were to respond to his words, she would end up telling him what she thought of him and his morals. She would not do that. He was her future husband, and she owed him loyalty for that, if nothing else.

Reaching the breakfast room, they sat across from each other and waited until she was served and Michaels had left the room. Ricci hadn't come here to kiss her and then insult her. No, she knew he was here for money, but he would start with the same words. He always did.

"Genna," he said, his dark eyes turning soft and pleading, "we are to be married. You can allow yourself to respond to my lovemaking."

She took several bites of eggs, then some toast, and then sipped her coffee. It never changed. He was in need of funds and thought to get them from her the only way he knew how. He would try to make love to her and when that failed he would become angry and then conciliatory. How many times could she tell herself that he was not bad, only immature?

With a sigh of resignation, she asked, "How much do you need?"

He didn't pretend to misunderstand her. That was *something* she could admire about him.

"Ten thousand francs. I lost heavily last night."

"Ten thousand?" This was more than normal. She knew he was living beyond the allowance she gave him as stipulated by Luigi's will, because he had asked for five thousand francs the week before.

"Well," he whined, "'tis your fault. If you had not left Madam duPree's early last night, I would not have gotten bored and gone in search of other entertainment. Then I would not now be needing so much."

If she hadn't left early last night, Jason might be

dead by now. Her knuckles turned white around her fork. "Ricci, I doubt my leaving caused you to become so badly dipped. But," she raised a hand to stop the protest he was starting, "I will write a draft on the bank." It was easier this way.

He smirked, but she could see the resentment lurking in the depths of his eyes. He hadn't taken well the fact that Luigi had left all the unentailed monies and property to her, even the palatial palace in the middle of the plains surrounding Venice. No matter how Ricci tried to hide it, he resented her holding the purse strings. She couldn't blame him.

Having gotten what he came for, Ricci left shortly after, and Genna fled to the library. With a sigh of relief, she leaned back into a huge leather chair. Rich mahogany paneling and thick green curtains kept the room dark and necessitated the use of two silver candelabra on her desk. But the solitude was worth the twilight. And there was a cheery fire crackling in the hearth, brightening her mood and sending tendrils of warmth to keep back the edge of chill that still hung on from the night.

Paris in early March was uncomfortably cold. She had long since forgotten the frost that laid over Scotland during this time of year. But maybe she had never noticed it because of the warmth her parents felt for each other and for her, their only child. The memory was bittersweet. Their love had led her to believe that she would one day have such happiness.

She pushed the disillusionment aside. The bill for her mother's Swiss sanatorium was due.

Quickly, she wrote a note for her secretary, reminding him to pay it.

Rising, she pulled her shawl closer. It was past time she checked on her patient. A knock stilled her.

"Genna," Aunt Hester said from the crack in the door that rapidly widened to admit the older woman's round form. "Is that . . . that *creature* still here?" A shiver set her chest to quivering like *blanc mange*.

Genna's mouth quirked upward, thinking immediately of Ricci but knowing her aunt meant Jason. Her amusement fled as Hester advanced into the light from the fireplace and sconces. Hester's eyes were haggard and red from lack of sleep.

"Oh, Aunt," Genna said, hastening to take the other woman's hand and lead her to the leather chair she had just left. "Here, the fire will warm your cold hands. I'll ring for tea."

"Yes, that may help," Hester said in a trembling voice, "but getting rid of that scoundrel will do much better. I hardly slept a wink last night for fear of being ravished in my bed."

Genna closed her lips firmly over the laugh that threatened. 'Twas not the time to make light of Hester's fears. Taking a seat nearby, she said, "Dearest Aunt, the scoundrel's name is Jason, and he's too weak to even get out of bed, let alone attack you. But to make sure, I've had Michaels post extra footmen, and Alphonse is with the patient right now."

"Humph! That Jason, as you call him, is a tall

man. I am sure that Alphonse won't be able to stop him if something happens. He simply must go!"

Michaels entered with a tray and talk stopped until he was gone again. Genna poured a strong cup of tea adding three spoons of sugar and plenty of cream.

"Here, dear," she handed the cup to Hester. "I understand your worry, but the man is sick. I'm very sorry you didn't sleep well, and I wish it weren't so, but I can't consign him to the street. I just cannot." Her eyes pleaded with Hester for understanding. "And more so, he was attacked."

She noted Hester's eyes widen with shock and her pudgy fingers shake as she reached for her tea. Her aunt, the poor dear, looked years older, but Genna could not throw Jason out.

"I thought as much," Hester said after a deep sip of tea.

"Yes, but you see, dear," Genna said, determined to get this unpleasant conversation behind them, "it means that someone is after him or thinks him dead. And we don't know who his attacker is, so it would be best if we told no one about him."

Hester reached for an iced cake and bit into it before replying, "It would be best for him to go back to the gutter you pulled him from." She finished the cake with a snap of her teeth, then sighed at the stricken look on Genna's face. "Luigi would not like this. For that matter, Ricci will not like this."

"You mustn't tell Ricci," the words catapulted out of Genna's mouth. "He is such a tattlemonger that before tomorrow is over the whole of Paris would know. That would endanger Ja . . . I mean, us. The person who attacked Jason might attack us."

The thought of further danger whitened Hester's face, but she nodded her understanding. "If only you would throw the bounder out," Hester sighed.

Genna declined to reply. They had been over this, and she had made up her mind. For better or worse, she had committed herself to Jason's care until he no longer needed it.

Hester took another sip and a bite of another cake before sighing. "Then we must leave. That will solve this dilemma you find yourself in about this man. Leave a servant to care for him. Besides, 'tis time we went to visit your mama. Heaven knows we would have been gone by now if it had not been for Ricci always forgetting to make the arrangements, even after he insisted on doing so. *I* think 'twas so he could get a bank draft with the excuse that he needed to pay some of the travel arrangements early. Humph! I am sure he spent the money elsewhere."

"As am I," Genna murmured. "But you're right, dear. We should have gone earlier. However, I've instructed my secretary to start the arrangements. He is also to look for passage from Switzerland to Italy." She didn't tell Hester that the plans were to be tentative so that she shouldn't be forced to leave before Jason was ready to travel on his own.

"Italy!" Hester set her cup down with a clink. "I had hoped you would return to Scotland."

"For what?" Genna asked gently. How many times had they had this conversation? "There's nothing for me in Glenfinnan. Papa was impoverished when he died. All the land and the title have gone to his heir, a distant cousin I don't know and who doesn't care what happens to me. No, my place is in Italy now."

"There is nothing for you in Italy, except a big mausoleum of a house and a future marriage to a man who will parade his mistresses in front of you and will squander your money faster than fat goes through a goose."

"Mmmph!" Genna choked on the tea she had just sipped. When she recovered her breath, she said, "Aunt, your language."

Hester had the grace to look embarrassed. "'Tis true."

"No, I must differ," Genna said calmly. "My mother's family is in Italy, while I have no Scottish relatives I care about besides you, and you are with me."

"Your mother's family will not receive you."

It was a direct blow, and they both knew it. Genna's face blanched, and she looked at the fire so Hester wouldn't see the tears that threatened to fall. She had thought that disappointment was behind her. After all, it had happened before her birth.

Her mother, Francisca Gallucci, was the only daughter of a wealthy Naples family. She had run away with a handsome, poor Scottish nobleman and been not only disinherited, but had her name stricken from the Gallucci family Bible.

Genna didn't want to discuss it further. "You're right, Hester," she said as easily as she could, rising from her seat. "However, Venice is my home now. 'Tis where I'll live after my marriage. And 'tis where I'll go after visiting mama." She smiled to soften the next words. "If you'll excuse me, I must attend to my patient."

Hester, a grimace of sympathy puckering her small mouth, watched her only niece until she was out the door. Hurting Genna was the last thing she wanted to do, but the child did not belong married to that Ricci. She should marry a good Scottish lad this time. But first, she should get rid of *that person* in the Gold Room.

Jason silently fought his way out of the nightmare. The dead men surrounding him began to dissipate as reality impinged on his senses. Someone was in the room with him. The rustle of a page turning, the yellow glow of candles and the warmth of a roaring fire played on his heightened awareness.

How long had he slept? The last thing he remembered was playing whist with the lackey, Alphonse. During the course of the game he had learned that, despite his French name, Alphonse was Italian. Being in Paris didn't sit well with the wizened little man, but the mistress had come here, so the lackey had come. It had been more than money that had brought the servant, it had been loyalty.

Jason's curiosity was whetted even more. What

manner of woman elicited such loyalty from a servant? And was she Italian also? She spoke very good French, if she were. Did she speak English? It would be nice to be able to speak his native tongue in safety again.

He turned his head to see who was sitting with him this time, hoping it was her. It was.

The flickering light from her reading candle cast shadows on her cheeks and under her chin. Her bosom, ample and shapely, narrowed into a tiny waist that only accented her generous curves, making the blood run hot in his loins. He grimaced, silently chastising himself. She'd saved his life, he owed her more respect than to lust after her when he couldn't offer any more than one night's passion.

"Mademoiselle?" His voice cracked, making her start. Was he always going to make her that nervous? She raised startled eyes, the mahogany brown of her irises making them glow like amber. They made him feel special. *"Parlez-vous Anglais?"*

He held his breath, disturbed by his daring. He was being a cursed fool, to jeopardize his mission like this, but there was no going back now. And she already knew his name and had informed him that it was English. Besides, he trusted her.

"Yes," she answered. "I'm half Scottish."

The dulcet tone of her voice washed over him, helping to mitigate his surprise and joy at her answer. He was taking unheard-of risks, but surely someone with a voice like hers would not betray him. Besides, speaking English was such a small thing to reveal, and she was part Scottish. The Scots were a fiercely proud and loyal people. Perhaps her sympathies would lie with his cause. He dared not ask yet, but it was something to consider.

"Which half is Scottish?" he questioned, wanting to know more of her, wanting to establish some sort of understanding between them.

She studied him, multiple emotions flickering in her eyes before saying, "When you're ready to tell me about yourself, then I shall tell you more."

He wouldn't tell her anything, and she knew it. The minx! Even as the situation irritated him, it increased his admiration for her. She might be softhearted where a sick person was concerned, but she was no one's fool.

He watched her lay the book down and rise, coming toward him. Her copper hair was swept up in a knot and then allowed to drape down and caress the creamy whiteness of her neck. She had thick, short lashes that accented the tilted corners of her eyes, making her exotic when compared to the English rose so popular with most of his countrymen. He wanted to drown in her eyes, even as he wanted to feast on the rest of her. Lush curves flared with the rise and fall of her bosom, making his own breath come in ragged draws. The high lines of her gown emphasized the voluptuousness of her hips as she came closer. She reminded him of a Greek statue he had had once seen of Juno, Goddess of Motherhood, full busted and ripe for a man's loving.

Her cold hand on his forehead was like a splash

of ice water. He was an idiot. The woman had saved his life, not taken him to her bed.

"You're hot," she said, moving her fingers along his cheek. "I hope you aren't getting a fever."

Her brows puckered, making him want to reach up and smooth them. "I'm a burden to you," he said, wanting to see her smile instead of worry.

"I wouldn't have it otherwise," she said. "You're injured," she sighed as though it vexed her but there was nothing she could do about it. "I've a weakness for people or animals in need."

"I'm glad," he said, taking her hand from where it rested on his cheek and kissing her palm. The silken coolness of her skin eased the heat of his lips, even as it inflamed his senses. His heart was thudding like the hooves of a thousand horses. Could she hear it?

She jerked her hand back as though he had burned her. He could see her retreating from his small advance.

"I imagine you are," she said dryly.

He chuckled and changed the subject. "Your lackey is Italian. But you speak French and English, and your English is much better than your French. What's your Italian like?"

He could see the speculation in the scrutiny she subjected him to. It wouldn't surprise him if she refused to answer him until he told her something more. Already, he could see she was spirited as well as compassionate.

"My Italian is like my English," she said, with a squaring of her shoulders that made her bosom jut and his pulse soar.

This isn't going to work, he thought. He was too weak, and she was too caring for him to be this aroused just by looking at her. She wasn't even being provocative. Perhaps if he closed his eyes. . . .

"Are you in pain?" she asked anxiously, laying her hand on his chest.

Even the blanket covering him wasn't enough to blunt the rush of excitement her touch caused. He was being stupid. He had heard of men who fell in love with their nurses, but he had never thought himself the type to be so easily gulled.

"No," he finally said through gritted teeth. "I'm in no more pain than when I awoke. What time is it?"

"Going past five," she said, moving her hand away.

His sigh was gusty with relief. "What are the chances of getting something to eat?" Now that she no longer touched him, his stomach claimed his attention.

When he glanced at her, she had a most knowing look about her. Surely, she didn't know how she affected him. He wasn't that gauche.

"I was wondering when your stomach would start," she said. "'Tis always the way. Even Luigi, as weak as he was, always thought of his belly."

Her words were a shot in his gut. She'd nursed another man. Had the man died? For a fleeting moment, he hoped so, then condemned himself for the selfish thought. But he had to know.

"Who is Luigi?"

"My husband," she said softly.

His fingers felt like ice. Another man made love to her, burying himself in the ripe bounty of her body even as he experienced the rich warmth of her affection. He wanted to strangle the man who had that right.

He told himself not to be a fool, it didn't matter. He would be gone in a day, two at the most. He had to get to Brussels. She was only a beautiful woman to whom he owed a debt of gratitude larger than anything he could ever repay.

"I'm surprised that your husband allows you to nurse me," he said as lightly as he could.

This time she actually laughed, a soft, melodious sound. Irritation narrowed his eyes at the sound. How could she be so caring for him and then laugh about something that would bother him, were she married to him and nursing another man?

She must have seen his frown, for she hastened to add, "I'm a widow."

How could she laugh about a husband who was dead? He didn't know what to make of her or his own confused response.

"You're certainly unaffected by your husband's death."

He saw her lips tighten at the censure in his voice. He knew it wasn't his place to criticize her, especially after all she had done for him, but he could not understand the emotions rampaging through him. Never before had he failed to control what he did and said. His life was forfeit otherwise.

"My husband has been dead a year. Not that 'tis

any of your concern," she said so icily that it would have frozen him had he not been so relieved to hear that she was a widow of some time.

She turned her back to him and moved away before he could reply. The orange glow of the fire silhouetted her stiff form. The straightness of her shoulders, more than anything she said, told him how much he had upset her.

"My apologies," he said, his voice a deep rumble in his chest. "My manners have gone begging it seems."

Returning to his side, she said, "'Tis no wonder with that wound you have suffered. I shouldn't have become so upset over such a trivial matter."

"No, no, I shouldn't have ventured to say anything, let alone censure," he said, anxious not to have her blame herself for his faux pas. "I'm too much in your debt, in addition to it being none of my concern."

"Methinks you doth protest too much," she paraphrased Shakespeare smilingly.

It lightened his heart to see her thus, and he knew he must look like a fool with such a grin splitting his face. He was getting weak. "We must stop this disagreeing," he said. "'Tis the second time we haven't seen eye to eye."

"Only the second?" she said in mock surprise. "I beg to differ. There doesn't seem to be anything we concur on. I dare to say that we won't agree on this next thing, either."

"Which is?" He was enjoying their repartee and wanted it to continue.

"Your dinner."

"My beefsteak and ale?"

"Ha! You mean your porridge and broth."

His eyelids sank to half-mast as he took in the enticing picture she presented with one hand on her hip and the other pointing at him as though he were a disobedient child.

"Managing little baggage, aren't you?" he said, eyeing her. "Although you aren't that small. I wager you would top my shoulder."

"That isn't saying much, since I don't know how tall you are. But you're not going to change the subject. 'Tis light food you shall have."

"Only if you'll feed it to me."

He capitulated so quickly, he could see that she was surprised. She had obviously expected a fight, but he didn't want to fight her. He wanted the warmth of her body next to his, and the intimate contact of her fingers as she fed him.

"And you call me managing? However, you're very likely too weak to feed yourself, so I shall have to do it."

"Don't smirk so, 'tis not becoming."

"Just so," she said, moving to the door. "I'll be back shortly."

He put a hand out to stop her. "Why don't you ring for a servant?"

"You should know why. You have a secret that you'll not share. 'Twould do you no good if the servants were to all see your face. They gossip, and if one of the English or even French households is missing you, my servants would be sure to find out and possibly tell where you are. I don't want that danger to my people. But I believe I told you something of the kind last night."

When he thought on it, he could vaguely remember her saying something of the sort, but he had been so drugged that it was hard to fish through the fog to what had actually happened.

Then before he could reply, she was gone.

Chapter Three

"Ouch!" Jason said, his head jerking back just enough to spill the hot beef and barley broth on his chest.

"I am sorry," Genna said, refusing to meet his eyes. If she hadn't been so aware of his lips closing around the spoon, and curious to feel their firm pressure against her own, she wouldn't have been clumsy.

This was a sick room, and he was her patient. No matter that he was covered only by a sheet while she sat in a chair pulled so close that she could feel the heat radiating from him.

Was he still naked under the cover, or had Alphonse gotten him some breeches? She didn't know, but the thought persisted in nagging her. A blush turned her cheeks peach, and her fingers shook as she snatched up the napkin and began to dab at the broth beaded up in the dark brown hairs starting just below Jason's Adam's apple.

A trickle made it through the tangle to edge

downward, and the damage was done. The soup had spattered the bandage wound tightly around his torso. It would have to be changed.

Jason caught her wrist. "Enough. The broth is gone, and I'm all right."

His eyes were dark green with flecks of gold ringing the pupil, a color she was beginning to realize they became when he looked at her. She felt herself flushing. Just a glance from him set her heart beating faster.

In a voice cracking with strain, she said, "If you'll release me, I'll stop."

For a moment she thought he wouldn't do so. His gaze shifted from her eyes to her hand he held, and his mouth tightened into a thin white line.

"What's this?" he asked, opening his fingers and moving his thumb along the bruise that ringed her wrist. "Did I do this last night?"

His anger surprised her. "'Tis nothing," she said, trying to pull her hand from his grasp.

Instead of releasing her, he bent his head to kiss the discolored flesh. Tingles darted from the touch of his dry lips against her sensitive skin. When she pulled again, he let her go. It was all she could do not to rub where he'd touched her, it burned so.

"I didn't know my grip was so tight."

The words were lightly said, but his eyes were tender, making the breath catch in her throat. Did she matter to him? It was a foolish idea and she dampened it immediately. She had only just met him yesterday and under inauspicious circumstances to put it mildly. For all she knew, he could be a murderer.

"I bruise easily," she muttered, taking the bowl and spoon to a table in order to distance herself from him.

"I would never hurt you willingly," he said.

His voice was deep and rough, and it made her want to cast doubts to the wind and touch him again. She couldn't. Her doubts about Jason aside, there was still Ricci to think about. Ricci with his wet lips and womanizing ways. Ricci who was her betrothed and who deserved her loyalty even if he didn't have her respect.

"That's comforting to know," she said, trying to make her voice light, hoping to break the tension that stretched between them like a well-tuned violin string. "My aunt is convinced you'll attack us as we sleep. Now I can reassure her."

He must have caught her need to turn the conversation, for he said, "Ravishment is something I try to avoid. There's too much danger of being scratched or bitten, neither of which I enjoy."

From the safety of the doorway, she darted a glance at him to determine if he jested. His bluntness was acceptable as banter between couples flirting. But that was in crowded rooms, not a bedroom with no chaperon.

His lips were curved just enough to tell her his words were meant as a jest—if she chose to take them as such. However, the angles of his cheekbones were sharp and drawn as they had been the night before when he was in great pain. Only it wasn't pain she saw reflected in his eyes; it was hunger, such as a man feels when he wants something and knows it cannot be his.

Did he want her? Shivers ran her spine at the thought, but reason dampened them. He wasn't the man for her. She knew nothing about him . . . and there was Ricci. Always Ricci.

"I must go," she blurted. "I'll send Michaels to change your bandage. I'm sure you don't wish to smell of beef broth. 'Tis definitely not the preferred scent when contemplating seduction," she added, determined to keep their conversation light.

"Coward," he murmured, but his eyes held laughter now.

Genna whisked out the door, closing it firmly behind herself before collapsing against it. Taking several deep breaths, she chided herself for a fool. What did she know of the man? He was probably British, since he wished to speak English, but he spoke French like a native. He had been stabbed and left to die. Whatever he had done, he considered himself honorable in spite of it. Her mind warned against him, but her body responded to him like parched earth to the first rain of summer.

It was late afternoon, the sky almost dark with the threat of rain, when Genna dismissed her secretary. Ricci would be here soon to take Hester and her to dine at the Palais-Royal, the only well-lighted place in the city. Even though she wanted to cancel, she couldn't. She had given her word.

Papa had raised her to believe that a woman

should hold her honor above all else. He had insisted that there were times when honor would be all a person had left.

A knock on the library door drew her from that dismal line of reasoning.

"Enter." She finished twisting the cap tightly on the bottle of ink before looking up. It was Michaels.

"Milady," he said, in clipped British accents, his dark dress immaculate as befitted a proper English butler, "the, ahum, gentleman in the Gold Room is hotter than perhaps he should be. I think he must be coming down with a fever and should see a doctor."

"I'll look in on him before dressing, but no doctor. At least not yet." She kept her tone cool and impersonal even though her pulse pounded with dread. This is what she had feared would happen; why she had wanted to call in a doctor. Surely Jason couldn't have done anything that was worth the risk of his life, but she had allowed him to keep her from summoning anyone. She prayed Michaels was wrong.

When she entered Jason's room, the curtains were drawn once again. A fire roared in the grate and several candles sent flickering light over the bed. Alphonse sat in the chair she had used while feeding Jason.

Her skin heated at the memory of her patient reclining, his chest bare, his lips moving over the spoon as she imagined they would move over her. She was thankful that the dimness would keep her embarrassment from showing.

Jason lay on the bed, his back toward her. The bandage appeared fresh, but the sheet rode his hips, threatening to go lower as he twisted to face her. She found herself fascinated with the idea even as she admired the expanse of muscled shoulders his partial undress revealed. It was unseemly.

She forced herself to study his face for signs of fever. His eyes were alert and teasing, his voice strong as he said, "Ah, my fiery angel. Is it time for me to be fed again?"

When he spoke, his teeth gleamed strong and white, reminding her of a caged tiger she had seen on display once. He could very easily be a preying hunter if civilization didn't fence him in. Her pulse quickened at the thought, for she was not at all sure that he *was* fenced in.

"Michaels says you have a fever. I've come to see."

"'Tis nothing," he muttered, turning his head from the hand she put out toward him.

"Would you behave as a child?" she scolded, knowing that she couldn't let him win again.

"Would you behave as a shrew?" he countered, turning back to face her.

"If needs be," she said, placing her cool hand against his forehead. He was warm, but not dangerously so. Perhaps Michaels had exaggerated. She certainly hoped so, for she couldn't see herself convincing this strong-minded man that he should have a doctor check him.

"See," he said smugly as her fingers lingered on his flesh, "I don't have a fever. Or at least, not the kind Michaels thinks."

Genna heard Alphonse's growl in the twilight surrounding her and Jason, but the sound was merely an undertone to her conversation with Jason. She knew what Jason was referring to, for she could see the desire sparking his eyes. She should ignore it.

But she found herself greedy for his admiration. Soon she would be married again, and then she wouldn't be able to experience this exhilarating emotion that tightened her stomach with anticipation and sped her heart with longing. Jason would be an incident in her past, and nothing in her future.

Besides, this was only banter, and he was too weak to do more. She was safe from him, but from herself? That was a question she didn't want to think on.

She trailed her fingers down the side of his face and lingered on the rough stubble of his cheek. Delicately, lightly as a spring mist, she laid her palm against him, ostensibly testing for fever.

"You're warm to the touch," she murmured, her eyes meeting his and acknowledging the attraction between them, "but I don't believe you're dangerously ill."

"No," he said, his voice deeper than she had heard it before, "but I am dangerously pressed in other areas . . . Genna."

The way he lingered on her name was as personal as a caress, sending shoots of pleasure through her like the tendrils of growing plants in the warmth of a spring day.

"Milady!" Alphonse's raised voice intruded.

Blinking, Genna dropped her hand from Jason's face and twirled around to face Alphonse. Anger tightened her fingers into a ball. He had no right to interrupt them, but then they had no right to display their emotions so blatantly in front of him . . . or to each other. She was engaged. And God only knew what Jason was.

"I must dress for dinner," she said, moving toward the door, anxious to be gone before she said or did aught else to encourage the man or herself. Yet, she couldn't forgo a glance at Jason before closing the door. His face was shuttered, his eyes closed, and his lips compressed. The vein in his neck throbbed.

Jason threw his arm over his eyes to block out the sight of her. He was ten times a fool, but he wanted her, wanted her with an intensity he had never felt before. Just the swish of her hips as she moved from the bed enticed him and tightened his loins to bursting point.

She didn't deserve his lust when he could not make her an honorable offer. There was no room in his life for the complication of a woman. He must reach Wellington, and nothing must come between him and that goal. The information he had been knifed for was too valuable for him to linger any longer than needed to gain enough strength to travel.

"I am warning you," Alphonse said, breaking into Jason's anguished thoughts, "if you do anything to harm her I will kill you myself."

Jason studied the old man. The threat would

have been ludicrous, except that Jason saw the devotion lighting the lackey's eyes from within.

"She has nothing to fear from me," Jason said tiredly, beginning to feel the effects of a long day and a wound barely starting to heal. His lower lip curled in disgust. "I'm weak as a kitten."

"See you stay that way where she is concerned," Alphonse threatened, before moving the chair by the bed toward the warmth of the fire.

Jason hoped he could continue to want Genna from afar, but he didn't know how much more contact with her he could stand before he seriously tried to seduce her. She was all women to him. Her compassion and caring beyond what he had believed possible, and her graceful movements accenting the full lushness of her figure. Every fiber of his being called out to touch her and love her. He longed to ignite a flame in her to match the one that continued to flare in him no matter how he tried to bank it.

He didn't know much more about her than she knew of him, yet he felt they belonged together. There was nothing to keep them from learning about each other. Nothing but the threat of war, he thought sardonically. And his duty to get to Wellington.

He must warn her to prepare to leave Paris. The information he carried indicated that Napoleon would soon escape Elba. When that happened, no place in France would be safe for an unprotected woman who had even one drop of British blood in her veins. If he didn't have to make such haste when he left, he would escort her. But again, his duty must take precedence over his desire.

A grimace twisted his mouth. *Duty*. It had always had been with him. He had been steeped in it from the cradle. Duty and Honor, the motto of his family, the code of his life. Now it stood between him and the woman he longed to be with. Again it would win.

It was late that night when Genna and Hester returned home. The earlier thunderclouds had dispersed, leaving the sky clear and sparkling with stars like brilliants and a moon like a silver piece, but the cold was pervasive. Genna hunched down into the sable of her cloak, remembering the night before and Jason's arrival into her life.

Just the thought of him warmed her. Was he all right, or was his long, lithe body wracked by feverish shudders? She didn't know, but she hadn't been able to leave earlier for fear of arousing Ricci's ire and possible curiosity.

She didn't want her betrothed to wonder about the extra footmen she had hired or to miss Alphonse's constant presence at her side. Ricci was such a gossip that he would quickly spread the information to every salon and drawing room. 'Twas bad enough Hester knew, but that had been necessary. She could only hope her aunt wouldn't speak for fear of endangering her own safety if naught else.

Stepping from the couch, Genna waited for Hester to disembark, before going to the front door where Michaels waited with a lighted candle to take their cloaks.

"Michaels," Genna scolded, "how many times must I tell you not to wait up for us. With all the lackeys who accompany us, there is no need for you to keep late hours. We're safe."

"Milady," Michaels bowed, but his voice was implacable, "I am your butler, and as such, I shall be here whenever you return."

Genna shook her head in exasperation, but knew it was a matter of pride with Michaels. They had been down this path often enough. "As you wish," she said handing him her cloak and turning to Hester. "I must check on my patient, so I'll wish you good night now, dear."

"Humph!" was Hester's answer. "Instead of making sure that scoundrel will live to ravish us in our beds, you should be thinking about what we learned tonight."

Genna paused, realizing that Hester needed to be reassured of their safety if they were going to remain in Paris. "You have a valid point, dear, but everyone agreed that just because Napoleon has escaped Elba doesn't mean that he's headed for Paris. Why, even Louis seemed unafraid."

Hester snorted again. "That fat excuse for a king? I should think he would be quaking in his diamond studded shoes. But no, he is not, so neither is anyone else."

Genna gathered her patience, wanting to rush to Jason, but knowing that Hester wasn't ready to go upstairs and sleep peacefully. "Dearest Aunt, when we hear that Louis has fled, then I promise you that we'll do the same. In fact, I shall tell

Alphonse and Michaels to prepare for that eventuality."

"Well," Hester said grudgingly, "I suppose I shall have to be satisfied with that."

Genna shook her head and swallowed the irritation caused by Hester's last words. Her aunt meant no harm by them, she was only speaking her mind.

Then, not seeing any reason to worry about Napoleon's escape yet, Genna put Hester and her worries out of her mind and mounted the stairs, eager yet fearful of what she might find. If Jason had a fever, all she knew to do was sponge him with cold water.

She opened the door with trembling fingers and peeked in. The fire was dead and no candles were lit. Alphonse was asleep, sprawled in the big chair by the mantel, his feet straight out in front of him.

"Please, don't be feverish," Genna prayed silently as she took a deep breath and moved toward the bed.

She didn't want to light a candle and chance waking Jason or Alphonse, both of whom needed their sleep. Jason was a darker area in the shadowed bed, and she squinted her eyes trying to see better. He lay on his back with one arm flung across his eyes.

Stopping at the edge of the bed, she listened. His breathing was slow and even, not the labored gasping of someone about to expire. A sigh of relief slipped between her parted lips.

But just to be sure, she leaned forward to touch

him. Her heartbeat thundered in her ears. What if he woke up while her hand was on him? There was something incredibly intimate about putting her fingers on his cheek while he slept, something only a lover would do.

He felt warm when he should have been cool in the cold room. Worry began to gnaw at her. She laid her palm on his forehead to be certain. His skin was dry, but surely not critically so. And he was sleeping peacefully. He might sleep the whole night if left undisturbed. At this moment he needed sleep more than he needed someone poking at him.

She should leave him, but found herself reluctant to end the contact so quickly. She skimmed her fingers down the side of his face and lingered at the contoured firmness of his mouth. Did he want to kiss her? She wanted him to, even as she told herself it wouldn't be right.

There was movement under her fingers. Was he awake? When she bent closer to see, his eyes were shut. His lips were curved in a spare smile, and she wondered if he were dreaming and, if so, what about? Was she in it? She was being silly.

It was time for her to go. She was so tired, she was beginning to imagine things that were impossible. However, she couldn't resist one last sweep of her fingers along his skin.

Early the next day, Genna donned a cream colored muslin morning dress with cascades of ivory lace falling from the neckline just below her chin. She would check on Jason and then eat a quick breakfast.

When she reached his room, raised voices met her ears. She opened the door hastily, hoping that no one was hurt.

Jason was propped up in bed, his face red with anger. Alphonse stood at the foot of the bed, his feet shoulder width apart and his fists on his hips.

"What is this?" she asked calmly, hoping to dispel some of the tension.

Jason turned to look at her, his features softening momentarily before firming again as he said, "I'm fed up with coddling. 'Tis time I dressed, but your servant will not give me my clothing unless you tell him to."

Genna looked at Alphonse, and said, "Alphonse, you may go now. It was a long night and it appears that our patient is well enough to fend for himself this morning."

For a moment she thought Alphonse would refuse, then he jerked his head in a short nod and strode past her. She turned her attention back to Jason.

"You've upset him," she said, moving closer to the bed.

"'Tis not hard to do, I wager," Jason said, some of the fury draining from his bunched muscles. "And over something as trivial as giving my clothes back to me. When may I have them?"

He spoke as though it was the most natural thing in the world for him to get dressed and resume his normal activities. She shook her head at his stubbornness. There were still grooves of pain between his eyebrows, and when he leaned back into the pillows, she marked the tightening of his mouth.

"Your clothes have been burned."

"What!"

She flinched at the burst of wrath that flared in his eyes. He would make a formidable enemy, but he wouldn't intimidate her. She shrugged, setting the lace under her chin fluttering.

"They were filthy and covered with more blood than any laundress could remove. Had I given them to my staff to clean it would be all over Paris by now that I'm harboring someone who bled like a stuck pig. You wouldn't wish that."

"'Tis true," he said. "Still, I would be dressed. There must be a servant who is my size. Bring me some of his breeches and a shirt and coat. Surely you didn't burn my boots, too."

"No, your boots are in the wardrobe," she finally said, sensing that anything else would be like waving a red flag at a bull. And besides, how far could he get with only boots on?

He must have sensed her hesitation, for he said in the tone of someone who knows he's being duped. "The clothes. Or are you going to refuse like your lackey did?" He ran his fingers through his thick hair, tumbling it over his forehead.

"When you're better," she said, dreading his next words.

His eyes narrowed, and his hands clenched the sheet tightly, the knuckles white. Softly, he said, "Do you wish to see me naked?"

Apprehension aborted the step she had started to

take nearer the bed. And, yes, a faint tremor of anticipation. She had only seen Luigi thus, and now she found herself wondering what Jason would look like. He was young and muscular whereas Luigi had been old and his body weak. Yes, she did want to see him, but knew they were treading on forbidden ground. They weren't for each other. This shouldn't be happening to them.

She kept her voice steady as she said, "Do you wish me to see you naked? 'Twould not be the first time I've seen a man thus."

He studied her as though sifting through her words for their true meaning, then a wicked gleam entered his eyes and he mocked, "An experienced woman."

"A widow," she shot back, hurt by his implied criticism.

He nodded his head in acknowledgment of her answer and the feelings behind it, but he was relentless. "I want some clothes."

"When you're better," she said, relieved that he seemed willing to forget his threat.

More swiftly than she thought possible, he sat up in bed, pulling the sheet with him. Before she could reach his side to push him back down, he was on his feet by the bed, his loins covered, but his chest bare except for the bandage. He swayed, putting out a hand for balance. The sheet slid precariously down until it barely covered him, and his eyes stared defiantly at her, daring her to refuse him again.

"Fool!" She rushed forward, wrapping her arms

around his waist to support him. "You're too weak to stand, let alone get dressed."

He smelled of lime and basilicum powder. It wasn't unpleasant, and she knew she would always associate those scents with him. Even as she held him, the heat of their bodies strengthened the scents until it was all she could do not to lift her head and kiss the lips so near her. He was sick, and he was bullheaded.

"Damnation, woman! You're not my nursemaid," he roared, teetering to the side before allowing himself to lean into her. The near fall sobered him, making his next words slow and measured as though he talked to an idiot. "'Tis not for you to decide. I've something of the utmost importance to do, and I cannot do it in bed. The sooner I'm up, the sooner I'll recover. I know."

"Hah!" She took a deep breath, for he was no featherweight and holding him up was beginning to weary her. If he lost his balance completely, they would both tumble down. "You're a heavy oaf, and I *am* your nurse. And you are behaving just as I would expect you to."

His eyes opened wide to pierce her with his disbelief. "As you would expect? Why, you don't even know me."

"I know enough to realize that you're stubborn and opinionated and overbearing. I also know enough to understand that you'll insist on pushing yourself beyond what you're ready to do. I don't intend to let that happen." Determination firmed her jaw and gave strength to her arms around him as she met him look for look.

He laughed and the force of it sent them toppling.

"Oh, no," Genna wailed, leaning backwards, hoping to right them before they landed on the bed and hurt him.

"Ooooph!" The wind gusted out of his lungs as they hit with Genna on top, her arms still wrapped around his waist.

They were a tangle of limbs, her body plastered the length of his, their legs entwined like lovers. Where their skin touched, currents of sensation flowed through her in ever increasing force. She felt the ripple of his muscles beneath her and saw the pain flickering in his eyes before he closed them.

She longed to kiss the skin so close to her lips, to taste him just this once, to satisfy the hunger that had been growing in her since he called her a fiery angel. But she couldn't. Jason was hurt and she was promised to another man.

She pushed against Jason's shoulders, trying to raise herself away from the intoxicating closeness of his skin. His arms around her waist tightened, keeping her lower body on his, but allowing her chest to lift. Her breasts rubbed lightly along his bare torso, causing her nipples to harden. She knew he realized what was happening to her, for his eyes were now open and blazing with a golden fire.

"Genna," he whispered, his voice husky.

She could feel him shudder under her. It would be so easy to lower her lips to his. It was what she wanted. What he wanted.

"We cannot," she managed between lips that felt stiff and dry. "'Tis not right."

"And I'm too weak," he added with a wry grin, the anguish he felt seeping out in the strain of his voice.

This time, when she pushed against him, he released her. Standing, she smoothed her skirts, giving herself time to regain her composure before looking at him.

His eyes were dark with pain and something else that she knew she must forget ever seeing. Ricci was like a bared sword between them.

"Men," she murmured around the constriction in her throat that was just beginning to ease. "Forever thinking of their nether parts. 'Tis a shame their brains can't be put to better use."

"You had best go," he said. "You were right. I'm not ready to be up and about."

The bitterness in his words wrung her heart. There was so much she wanted to share with him. So much she wanted to find out about him, but didn't dare.

"I'll send Michaels to check your bandage."

"Yes," he said, "that would be safer."

Worry for him drew her brows together. Though he hid it well, she knew that their fall had seriously hurt him. It might have ripped the stitches, in which case, the wound would need to be sewn again. It would be harder this time. She cared for him, and the agony he would feel if she should have to sew him up would make the task very hard on her. And too, it would delay his recovery, something he wouldn't take kindly. For his sake, she didn't want him to suffer more.

She paused at the door, wanting to talk to him about it, but knowing that it wasn't the time. It would only make the situation more awkward than it already was. He spoke instead.

"Someday I'll put everything I own to better use, Genna. God willing, it won't be long."

Chapter Four

"Oh, no," Genna moaned, her right hand resting on Jason's brow. He felt like a firebrand. "Why did I leave him today?"

"'Tis not your fault, milady," Alphonse stated. "He was not hot this morning."

Genna looked at Alphonse's set face. "I should have stayed with him. Perhaps he would not be worse now."

Pulling himself up to his full five feet four inches, the lackey said, "Are you saying I do not know how to care for a sick man? Are you saying that I allowed him to worsen?"

Stricken that Alphonse thought she would blame him, she reached impulsively across Jason's still form to rest her hand on the lackey's arm. "No, Alphonse. I don't blame you."

"Then why are you blaming yourself?"

Her gaze slid away from the older man's eyes. Why did she blame herself? Because this strange, stubborn man who would not even tell her his full name, let alone why he was in Paris, was becoming an inseparable part of her daily thoughts and actions.

Forcing herself to meet Alphonse's eyes, and set on refuting the emotions rioting in her bosom, she said in a self-mocking tone, "Because I'm always so stupid. You know how I agonized over every little setback of Luigi's, even when we knew there was nothing that could be done."

Alphonse grunted acceptance of her words.

"No!" Jason shouted, capturing their attention. His body spasmed into a vee that brought him sitting upright in the bed. His eyes stared ahead at a scene only he could see. "I must get through. I must!"

"Jason!" His name was one long breath flowing out of Genna as she lunged forward to push him back. The accident yesterday hadn't broken open his wound, and she didn't want him to do so now. The fever devouring him was dangerous enough without that complication.

"He needs a doctor," Alphonse stated.

She turned eyes blinded with unshed tears toward the lackey. "I know," she whispered, the words catching in her throat. "I know."

By putting all her weight behind her shoulders, she maneuvered Jason back onto the bed, but his breathing continued loud and rasping. His arms twitched and his head twisted from side-to-side. His eyes were shut so she couldn't see the suffering in them, but she could discern it easily enough from the creases around his mouth and the taut cords of his neck.

"Jason, Jason," she murmured, smoothing the damp blond hair from his forehead. "'Tis all right. Everything is fine." Over her shoulder, she told Alphonse, "Get me a moist cloth. We must cool him off and this is the only way I know."

"He should be seen by a doctor."

If only she could send for the doctor, but she knew Jason wouldn't want that. He would rather die than risk revealing whatever mission had precipitated him on this dangerous course.

"No, Alphonse. No doctor."

The lackey stared at her, and she knew he was trying to force her to his will. Finally, realizing that she meant to stand her ground, Alphonse broke the deadlock of their gazes.

"If you insist, milady." The title was grudgingly given. "I think 'tis a mistake, but 'tis one you will not change."

"I dare not," she said softly, wanting her old friend to understand, but willing to continue as she had begun whether Alphonse understood or not. In the short time Jason had been with her, he had become more important to her than she dared admit . . . even to herself.

"Then I had best get fresh water, this has turned tepid." Without another word, Alphonse left the room.

Genna's attention immediately riveted on the man in the bed. He was calmer than minutes before, but his skin was still flushed and dry, like fine parchment.

Taking a deep breath to still her speeding pulse

and steady her shaking fingers, Genna prayed for Jason's well-being. In the deepest recesses of her heart, she asked nothing more than to have him live; knowing she could never be more to him than his nurse and he could never be more to her than her patient.

Careful not to disturb him, she began to run the cloth over his heated face.

Hours later, the household long since gone to bed, Genna stared at Jason's prone figure. Her eyes were gritty and swollen from lack of sleep, barely allowing her to make out his silhouette against the feebly flickering flames of the fire. His features were calm and reposed, almost as though he were laid out. At the idea, the breath caught painfully in her chest.

She had done everything she could think of: dribbled water between his lips, sponged every part of his body, taken all the covers off him and when that didn't work wrapped him in every blanket she could find. Still, he was eaten up with fever.

Rising, she walked on feet made unsteady by exhaustion until she could prop herself on the edge of the bed.

"Genna, my beautiful, fiery, Genna."

Jason's voice was soft, a thread of its former strength, but it took her by surprise. He was supposed to be sleeping. She inched closer, unsure of what he had said and wanting to know for sure. Had he really called her beautiful, or was it her imagination?

"Genna."

Her name, spoken with all the longing of a man thirsting for the water of life, sent waves of heat coursing through her body. Did he care for her?

He opened eyes glazed with fever, the pupils dilated until there was a barely discernible ring of moss green around them. "Beautiful Genna."

His lids lowered as he sighed. Alarm shot through Genna. Leaning forward until her ear rested against his chest, she listened. His heart beat strongly, reassuring her that he still had strength to fight his illness.

For long minutes she allowed her head to rest against his breast, rising and lowering with each breath he took. The wiry texture of brown hairs covering his exposed torso tickled her cheek; the smell of basilicum she had used on his wound and lime water she had bathed him in assaulted her sensually to leave her intoxicated by him.

Lifting her head, she studied his face, feature by feature, reveling in the sense of fierce longing he aroused in her. When his eyes opened and his hand rose to cup the back of her head and pull her lips down to his, she didn't resist.

Their skin touched, the bare brush of flesh on flesh. Ricci and her promise to Luigi were forgotten. All she knew, all she wanted was inexplicably bound to the man whose lips held her captive. Her world, her very existence revolved around Jason and the exquisite pleasure his slightest kiss gave her.

His mouth on hers ignited a flame in Genna that grew to a conflagration that spread through her entire body, dancing along every nerve and making her light-headed. She wanted it never to end.

It was over too soon.

Jason fell back, his eyes closed. Genna looked in wonder at this man who could fire every sense in her body with such an ephemeral touch.

"Jason?" Her voice was a whisper, but her question held all the longing he had torched in her heart. After endless seconds of waiting, she realized he had fallen asleep. She smiled wryly. How typical of a man to sensually awaken a woman and then fall asleep before she was satisfied.

"Milady?"

Alphonse's voice came from the door Genna hadn't heard open. Turning, one hand at her throat, she bolted from the bed, her cheeks stained coral.

"Yes?" The word was breathy with the desire Jason had evoked in her.

"Milady, you should rest." Alphonse advanced into the room, his alert brown eyes taking in everything as his frown increased. "You should not even be in this room."

Blushing more deeply, Genna forced herself to meet the appraising look in Alphonse's eyes. "I can't leave him. Propriety is for those who don't have a life at stake." At his raised eyebrows, she firmed her jaw. "Jason is in danger of dying because of this fever. He must be tended."

"Then I will do it."

It was a bald statement, and she knew he was only speaking for the best. But if Jason regained consciousness, he would expect her to be here, and she wanted to be here. She shook her head. No one else could be allowed to care for him.

Mouth thinned, Alphonse added, "Then at least get some rest. An hour. I will take good care of him." When she lifted her chin to say no, he continued, "You will do him no good by making yourself ill, and you have already been here for twenty-four hours with no break."

Genna took a deep gulp of air, trying to calm the riot of sensation that still moved through her veins like champagne. Alphonse was right. She did need rest and something to eat. She hadn't eaten since this morning, and she would be gone too short a time for Jason to awaken in his present condition.

"I'll go get some breakfast and clean up a bit. Then I will return."

"You need to sleep."

Again he was right, but Genna feared to leave Jason. What if he should become worse while she was gone? But if she collapsed from exhaustion, she would be no help to him either. Her gaze moved back to him where he lay peacefully on the bed, and her heart swelled with longing for him and desire for his well-being.

"Milady," Alphonse persisted.

"You're right, my friend," she finally acquiesced. "But only for a short time."

The winter sun was setting at three in the afternoon when Genna returned to the sick room. She would have returned sooner, but Aunt Hester had needed soothing. Even as she had calmed

Hester's anxieties about the *scoundrel* ensconced in the Gold Room, Genna had tried to belay her own fears for that *scoundrel's* safety. Was he worse?

Entering the Gold Room, she was startled to see Alphonse bent over a thrashing Jason. "Oh, dear!" She sped toward the bed.

The room was hot, and Jason's words poured from his dry lips in an agitated stream as he twisted in Alphonse's grip. "No, no, nothing must stop me. I have to reach Brussels. I must see Wellington." Jason panted, wrenching his hand from Alphonse's grip and levering himself up on one elbow, his eyes wide open and staring.

"Shhh, Jason, nothing will keep you from Brussels." Genna pushed on his torso, careful not to touch his bandage, but determined to get him lying down once more. It was an impossible task.

For the flash of a second, Jason's eyes seemed to focus on her and then he was gone again, straining against her efforts to keep him still. "You don't know," he hissed as though talking to a person standing at the foot of the bed. "I have information about Napoleon that Wellington must have. 'Tis imperative."

Genna felt the blood drain from her face, and her gaze met Alphonse's over Jason's head.

The lackey rolled his eyes, and he said softly, "I knew something was wrong. He would not have covered the wound otherwise."

"Dear God," Genna murmured. "A British spy. No one must hear of this." Even as she spoke the words, she searched Alphonse's countenance for his willingness to remain silent.

"I will not betray him, my lady. But you had best be careful who you let in or near this room while he is in this condition. We were watchful before, but now it had better be only the two of us."

Alphonse's pinched mouth and dark eyes told Genna more than any words could have just how hard it was for him to say that. It now meant that, like it or not, he must agree with her when she said no one else must care for Jason.

Exerting more pressure, the two finally got Jason lying flat, but they couldn't stop the restless turning of his head or the sightless seeking of his eyes. Words continued to tumble from his mouth in a torrent that began to defy understanding.

"'Tis just as well he is nigh incoherent," Genna said, leaning heavily against the side table to catch her breath.

"He should be dosed with laudanum," Alphonse said. "That would quickly quiet his tongue."

Askance, Genna asked, "Do we dare? With his fever and all?"

"Do we dare not?"

She shuddered. "As usual you are right. There's always the chance that someone will stumble in here and hear him, no matter how vigilant we are. If that happens, he could very easily reveal himself to be a British spy by his ranting. That's more dangerous than any fever could be."

An hour later, the room was in shadows, the fire the only light. Alphonse had left thirty minutes earlier and Genna hadn't wanted any candles lit.

Gloominess reflected the dark turmoil in her bosom. What was she to do?

Laudanum administered, Jason was dozing fitfully, but, thankfully, quietly. The fever was still high, but at least the betraying words were stopped. She now knew for certain he was a danger to her household. Still, she couldn't condemn him to certain death on the streets.

Something about him, perhaps his honor and strength of purpose, reflected her own values. Spy or ordinary man, he was beginning to mean more to her than any other person in her life. She laughed, a hollow, almost bitter sound.

Her gaze returned to Jason, drawn like a bee to honey. Standing, she moved so that she could look down on him. Unbidden memories of their kiss played across her mind's eye. The flickering aftereffect of sensation rippled along her nerves, reminding her of the heady bliss she had found in his embrace.

A sob of frustrated indecision escaped the tight line of her lips. It was no good, standing here looking at him. There was nothing for it but to continue as she had begun. She must nurse him back to health. Then she must send him on his way, whether her heart broke in the process or not. They were not for each other.

A groan from Jason drew her from her unhappy thoughts. All recriminations vanished. The only thing that mattered was that Jason needed her.

Several rapid steps brought her to his side. She put a hand on his forehead and gasped in delight. He was sweating. He was actually sweating. He would be all right. The fever was breaking.

Falling to her knees by the bed, she took his hand and cradled it against her cheek. Everything would be all right. With time to rest and recover his strength, he would soon be able to go his way. The idea brought immediate sadness, but she pushed it away. It was best for Jason.

Her emotions once more back to her normally practical level, Genna wiped the freely flowing perspiration from Jason's face and upper chest.

"Thank you," he said, the rasping quality of his voice sending chills through every limb of her body. She hadn't realized he was awake.

Striving for a coolness she didn't feel to hide the strong emotions he evoked in her, Genna replied, "'Twas nothing. I would have done it for anyone."

"Don't belittle your concern," he said, his brows drawing into a straight line of irritation.

Unable to resist the urge, she reached out and smoothed away his harsh scowl with the tips of her fingers. "I won't belittle what I've done because it has helped you."

He caught her hand and brought the palm to his lips. The feel of his fever roughened lips moved like piercing threads over her sensitized skin, and sparks of longing licked up her nerves making her shudder. Without meaning to, her fingers caressed his bearded cheeks as he continued to nuzzle her hand.

Unable to break the contact, her eyes met his in mute appeal. What she saw in their gold flecked depths made the breath catch in her throat.

Desire stared out at her, defiant and, yet, pleading in its intensity. But there was more. There was tenderness, and that scared her more than any threat to her life could have. It threatened her very soul.

She was engaged to another man. She had given her word to marry that man regardless of whatever else happened. She would not succumb to the longing Jason aroused in her.

Briskly, she pulled away from him, breaking their physical contact and emotional commune. Several steps back and she felt sufficiently far away from him that she could turn and look at him again.

"Well, Jason, what shall I so with you now?" She willed her voice to calm authority in spite of the bewilderment she saw in his eyes before it quickly turned to wry amusement.

"Run away from me?" His lips twisted into a small smile.

"Shouldn't I?" She couldn't help the ironic lift of one brow. More than any other man, he was the most disruptive to her way of life.

The lightness left him, leaving his face harsh and angular. "Probably."

A sigh escaped her as she contemplated him and the problem he presented. He was a British spy whom she trusted, but whom she couldn't allow to remain longer than necessary to heal. As long as Jason stayed, her people were in danger from the French and the person who attacked him.

Since he was staying, she felt she should confront him with the information he had let slip during his delirium. Perhaps now he would tell her what he was doing.

And then what? She would never throw him out. Her lips curled in self-derision. "Jason, you spoke in your sleep."

Immediately, his expression turned wary, his lashes shuttered his gaze. In a low drawl, barely loud enough for her to hear, he said, "I don't suppose I talked about the weather."

Audacious! Genna wanted to feel only anger at him for his flippancy, but his very bravado disarmed her. She chuckled, her hands relaxing to her sides. "No, you did not."

The muscles in his shoulders bunched, and his hands gripped the sheet on his hips in a hold that wrinkled the linen. He didn't pretend to misunderstand her. "Are you going to turn me over to the authorities?"

Pain at his immediate assumption that she would betray him tore through her like a jagged knife, and she spoke before thinking. "How can you even think I might do so, let alone say such a thing to me? Haven't I already risked everything I hold dear by keeping you here, even though I knew nothing about why you were attacked? What have I done to make you distrust me?"

The agony his doubt caused her was so great that Genna had to twist around on her heel to keep him from seeing the tears of disappointment clouding her vision. After all she had done, all the feelings he had awakened in her and she, likewise, in him, he thought her capable of doing so dastardly a deed.

"God," his agonized groan stopped her from leaving the room. "Genna, my fiery angel, I never meant to hurt you, but I had to ask. I had to know for sure."

Her back still to him, she gulped back the sob pushing its way up her throat. All her life she had been reasonable, because she'd had to be. She had to accept her forced marriage to Luigi then her subsequent betrothal to Ricci in order to keep her mother in the Swiss sanatorium so necessary for a consumptive's continued health.

Now she had to be reasonable about Jason. He was right. He had to ask the question, no matter how much it might hurt her. He was the one jeopardizing his life. She had to accept his need and let go of the pain he had caused her.

Taking a deep breath, she said, "I understand. You had to know. 'Tis all right."

But it wasn't, not quite. There was an ache in her heart that her mind's practicality couldn't soothe.

As though sensing the lie in her words, he said, "Genna, please come here. It isn't all right, and I wish I could unsay the words, but I cannot and I would not. What I do is more important than either one of us. I'm sorry."

She squared her shoulders and turned to face him. "I know that. And for your ease of mind, I'm half Scottish with not a drop of French blood or loyalty in me. I don't know why you're a spy or what you found out that is so important that someone tried to kill you, but I won't betray you."

His head dropped back onto the pillows and his

eyes closed, his body relaxing as though a great load had been lifted from him. "Thank you."

Genna realized that was all he was going to say, and her own emotions were too raw for her to pursue the discussion further.

"I'll leave you alone to rest," she said to his still form, as eager to leave and relax her rioting emotions as she had been earlier to stay by his side.

Instead of answering her, he turned until his eyes met hers. What she saw in his expression made her sadder than she had felt when Luigi died. Jason's face held such longing and regret that it scared her because she knew it was a mirror of her own countenance.

Without another word, she fled the room and ran from the promise of him that could never be fulfilled.

Blinded by her anguish, Genna bumped into Ricci before she realized he was there. With a start of surprise, she gasped, "What are you doing here?"

His eyes narrowed and one hand locked around her right wrist, holding her painfully close to him. "Tut, tut, my dear, that is no way to greet your betrothed."

Twisting her hand, she tried to free herself, but he only held her tighter. To fight him was useless, so she stilled. She couldn't, however, stop registering the way Ricci's fingers bit viciously into her wrist. Jason had confined her the same way just days before but with no intent of harm. She had to stifle the sob brought on by the dissimilarity between the two men. Ricci cared nothing for her and relished any pain he might cause; Jason hurt as badly as she did when he harmed her.

But it was the realization of just how truly cruel Ricci was that purged Genna's mind as nothing else could have. She pulled dignity around her like someone else would don a fine dress. "I didn't expect you to call at this hour of the night. Usually, you are otherwise detained."

If he heard the sarcasm in her voice, he ignored it. He did release her hand, but advanced on her until Genna's back was up against the hall wall. She lifted her chin and stared him down, determined that he wasn't going to intimidate her.

With pointed deliberation, he said, "Had you been attending the normal social gatherings, I would not have had to curtail my pleasures to hunt you down. However, you are my future wife and I do owe you my services as protector."

Protector was the last thing she would have called Ricci, and it was all she could do not to laugh in his face. However, she managed to keep any telltale inflection from her tone. "Why should I need your protection at this hour of the night? And how did you get in?"

He sneered. "I came in the front door after banging on it until I woke Michaels up. I told you long ago that your butler is worthless. When we are married, I will get rid of him and that housekeeper. But that is not what I came to say."

Genna closed her eyes to keep him from seeing the dislike in them. She wanted to tell him pointblank that he would have no control over whom she kept when they were married, but knew better. As her husband he would be able to dictate everything. It was a bitter pill to swallow.

"As I was saying," Ricci continued, "as your only male relative, it is my duty to take care of you. Louis has fled Paris. This city is no longer safe for anyone with ties to Britain. We must leave immediately."

"But I can't," Genna blurted.

Chapter Five

"What do you mean, *cannot?*" Ricci hissed in her face.

She couldn't go now, not before Jason was well enough to travel. If she moved him, he might suffer a relapse. If she left him alone, the chance that he would worsen was very good.

His voice deceptively quiet, Ricci repeated, "What do you mean, cannot? I am your betrothed and if I say you must go, you will go."

Genna's attention focused on him, his dark eyes filled with the loathing he felt for her and his breath laden with the sweet smell of cognac that made her want to gag. Time stood still as she contemplated the twisted cast of his features, the rictus of his mouth, and the pomaded gleam of his black hair in the flickering light of the wall sconces. She had always known Ricci was spoiled, now she began to think he might be evil.

As suddenly as he had grabbed her, he released her and she sagged against the wall. His abrupt action shattered her train of thought, and she shook her head to clear it of the mental picture of Ricci as a villain. Fatigue was making her imagine things.

When she looked at him again, Ricci was just Ricci, a spoiled young man, no different from any other indulged aristocratic youth. It was just her misfortune that he was her cross to bear.

"I asked," Ricci emphasized each word with barely concealed venom, "why you cannot leave Paris."

She blinked to give herself an opportunity to compose herself. It would do her no good to defy him again, and it might very likely cause him to start nosing around for a reason. Then he would find Jason and she couldn't allow that.

Pushing away from the wall and taking several steps away from Ricci, she prevaricated. "You took me by surprise, that's all. What I meant, is that I don't perceive how I can leave Paris immediately. And how do you know that Louis has left Paris?"

He nearly snarled at her. "How dare you question me? Luigi may have allowed you to run his affairs, but he was an impotent old man. I am not, and you will do as I say."

Her hackles rose, and it was on the tip of her tongue to give him the verbal lashing he so richly deserved.

"Pardon me," Alphonse interrupted. He flashed a warning look at Genna before bowing deferentially to Ricci. "Milord, Conte, I could not help overhearing the conversation and I think it very wise of you to come immediately to the Contessa with this warning."

Alphonse's words affected Ricci like balm on an oozing sore, and Genna couldn't help but marvel at the change they wrought. A little deferential treatment and her betrothed became relaxed and suave. His personality was indeed mercurial, something she should be careful not to forget.

"No wonder my uncle valued you," Ricci said to the lackey, smugness settling over him like a mantle. Turning his attention back to Genna, he showed white, sharp teeth in the parody of a smile. "Had you been with me tonight, as was your duty, you would have heard the news about Louis the same way I did. The British ambassador announced that the French king fled last night around midnight."

Shocked dismay held Genna in its grip. If the British ambassador said Louis was gone, then it must be true. They must leave Paris immediately . . . but she dared not move Jason. He was too weak.

Hands clenched into fists in the folds of her dress, she managed to speak calmly. "Thank you, Ricci. We must prepare to leave as soon as possible." Not giving Ricci a chance to respond, she said to Alphonse, "Please go and awaken the servants. They must start packing at once, but only necessities. I will see to Aunt Hester." *And Jason.* Returning her attention to Ricci, she said, "We will meet you on the road leading to Brussels at first light."

Instead of leaving, Ricci stood his ground. "Do

you have funds for this journey?"

Genna regarded him as dispassionately as she could in her exhaustion and worry. Only Ricci would so crassly question her financial status. Curtly, she answered, "I have sufficient. Now I suggest that you return home and pack. We haven't much time before the French rally around Napoleon's banner again, and we must be gone before then."

Disgusted with him, and anxious to settle her own affairs, Genna twisted on her heel and sped into the dimness of the hallway toward Hester's bedroom without waiting to see Ricci's response to her words. She had neither the time nor the energy to waste on his selfishness.

Not wanting to alarm Hester, Genna knocked softly. When there was no response, she turned the brass doorknob and entered. The room was dark except for the small pool of yellow light cast on the peacefully sleeping Hester by a small candle the matron always kept burning by her bed.

Hastily, Genna approached the bed and gently shook Hester's plump shoulder. "Aunt Hester, you need to wake up."

Several more overtures and Hester finally opened sleep swollen eyes. "Wha . . . wha . . . Is that you Genna?" She peered around the room then back at Genna. "But 'tis not even light out. What outlandish start is this?"

"Dearest," Genna said patiently, "I don't want to alarm you, but you must leave Paris immediately. Louis has already gone and Napoleon will soon arrive."

Bolting up in her bed, her white lace and muslin nightcap askew, Hester moaned, "Oh dear, oh dear. What is to become of us with that devil loose again? He will murder all of us in our beds."

Genna swallowed a groan of exasperation. This was not the time to chide Hester for her fears. Her aunt was very likely close to the truth. "'Tis all right, dearest. Napoleon isn't here yet. We've time to escape, but you must get up this instant and pack a portmanteau with only essentials."

Hester bobbed her head up and down in agreement, her round face a study in fear. "Yes, yes. I will do so immediately."

"That's good," Genna said, infusing her voice with brisk matter-of-factness. It would do no good to allow Hester to wallow in her fears. "Be in the foyer in exactly thirty minutes. The servants will be there and the carriages will be waiting."

"Yes, yes," Hester mumbled, crawling out from under the morass of covers only to stop with one foot on the cold wooden floors. Her face wrinkled in concentration and she turned suspicious eyes on Genna. "You will be there, too, will you not?"

Genna met her aunt's gaze openly, knowing this was only the first of many battles she would have to wage in these early morning hours. Gently, but firmly, she said, "I will be there to say goodbye. But there's no time to discuss this. You must pack."

She turned and headed for the door, not wanting to get into an argument about a decision she had made without even realizing it. Nothing and no one would make her leave Jason. Hester's voice stopped her.

"'Tis that *man*. Do not bother to deny it. I knew the instant you allowed him into this house that he would be the ruination of you." Hester's complete body shook with angry convulsions as she stared her niece down. "I cannot force you to leave him, but you could be captured. You could be killed. Think about your mother and her feelings if something should happen to you. You are all she has."

Genna took a deep breath to armor herself against the anxiety Hester's words caused, but she couldn't shut out the possibilities Hester had so bluntly stated. She was all her mother had left, not to mention Hester's feelings, which the older woman had left unsaid. But Genna knew of the love her aunt had for her.

She hadn't considered her mother and aunt before; emotions swirled through her mind and heart. Jason would very likely die if she left him alone. And if she took him with them, he still might die, and he would also expose the others to the danger surrounding him. Either situation was intolerable, and in the end she could never leave Jason.

All Genna could reply with was a soft, "I cannot leave him."

"Humph! And you betrothed to marry another." Lips pursed in disgust, and brows drawn in worry, Hester turned away to start packing, but her final words drifted over her shoulder. "Love! You should care so much for your own blood."

Before Hester could inflict more verbal damage on her already ravaged nerves, Genna closed the door quietly behind herself. There was no time to wallow in the ramifications of her decision. In fact, there wasn't time for anything but preparations to see everyone hastily on their way. The others had a chance of reaching safety if they moved quickly.

Speeding down the hall, Genna pulled herself up sharply at Jason's door. More than anything, she wanted to look in and assure herself that he was doing well. But she knew that a moment would expand into minutes and then longer until she missed the appointed hour she had given her household. No, she would see her people on their journey and then she would come back. It was the only way.

The kitchen was a bustling hive of activity instead of slowing down for the night as it should have been. While the cook and all his helpers were French, the departure of Genna and her household meant they must leave also. But before being dismissed, they needed to pack enough provisions to last the group of fleeing English servants and Hester until they reached safety.

"Francois," Genna said, taking the chef's outstretched hands and squeezing lightly before releasing them and stepping backwards. "I will miss you dreadfully, but...." she shrugged much as the Frenchman would have.

"Milady, I know. My best wishes go with you." He put his fingers to his puckered mouth and threw a kiss. "You have been a good mistress, for all that you are half *Anglaise*."

"Scottish," she murmured, but his attention was already elsewhere. With a word of appreciation here and a nod of encouragement there, Genna made her way out of the kitchen and toward the hallway where her English servants should be assembling.

They were milling about impatiently when she arrived. In their midst, Aunt Hester stood like a large gelatin figurine in her serviceable green wool cape and plain hat and gloves. At the sight of Hester's sensible clothes, Genna let out the sigh of apprehension she hadn't realized she was holding.

Mounting several steps of the stairs, Genna turned back to face her people. A hush fell over the small group.

Genna looked around, making eye contact with each person before taking a deep breath. "As you know, Napoleon has escaped. What we just learned is that he's so close that Louis has fled Paris. However, the Conte di Ponti has given us enough warning that you should all be able to make Brussels safely. I have ordered all the horses but two to be put at your disposal. The carriages are loaded with the few possessions there is room for. Enough food has been packed for a week. When you reach Brussels, my secretary has been instructed to reimburse every one of you for a year's pay to help compensate for what you leave here."

Gasps of surprise, quickly followed by "Nay, my lady, ye mustn't," were silenced by her raised hand. She had to blink back tears at their refusal to take money they didn't feel they had earned, but she was adamant. She had brought them to Paris, her honor would not allow them to lose everything because they followed her.

"I brought you to Paris, I take responsibility for the loss of your possessions. There will be no further discussion. Now, all of you . . . my love goes with you. God speed."

No one moved. Bewildered, Genna stood where she was.

"Milady," Alphonse stepped forward, "are you not coming with us?"

Genna darted a glance at Hester, convinced that she was the one who put Alphonse up to this public questioning. Normally, he would have never done so on his own in front of other servants. Hester stood unnaturally straight, her eyes daring Genna to answer.

It hurt Genna to realize that she would have to be dictatorial, but she couldn't reveal her real reasons. Drawing herself up, head high, shoulders held regally, she said haughtily, "No, I will not be accompanying you. Much as it grieves me, I have unfinished business here in Paris. However, I will follow shortly."

At her display of aristocratic authority, the servants began to disperse quickly. Hester and Alphonse hung back.

"Genna," Hester remonstrated, "surely you are not serious about staying with that . . . that *man*. 'Tis unseemly, not to mention deadly."

"My lady," Alphonse insisted, "your aunt is correct. The man in the Gold Room has made his own bed, leave him to lie there."

"Both of you, I've had enough of your meddling." Anger spurted through Genna at their continued refusal to accept her decision. "*I* am in charge here, and you will do as I say."

Hester's face crumpled. "Oh Genna, child, we love you."

Immediately, Genna wrapped her arms tight around Hester's rotund figure. "I know, dear. I know." She wouldn't let the threatening tears fall. She would not. "But I must stay with him. I can't explain it. I only know that to leave him is more than I can do."

"I was afraid of this." Alphonse's sad voice came between the two women. "The way you look at him. Never have I seen you look at another that way."

Genna turned enough to put one hand on Alphonse's shoulder and their eyes met. "I knew you would understand, if only you tried."

"Milady, since you will stay, look in my room under the bed. There is a box. You may need what it contains."

Genna looked at him with raised eyebrows, but his eyes slid away from hers and he didn't elaborate. She knew from his refusal to explain that whatever he was referring to would upset Hester. Otherwise, Alphonse would have told her.

"What about Ricci," Hester interrupted, agitation making her voice squeak.

Worry puckered Genna's forehead. She had completely forgotten Ricci. "I don't know. I—"

"We will solve that problem when we come to it," Alphonse said briskly. "Possibly we will manage to miss him at the rendezvous."

Relief flooded Hester's features. "Yes, that would do nicely. I do not relish traveling with him anyway. He would whine the entire way. If there is anything I detest more than a whining man, I do not know it."

Hester's remark was like a ray of sunshine dispersing the shadows that had darkened Genna's spirit. "What a perfect solution."

For precious moments, the three basked in the comradeship of shared laughter before sobering.

"We had best be on our way," Alphonse said.

"Goodbye, darling," Genna said to Hester before taking Alphonse's hand. "Do not look so glum. I'll very likely beat you to Brussels."

Obviously puzzled by her choice of sanctuary, he asked, "Why Brussels?"

Genna lowered her voice. "Because that is where Wellington is supposed to go from Vienna to command the allied troops. There has been talk of nothing else all week. 'Twill be safer where the duke is."

He nodded his understanding before following Hester from the house.

Genna watched the small contingent of British servants and her aunt move into the fog-weighted morning. Swiping a hand across her eyes and sniffing, Genna closed the door.

"Oh," she said to herself, "I almost forgot." Opening the door, she removed the brass knocker. Now anyone looking at the house would assume that the residents were gone. She laid it on one of the marble-topped mahogany tables that flanked the entrance.

One last visit to the kitchen to ensure that the French servants were gone and then she would check on her patient. With luck, he would be sleeping and she would have time to decide how to tell him what had happened.

The house still around her, everyone gone, Genna stiffened her spine and lifted her feet as she made her way from the kitchen to the Gold Room. Each step she took on the wooden floors echoed hollowly, making her look behind herself in unfounded dread of what might be there. With the servants gone, there was no one to ensure the house wasn't broken into. She and Jason would have to be careful of that danger as well as the more obvious one of someone looking for him.

She sighed, and forced the worry away as she entered Jason's room and closed the door quietly behind herself. Jason was once more sprawled across the wide bed, the covers thrown off baring his skin to the cold air.

Exasperation made Genna shake her head. The man would be the cause of his own demise if he did not learn to sleep with the blankets on him instead of on the floor. Quickly and efficiently, she covered him without awakening him.

Late the next evening, she checked on him for the one hundredth time that day, only to see him still sleeping. She'd tried to keep her ministrations to a minimum and her noise nonexistent, but now the fire was out and the room was colder than she thought safe for his condition. She had to get the room warm. With economical motions, she knelt by the fire and began to prod the glowing coals into life.

"How many times must I tell you to let a servant do that?"

Startled by Jason's deep voice, she almost dropped the brass poker. Angling around, she frowned at his order. "And how many times must I tell you that wouldn't be wise?"

"Then let Alphonse do it." He grinned and pulled the blanket up around his shoulders.

His action in covering himself was strangely erotic to Genna, implying a wealth of possibilities that blatant exposure never could. It conjured a picture of Jason as he had laid in the bed that first night. The sheet had barely covered his hips and done nothing to hide the contours of his strong thighs. His torso had shown completely, the lean muscling of his ribs and stomach a sinewy ripple.

She felt a flush mounting her cheekbones that she was helpless to stop because she couldn't stop the memory. This man and everything about him inflamed her blood.

"Let Alphonse start the fire."

For an instant, his words meant nothing. She was still engrossed in remembering.

"Well?" he asked, asperity a heavy hand on the word.

Blinking, she concentrated on his question. "Alphonse? Because Alphonse isn't available. That's why."

Then she realized what she'd said. She was a fool

to have allowed her reaction to him as a man affect what she told him and when. After he had something to eat would be soon enough to let him know the others were gone. To keep him from seeing the consternation in her face, she turned her attention back to starting the fire.

"Why isn't Alphonse available?" Jason persisted, rising up in bed.

She ignored his question and took one last, nervous poke at the coals. The fire started. Satisfaction gave Genna the needed resolve to rise and dust her hands off on each other before turning to Jason. "I'll get you some hot soup."

"Not until you tell me why Alphonse couldn't have started the fire."

She glared at him. "Why are you always so difficult?"

He would badger her until she told him, and she didn't relish a battle of wills right this instant. Too much had already happened, and her reserves of stamina were severely depleted. She might as well tell him and be done with it.

Taking a deep breath, she squared her shoulders. "Alphonse is well on his way to Brussels by now."

"What!"

His voice was a roar matched by the fire behind her that was finally blazing with a vengeance of snapping sparks. One step backwards from Jason's intensity, and Genna felt the heat licking at her skirts. She was caught between two elemental forces, and she didn't know which she dreaded most.

Calmly, her hands clenched together in front of her to still their tendency to shake. She walked toward the bed. "Napoleon has escaped Elba and is on his way here. Louis fled two days ago. Alphonse and the rest of my English servants are on their way to Brussels."

Before she could add the rest of the story, Jason collapsed back onto the pillows and groaned. The sound was like that of an enraged bull or someone in great pain. Genna ran the remaining distance separating them, her heart pounding in fear that he had suffered a relapse.

"Jason, oh, Jason," she said, agony squeezing her chest.

Reaching for him, she was shocked motionless when his hand fell away from his forehead and she saw his eyes. Dangerous slits, they blazed with anger and potential violence. The muscles in his neck were knotted, and his shoulders were bunched with restrained fury.

Her arms dropped to her sides and uncertain of what was happening, she asked softly, "Jason?"

His fist slammed into the pillow, ripping the linen casing and sending feathers scattering in the air. "Damnation! The whole world knows about Napoleon's escape. The most important information I've gleaned in ten years, and I couldn't deliver it in time."

Now she understood. He was berating himself for what he percevied as his own failure. Tentatively, she put a hand on his arm. "'Tis not your fault. You've been unable to even get out of your bed, let alone reach Brussels."

He shook her hand off and squeezed his eyes shut. In a suddenly weary voice, he said, "Go away. I need to think about what to do next."

The straight, unyielding line of his thinned mouth brooked no interference. Hurt, and undecided on what was best, she took one step back toward the door. He needed her. "I won't leave."

For an eternity, he lay motionless, his eyes shut, the sheet draped across his hips. Even the tapering strength of his waist and thighs did nothing to distract Genna from her determination to be here for him. Emotionally, he meant more to her than any admiration from his masculinity.

"Blasted woman," he finally growled, a lopsided, rueful grin twisting his well-defined lips. "You've more pluck than many a man I've met."

She chuckled, relieved at his release of self-directed anger and more thankful than she cared to consider that he had allowed her to stay. "Probably because I've nursed more stubborn, opinionated males than any man you know."

"Vixen." The word was an emotional catharsis, and his mouth softened and his back relaxed. Then his eyes, those moss green orbs that reflected his innermost thoughts, turned golden.

Genna's stomach tightened with the awareness of his closeness. Musk clung to him, heightening her perceptions of the crisp blond and sandy brown hairs curling over his upper torso and of the hardening of his one nipple exposed to the cold air. Somehow, she resisted the urge to touch that nubbin of bronze skin, a shade darker than the flesh surrounding it, even as she swallowed the words of love rising in her throat.

She was committed to another man, and she forbade herself to dishonor her promise because Jason aroused feelings in her that she had never known existed before. She had to be stronger than that.

Forcing herself to smile roguishly at temptation as he reclined on the bed, Genna said, "I may be a vixen, but you drive me to it. Now," she moved away from his disturbing influence and said briskly, "I'll get you some broth. You need to regain your strength quickly."

His eyelids drooped. "Genna, you said all the servants were gone." She nodded. "Then we're alone in this house?"

Unsure whether he was angry, she met his gaze squarely. "Yes."

"And Napoleon is on the loose."

"Yes."

"Why did you stay? I'm no one to you. Until several weeks ago you didn't even know I existed."

What could she tell him? She didn't understand herself. Against her volition, her fingers plucked at the lace on one wrist. "You're sick. If I left, you might not recover, or someone might discover you. . . ." She took a deep breath and willed her hands to fall gracefully to her sides. "Having rescued you from certain death in the streets, I've a commitment to ensure that you live. I would've done the same for anyone."

The air left his lungs in a sudden rush and his mouth hardened. "You've said that before. Then you had best work hard, for I intend to have the two of us out of Paris by tomorrow evening."

"That's much too soon."

His hands clenched into fists. "It's much too late. Every second we stay here, we increase our chances of being caught a thousandfold. We'll be gone by tomorrow evening. I would leave this instant, but realize that I must have some of my strength back if I'm to protect you on the journey. I am not so stupid as to hare off like a rabbit being chased by the fox."

She heard the irritation in his voice and saw the frustration in every tense line of his body. And even though she had no intentions of letting him make that long and cold journey in his current condition, she realized that now wasn't the time to argue with him.

"We will see," she murmured.

Chapter Six

"*What* are you doing?" Genna demanded, kicking the door shut behind herself.

Jason was in the middle of the room, a sheet wrapped around his hips, and a brass fire poker in his right hand supporting him as he moved hesitantly around.

"What does it look like?" he asked sarcastically. "You won't feed me anything but broth and refuse to bring me decent clothes. I intend to take matters into my own hands."

"Stubborn as a mule, that's what you are." She plopped the tray she had brought from the kitchen on a table and advanced on him, fists on hips. "It has only been six hours since you awoke this morning, and only forty-eight hours since your fever broke. You expect too much."

He rounded on her, anger delineating every muscle in his shoulders and arms. "I do not expect enough. Napoleon is on the loose. I *must* leave here and I won't allow you to stay here when I go, even though taking you with me will increase my travel time. And time is a commodity I've precious little of."

His fury buffeted her, and unconsciously Genna took a sliding step backwards. His cruel words, naming her a burden, hurt more than they should have. She should let them pass, realizing he was angry with himself and therefore with everyone else. But her own exhaustion and worry kept her from thinking clearly. Only the pain she felt at his rejection mattered.

"Then go! Go into the cold like a lamb to the slaughter. Leave me behind so that you won't be slowed. What am I to you? Nothing! Nothing, and I know it." One hand slashed down and in the same motion she twirled around and sped for the door. Her other hand swiped viciously at tears that would not be denied.

"Genna!"

Her name was a cannon shot. Fingers wrapped around the door handle, she stopped; chest heaving, eyes squeezed shut as she struggled for control.

"Genna."

The thump of the poker he used as a cane was followed by the heavy then lighter sound of his feet and another thump of the poker. He was coming after her. She should leave, now, before he reached her. He was everything she didn't need, couldn't succumb to. And he didn't even want her.

The poker fell to the floor with a muted clank and then his hands were on her shoulders. Shivers raced down Genna's arms, leaving gooseflesh in their wake, and her hand fell away from the door into a fist by her side. What was he going to do to her? What would she let him do?

"Please," she said, gulping back the sobs that were only now beginning to abate. "Let me go."

"God, I wish I could."

The anguish in his voice matched the agony in her heart. What were they doing to each other? She didn't know, but she couldn't allow this emotional turmoil to continue. Not answering him, she twisted the doorknob and pulled.

His right palm slammed on the oak door, thrusting it shut with a bang before returning to her shoulders. His fingers tightened on her skin and he tried to turn her.

"Genna, look at me."

Shaking her head vigorously, she said, "No. Let me go. We're both tired. You're sick and I'm very nearly sick from lack of rest. It's been a long day."

When she resisted his efforts to turn her, he pulled her back into his embrace. Taken by surprise, Genna tumbled until her spine pressed against his chest. The back of her head nestled in the curve between his neck and shoulder, and his chin nuzzled her temple, the whiskers grazing her skin like a fine bristled brush. The breath left her body in one long sigh of shocked delight. She felt as though she had come to rest after a long and arduous journey.

"Genna," he said softly, his breath moving the hair around her ear like a warm, tropical breeze. "I'm sorry for my temper. You didn't deserve my anger."

Lightly, oh so lightly, his mouth moved against her earlobe, and she felt her knees weaken and her balance become dependent upon the solidity of his chest against her back. His lips were like burning embers as they trailed down the side of her neck, causing her to arch her chin upward to give him better access to the base of her throat.

"That's right, Genna, move for me," he murmured against her heated skin.

Unconsciously, she turned into his embrace, her head thrown backwards as his tongue darted at the heated pulse where her collarbone rose from the lace of her bodice.

Somehow, she did not know how, she found herself cradled in his arms as he leaned against the closed door for support. His hands roamed over the knotted curves of her back, stopping short at the flare of her hips only to move back up to the tightness of her shoulder blades. He made her feel like a desirable woman.

"Genna," he said, "when you press yourself against me, all I can think of is making love to you."

His words sent sparks coursing through her body, turning her legs weak and her skin hot. She wanted him to make love to her; this instant, on the floor, if that's what he desired. She wanted him to take her.

His flesh against hers was tinder sending flames rushing through her body. Her stomach clenched in pleasurable ripples as his mouth moved gently across hers, and his tongue slipped along the heated contours of her lips.

Lifting his mouth a fraction from hers, Jason breathed, "You fit perfectly to me."

His words were fuel to the fire he had ignited. Genna raised her arms to run her fingers through the cool thickness of his blond hair, smoothing back the lock on his forehead before plunging again into the tactile silkiness. Then, lips parted, unable to resist the desire he kindled in her, she pulled him to her, completely surrendering to her longing for him.

They merged with an intensity that obliterated any lingering doubts Genna had. This man was all she wanted, all she needed.

Jason's tongue plumbed her depths, running along her teeth, making Genna moan deep in her throat with pleasure. She returned the caress, flicking her tongue with his like two flames dancing heavenward.

His hands slid lower until they cupped around her hips, and he pulled her closer. "Oh!" Genna gasped, feeling the fullness of his arousal hard against the soft swell of her belly.

Barely lifting his head, Jason grinned down at her. "I think I'm well, don't you?"

Flushing from arousal and embarrassment, Genna met his look boldly. "Perhaps, but just because you're capable is no reason to take the chance."

He kissed her lightly on the lips, nipping at her underlip before sucking it into his mouth. "You think not? I don't think I can continue this play without going deeper."

Unimaginable sensations churned in Genna as

he persisted in nuzzling and suckling her sensitive skin. The edges of her mind told her she should not be succumbing to him, but her body pressed closer to his, reveling in the firmness of his muscles. One hand strayed from his hair and began to toy with his left nipple. Her fingers rubbed against the nubbin and cavorted in the swirl of crisp hair surrounding it.

"Ge . . . enna." He took her mouth with renewed passion.

A gurgle of laughter welled up in her chest.

Without warning, Jason's head jerked up and his hands stilled their kneading of her hips. Bewilderment froze Genna against him. "What?"

Not answering, he shook his head and put one finger to his lips for silence. Genna watched him with apprehension. Gone was the intense look of the lover, and in its place she saw a dangerous animal poised for action. But what had wrought this change? Then she heard it.

Someone was moving stealthily down the hallway. The footfalls were muffled, but nothing could mute the sound of a door opening. Her heart began to pound in fast, agitated spurts. With astonished eyes, she looked at Jason.

He met her look and smiled, a grim stretch of his lips that boded ill for the person lurking outside. Pantomiming, he directed her to get under the bed. She balked, shaking her head no.

His eyes flared and his chin hardened. The fingers that had just held her gently bit into her flesh, compelling her to move. His mouth moved and silent words beat at her. "Damn it, get under the bed!"

Outside, the footsteps began again. Any second and they would be at the door behind Jason's back. Fear for his safety was a noose around Genna's throat. Then before she knew what he was doing, she found herself spun around and her shoulders pushed away.

She stumbled. Her hand flashed to her mouth, muffling her automatic exclamation. She wouldn't betray them. Reaching out to steady herself, she cast one last glance over her shoulder as she made her way to the bed.

Jason stooped and picked up the poker.

Sliding under the bed, the last thing Genna saw was Jason raising the poker and positioning himself behind the door. Whoever was searching the house would be met with a surprise. She squirmed around until she could see Jason once more.

Surreptitiously, the door inched open. The breath caught in Genna's throat, but she refused to close her eyes. If Jason needed help, she would go to him. No matter what.

The flickering light from the fireplace barely reached the shadowy figure slinking into the room. A man, dressed in dark clothes, stepped cautiously through the door. He took another pace forward. Then another.

A glint of flame flashed on the poker as it came down. There was a sickening crunch. The figure sank to the ground.

Genna scrambled out from under the bed. Fist in her mouth, she rushed to Jason who was bent over the man.

"What? Who?" The questions tumbled from Genna as quickly as the blood raced through her veins. "Is he dead?"

"Get the knife," Jason ordered, without sparing her a glance as he rifled through the man's clothing.

Searching the floor, Genna found a wicked looking blade at least ten inches long. She sucked in air. Was this the man who had attacked Jason before? Was this the weapon Jason was still recovering from? Faintness washed over her.

No! she chided herself. This was no time for frailty. Jason needed her. Forcing herself to take deep breaths, she steadied herself.

"Damnation!" Jason hissed. "There's nothing on him to give any clue as to his identity."

"Is he dead?" Genna asked again, wondering what they would do if he were.

Distracted, Jason ran one hand through his hair as he frowned at her repeated questions. "Does it matter?"

She gulped. The man would have killed them, but still. . . . "To me."

Jason sighed in exasperation. "No, he's not dead. Although it would be better for us if he were."

Startled, she stared at him. There was not a shred of remorse in his voice or face for what he had said. Was he a cold-blooded killer? What manner of man was he?

Cursing, Jason grabbed the poker and levered himself to a standing position. "Genna, don't look at me as though I'm a monster. This man will kill us if he gets the slightest chance. I don't relish having a danger like this in the same house where I sleep."

Still uncertain about Jason, and even more perplexed about the feelings for him that would not seem to die or even lessen even after what he'd just said and done, Genna managed to nod. He was right, even though his ruthlessness bothered her.

"Damn it, Genna. Stop looking at me as though I've just killed him. I have not! But I would if need be."

The harsh reality of his words slammed into Genna, like a fist into her stomach. She didn't know Jason. Didn't know him at all. Unable to meet the cold determination in his eyes, she turned her back on him and stared unseeing at the brightness of the fire.

Hands descended on Genna, and she was twirled around before she even realized Jason was behind her. Head flung back, she met his blazing eyes defiantly.

"Don't condemn me, Genna."

Silently, she listened to him, but could not bring herself to voice the words she knew he wanted to hear. It was all too new and too violent for her.

Without warning, he yanked her to him. His mouth descended on hers in a crushing, punishing caress. His teeth nipped at her lips, demanding entrance. When she refused, he bit her.

Gasping, she parted her lips and he surged in. His tongue plunged deeply, ravaging her senses.

He demanded a response from her, forced her to bend to his will until she lay like a limp doll in his arms.

When he at last gentled her defiance, the kiss softened. His hands rose and cupped her face gently. Showering tiny kisses on her forehead, cheeks, and chin, he said, "Be warned, I will do anything to protect you. Even kill."

Chapter Seven

Genna stared up at his hard visage, trying to see in him the man she was falling in love with. Where was the tender companion with the ready wit and caring compassion? Obliterated by the mask of the spy. *And it didn't matter.* Whoever he really was, she wanted him.

In this instant of time, she didn't care about her promise to Luigi. All that mattered was that she and Jason were together, and that they would survive together.

But she knew that was wrong. Her honor bade her to move away from Jason. Firming her chin, hoping to gain the strength of will to resist him, she moved away. Pointing vaguely at the still body, she asked, "Shouldn't we do something about him?"

"We'll tie him up and stash him somewhere where he won't be found easily."

After long, strenuous minutes, their assailant was packed away in the wardrobe and out of sight.

Genna wiped her brow with the back of her hand. "Is he the man who attacked you before?"

Jason lowered himself to the bed by supporting his weight on the poker. Even with Genna's help, hoisting their assailant into the wardrobe hadn't been easy. Much as he hated to admit it, even to himself, she was right. He wasn't ready to travel.

His mouth tightened as he answered her question. "I don't know. Possibly. I didn't get a good look at the person who knifed me. He wore a mask over the lower portion of his face."

"Oh. Still, how did this man find you here?"

Leaning back on the pillows, Jason took deep breaths, willing his body to relax and the pain to lessen. "I don't know unless he was able to follow my trail." He paused to reposition himself, wincing at the sharp pull on his wound. "I thought I was more careful than to drip blood, but perhaps not."

"Will there be others?"

He glanced up in time to see the worry puckering her brow before she turned away. Damn! He didn't want to involve her in this. But he had and it was too late to pull back. Whether he liked it or not, she was as deeply woven into the fabric of his mission as if she had been with him from the beginning.

"Genna, I don't know. Probably." Just answering her in monosyllables drained what little stamina he had left. "We need to leave soon. I need to have real food, not broth."

She twisted on her heel and stared him down. Any other time Jason would have enjoyed her show of spirit and even baited her, but not now.

"Either you bring me the food I need, Genna, or I'll have to descend to the kitchen and fend for myself."

"You leave me little choice," she muttered.

"No," he answered, his voice level and his head motioning in the direction of the wardrobe where they'd put the intruder after binding and gagging him, "*he* leaves you little choice. If he's nosing around here, then chances are high that others will follow."

Jason willed her to agree with him. He didn't have the strength to fight her as well as his body's weakness.

"I'll get you beef," she finally said, "and bread and cheese."

He could tell she would do it grudgingly, and he wished she would willingly help him to do what was necessary. But whether she did or not, he would prevail. "Good. While you're getting it, pack enough for a week."

"What?"

He raised one eyebrow. "You heard me. And change clothes while you're about it. Put on some maid's skirt and blouse. You'll need a heavy wool cape and gloves and sensible boots." He frowned, hoping to impress upon her the urgency. "I'll need serviceable breeches and a coat and cape. While you're getting the food, I'll search the servants' quarters." Under his breath, he muttered, "If only I had a weapon."

"You want a weapon?"

He studied her face, looking for the revulsion he

was sure she was feeling for him. "Yes, Genna. I need something in case we're attacked on the road. I can't count on always being lucky enough to hear someone sneaking up on us or on being able to hide until I can hit that person on the head."

"Perhaps I can find something," she said, consideration wrinkling her brow.

Hope that she was beginning to accept what he must do lightened his mood. "If you can, that would be welcome. And Genna," he paused, letting his gaze wander hungrily over her face, wanting to kiss the small worried pucker from her coral lips, "I hope to God I can protect you from the hazards ahead. I'll do anything necessary to get you safely to Brussels."

She sighed, her shoulders drooping slightly. "I know you're doing what you feel is necessary, Jason, and I'm sorry to be such a trial to you. I'll do better."

He stepped forward and pressed a kiss on her lips, fighting the urge in his loins to deepen the caress. "You are never a burden, Genna. I only wish we'd met under different circumstances."

He'd expected resigned understanding from her, not deep brown eyes that looked at him as though he'd just struck her a mortal blow. What had he done to bring this pain about? He lifted her chin so that he could gaze deeply into her eyes. "Genna, what have I done that you look at me this way?"

Instead of answering him, she shook her head free of his caress and left the room without a backwards glance. Jason watched her until the door closed.

Something was wrong, and he had no idea what. Bending to retrieve the knife that his attacker had intended to use on him, Jason pondered Genna's actions. He didn't think she was afraid of their journey, and she'd said she might be able to get him a weapon so it couldn't still be squeamishness about the violence he'd used to knock the intruder out.

He couldn't figure out what was wrong and he didn't have the time or energy to continue this train of thought. Right now, he had to move quickly. Soon the man would be rousing and the drapery cord binding the spy's feet and wrists wouldn't hold for long after that.

Using the poker as a cane, Jason moved to the door. He dreaded having to climb the stairs to the servants' quarters, but knew he must. Well, the sooner started, the sooner done.

In the kitchen, a mouse scuttled under the table, making Genna jump, one hand clutching her skirts high. The blood pounded painfully in her ears for several minutes before she could calm herself. Her reaction to the mouse was unwarranted; a sign of how distraught she was.

She had to admit that Jason was right. They were in more danger staying here than going. She needed to stop fighting him and help.

Efficient movements soon had a week's rations of meat, cheese and bread packed in oiled bags. On a plate she heaped all the rich food Jason could dream of and added a mug of warm milk to the bounty.

She put it all on a tray and started for the door just as Jason entered, using the poker as a crutch. In place of the sheet, he had on clothes found in some footman's chest. A slouching wool hat rode low over his brow, shading his eyes and casting a shadow over his square jaw. His own boots, scuffed but sturdy, showed beneath the heavy folds of a brown cape.

"Do I pass muster?" At her nod, he smiled. "Good. Then perhaps I can fool my enemies. Whoever they may be." Taking the hat off, he tossed it on the table beside his plate and dug in. Between mouthfuls he said, "I'm surprised you didn't fix gruel."

Genna's immediate response was anger that he would doubt her, but she curbed it, realizing that he didn't know her well . . . just as she didn't know him. "When I say I will do something, I do it."

Jason grunted his acceptance of that and continued eating. Five minutes later, he thought his stomach would split. He hadn't eaten a third of what Genna had served him, but he couldn't take another bite. It shouldn't have surprised him. This wasn't the first time he had been wounded, and he knew he was pushing himself too fast. Still, his weakness irritated him.

When he looked across at Genna, he noticed for the first time since entering that she still hadn't changed. Fury knotted his stomach, making it even harder for him to keep the heavy food down.

"Genna," he said so quietly that she had to lean forward to hear, "I thought I told you to change clothes."

Patches of angry color rode her high cheekbones, turning her skin to golden peach. "I've been preparing the food as you instructed. When I'm able to do two things simultaneously, one in the kitchen and the other in the bedroom, I will inform you."

Before he could apologize for losing his temper, she rose majestically, her back straight and her head held high. Jason knew he'd been wrong to chastise her so quickly, but his stamina was fading rapidly and he'd taken his frustrations out on her.

And he had plenty of frustrations where she was concerned. He smiled in rueful appreciation as he watched her swaying hips. How close he had come to burying himself in their lush fullness. If that spy hadn't come along when he did, Jason knew he would have taken Genna in the middle of the floor with no regard for anything else but the hard desire she evoked in him.

Memories of her in his arms rushed through his body until he ached with suppressed needs. She was more woman than he had ever encountered before, and he wanted her with an urgency that surprised him with its intensity. He had never desired a woman so completely, and under any other circumstances he would have claimed her totally.

But now wasn't the time. Their lives were at stake, and he was the only one skilled enough to get them out of France safely. They couldn't afford for him to be distracted by visions of making love to her.

Discipline took over, and Jason made himself eat more. He was finishing the last of the beef when Genna entered the kitchen.

"Damn," he cursed under his breath. Even dressed in a patched and torn wool skirt, a dingy muslin shirt that had seen better days, and a pair of scuffed riding boots, she was still beautiful enough to be a danger to them. Any man who saw her would gladly knife him in the back to have her.

"What's the matter now?" she demanded, arms akimbo.

He looked at her in frank disbelief. Didn't she know how alluring she was? If anything, the worn clothes accented the full swell of her bosom and the flaring womanliness of her hips. The urge to bury himself deeply inside her was so powerful that Jason had to look away.

"Did you find a cape?" he growled, hoping that a mantle would cover her sufficiently.

"Yes, and something even more important. Something that might even put a smile on your scowling face." Impudently, she strutted toward him.

Jason watched her with narrowed eyes, swallowing hard to keep down his rising arousal. "Damn," he muttered, fighting the urge to reach out for her and claim the heavy orbs of her breasts with his mouth.

Only when she shoved the box under his nose, did Jason realize she carried something in her hands. It was made of sandalwood polished to a satin finish and had brass fittings. Inside was a matched pair of Manton dueling pistols, their handles done in gold with the initials LP entwined.

He looked at Genna, one eyebrow raised in query.

"Alphonse had them. They were under his bed."

"How did you know?"

"Alphonse told me when he left. They belonged to Luigi."

"Your husband." Jealousy, fierce and primitive, ripped through Jason at Genna's mention of her dead husband. Just knowing that someone had made love to Genna was enough to tear Jason's guts. It did no good to remind himself that the man was no rival. He knew his response wasn't healthy, but the emotion still ripped through him.

"Yes, my dead husband. I would have gotten them sooner, but I honestly forgot about them." In a small voice, she added, "They would have been helpful with the man upstairs. You wouldn't have had to put yourself at such risk by hiding behind the door."

The remorse in her eyes overrode Jason's jealousy. Genna cared for him now, and he intended to see that it remained that way. "They might have helped. Probably they would've only made things harder."

Disbelief washed all over her, she asked, "Harder? I don't see how."

Jason sighed and ran a hand through his hair. Things were getting so complicated, and his wound was beginning to hurt again and they had to leave soon. "With the poker I could knock him unconscious. With the pistols I would have had to shoot him in order to be able to safely tie him up. I may be a spy, but I only kill when there's no other way."

Comprehension dawned and Genna nodded her head in understanding. "I see. If he'd been conscious and one of us had attempted to tie him up, he might have grabbed that person as a shield even with a gun aimed at him."

"That's always a possibility." Rising, Jason supported himself with his palms on the heavy oak parson's table. "But enough. We must go."

Genna ran to him and put her shoulder under his. Together they gathered up the bags of food and a bag with medicinals for Jason's wound. Then, donning their capes, they made for the stables in the back of the house.

Leaving Jason propped against the stable door, Genna entered and lit a candle. Relief flooded her when she saw the two thoroughbred mares in their stalls as she had instructed. Until now, she had refused to even consider what they would do if the horses hadn't been there.

Shortly, she had them saddled; one with a sidesaddle.

"We need two bags of oats," Jason said, his voice sounding eerie as the early evening mist floated several inches above the ground.

When she finally led the horses out of the stable, Jason's teeth were clenched together as he withstood the increasing ache in his side. It was all he could do not to slide down the door and sprawl on the cobbles. His reserves were about used up and there were still hours of riding ahead of them.

Then he got his first good look at the horses and groaned. "Bloody hell. We're in for it now."

Tying the provisions to the saddles, Genna glanced over her shoulder at him. "What do you mean? We're almost gone."

Jason rubbed his aching shoulder muscle just above the bandage, and tried to make his voice sound as though riding thoroughbred horses was the normal thing to do instead of the prerequisite of the wealthy. "We're almost gone from the house, but we still have to get through Paris. After that we must go through the countryside between here and Brussels which will soon be teeming with men loyal to Bonaparte. Riding horses that are worth more than an ordinary man could earn in his lifetime isn't the smartest way to stay incognito."

"Oh." Genna hadn't considered that when she'd given the order. "I was only thinking of speed."

Jason pushed himself off from the wall, staggering slightly before he reached the mare he was to ride. "I know, and that's definitely something to consider. We will simply exchange these at the first opportunity. In the mean time, they can get us swiftly gone."

He didn't voice his worries that the horses might precipitate an attack on them before they were even out of Paris. Genna didn't need that additional worry.

"Right now," he said, going back into the stable

and coming out with a worn blanket which he began to rip into strips with the knife, "we'll wrap these around the horse's hooves to muffle the sound. 'Twill help us move stealthily."

Immediately comprehending what he was doing, Genna took the pieces of blanket that he handed to her and began winding them around each animal's foot. When that was finished, she tied the bags of provisions to the saddles and guided her horse to the mounting block.

With an economy of motion, she hoisted herself up and hooked her knee around the horn. There wasn't much to her skirts, but what she had she carefully arranged to hide as much of her legs as possible. As it was, a good foot of her riding boots still showed.

"You would do better astride," Jason said, the strain of having mounted evident in his voice.

She knew he was very likely right, but there was nothing for it. "I know. But the servants took the other horses and the saddles. They left Lady at my request. The groom also left the saddle I use. Unfortunately, it's a sidesaddle. However, I won't slow us down."

"No," he muttered. "I'll be the one to do that."

Hunched down in the saddle, Jason urged his mare forward. One hand held the reins, the other gripped the knife taken from their visitor. While it was too early for members of the aristocracy to be about, it was late enough to be dark. There was no telling who lurked in the shadows or what they would do to get the expensive animals.

Overhead, thunderclouds added to the dampness and made the cold breeze bite deeply. Jason shivered, feeling the edges of his wound pull.

"Jason," Genna whispered, "I'll lead. I know the way out of Paris."

Jason considered. He didn't doubt that she knew the way, and it was highly unlikely that anyone attacking them would do so from the front. He pulled his horse back to allow Genna to pass him. "Go ahead."

At his nod, she urged her mare into a canter. Jason followed suit. Even though it was one of the more comfortable gaits a horse had, it jarred his wound with every step. Jason gritted his teeth to prevent the groan rising in his throat from escaping.

As painful as the ride was, he didn't relax his vigil, his eyes darted back and forth. Every half a block he turned in the saddle to study the area behind them. . . . Nothing.

By the time they left the main stand of houses and shops behind them, he was clenching the reins so tightly that his shoulders ached. Yet, even now, with only an occasional building, he knew they couldn't let up. He didn't hear anyone following them, but that didn't mean no one was. Many a time he had wrapped his horse's hooves to muffle the sounds, just as they had, and pursued his quarry unsuspected.

At last, when they had seen no buildings for a count of five thousand, Jason caught up to Genna and signaled her to stop. The horses weren't winded, but Jason felt as though he had just raced from London to Brighton, setting a new record.

Surreptitiously, Jason pocketed the filched knife in the specially made sheath in his boot, which he'd found empty when he put the boots on. He'd realized that Alphonse must have taken the knife when he undressed him that first night.

Then, eyes constantly scanning the surrounding country, he said, "There's barely enough light to follow the road, with the clouds obscuring the moon. But that's good for us."

Genna snorted. "So long as we don't become lost."

Unable to determine her feelings from the abrupt words, Jason peered through the darkness separating them. Beads of moisture were gathering on the edge of her wool cape where its hood hung over her forehead. He couldn't see her eyes, even if there had been enough light.

Giving up on subtlety, he baldly asked, "Are you afraid?"

"Yes."

The curt word was rife with unspoken emotions and his heart went out to her. How could he comfort her? He wasn't even sure he should try. They might be out of Paris, but they were far from Brussels. Every turn in the road might confront them with French troops or even French peasants loyal to Bonaparte and ready to take prisoners or worse. All he could do was speak honestly and not belittle her feelings.

"You're smart to be fearful. 'Tis the ones who are too cocksure to worry who end up not making it."

"Thank you," she said quietly.

More than anything, he wanted to reach for her and draw her onto the saddle with him. He couldn't. They were wasting precious time as it was.

"You're welcome. But enough of that. We must ride like Bonaparte himself is after us for as long as these horses last." But how long would *he* last? It was a question he didn't want to face.

Genna kept pace with Jason, one hand on the reins and the other gripping the folds of her cape tightly around her neck and face. Clouds skated across the full moon making shadows dance on the uneven terrain they traveled. Every once in a while, she heard the lonely hooting of an owl or the crackle of an animal moving through the bracken lining the road.

She didn't know how far they had come or how far they had to go tonight before Jason would allow them to rest. Her fingers, even in the fur lined leather gloves she wore, were cold to the point that several times she lost hold of her cape.

Her back was beginning to ache from the sidesaddle, and it would be hard for her to dismount. She pushed her discomfort aside. If this mad run was difficult for her, it would be much more difficult on Jason.

The moon was low in the sky when Jason at last raised his hand and Genna was able to pull in her mount. Vapor rose from the flaring nostrils of both mares and their sides expanded and shrank like bellows. It wasn't a minute too soon, Genna decided, patting the sweat streaked neck of her horse.

"'Twill be daylight in a couple hours," Jason said, his breath puffing like smoke. "We must find shelter and get some sleep. Tomorrow will be tougher."

Genna laughed harshly. "Shelter? When we can barely see far enough ahead to keep the horses from stumbling in a hole?" Only after the words were out, did she realize how like a shrew they made her sound. Jason didn't need her temper on top of the other problems plaguing him.

Guiding her horse next to Jason's, she reached for one of his hands where it rested on his knee. Even through the thick gloves he wore, she could feel how he shook. Contrition at his discomfort and indignation at his determination not to call it quits sooner gave an edge to her voice. "You've pressed yourself too hard."

"I had . . . no . . . choice."

His breathing was labored, but he sat his saddle straight. Admiration swelled her chest as she looked at him. "You stubborn, bullheaded man. How can I get you well when you take so little care of yourself?"

"Show me another alternative, and I'll let you rule my every action."

Even though he said it lightly, the truth of his words was irrefutable. They weren't safe yet.

"Come along," he said when she didn't reply. "I think there's a branch in the road. Perhaps 'tis the path to a farm house."

Genna doubted it, but didn't want to darken their mood further. Gently urging her mare on, she followed Jason down the lane that was little bigger than a foot path. If there were shelter to be had, however meager it might be, she wanted it.

The clouds that had threatened rain all night finally let loose their burden. This was all they needed, Genna thought sourly. Luck being what it was, Jason would now catch an inflammation of the lungs.

"I see something," Jason said, his mare breaking into a trot.

Genna couldn't believe her eyes, but there it was. Yellow light flickered between rain drops. Perhaps they would have shelter; a nice warm bed and something hot to eat. The self-delusion lasted only as long as it took for her to see Jason veer to the left and go around the house.

When she caught up with him, he was dismounted and struggling to open the wide doors of a rickety barn. The stubborn fool!

Lady wasn't fully stopped before Genna threw herself from the saddle to aid Jason. She landed with a thud and her right leg gave out.

"Oh!" The exclamation of pain tore from her as her ankle twisted. The last thing they needed was for her to have a sprained ankle.

Jason was immediately beside her, his arm circling her waist. His warm breath fanned her cheek as he bent close to gaze into her face.

"Are you hurt?" he asked. "I would carry you, but...."

Tears were very near the surface as Genna struggled to stand unaided. He was too weak to support her. He should be in the barn, not out here worrying about her.

"I'm fine," she stated, using all her effort to keep her voice from catching. "We need to get inside. You'll be soaked through, if you aren't already."

"The door is open enough for us to squeeze through with the horses single file. We should be able to get two or three hours of sleep before the farmer is up."

Dazed, hungry, cold, and angry with her own incompetence, Genna numbly followed him. Only after the horses were taken care of and she and Jason were chewing on dry, cold beef did Genna think further.

"Must we leave so quickly? You need a good night's rest. If you don't get some sleep, I can't vouch for your getting better."

Worry for him was like a canker in her heart that refused to heal. Somehow, some way, she had to ensure that he mended. She had risked so much and grown to feel so deeply for him, that the mere inkling that he mightn't recuperate was more than she could bear.

"We must be gone before light and the farmer is up and about. The fewer people who see us, the harder it will be for anyone to trace us." Jason grunted as he rose and began piling hay into one mound. "There are several routes from Paris to Brussels and we could be on any of them." He grinned at her over his shoulder.

He was right and she knew it. "Why are you only making one bed?" she asked, watching him. The blood in her veins began to course through her, warming her in spite of the cold.

He rocked back onto his haunches, his brows

pinched by pain and exhaustion. "We haven't enough blankets to keep both of us warm if we sleep parted. So...." He trailed off, straining to see her reaction in the pale light cast by the moon which streamed through the one opening in the upper story. "But first, let me see your ankle."

Again, he was right. Genna took a long shuddering breath, realizing that they would be spending the night lying together. Then her common sense asserted itself. Both of them were ready to drop where they were, neither would have the drive to do more than sleep.

Frowning, he squatted in front of her and pulled off her boot. Then he began to probe for any swelling or damage. His hands were gentle on her swollen flesh. In spite of all Genna's silent reminders that they were in no position to be amorous, she couldn't stop the tingling warmth his touch evoked.

As he examined her, she closed her eyes to block out the concern on his face. She was no young virgin without experience of a man's touch; she was a widow who had endured a man's pleasure as her duty. Still, this intense reaction to Jason's touch was new; it had been from the start.

"There doesn't seem to be any damage," he finally said. "Now we'd best get what little sleep we can."

He was so pragmatic that Genna bit her lip embarrassed by her own susceptibility to his slightest caress. He was so pragmatic that she could be no less.

Together they snuggled into the hay and piled

their capes and blankets on top. Genna took herself firmly to task when Jason's arm brushed against her bosom, causing her nipples to harden and her breasts to swell. And when his hand went around her waist and pulled her flush to his chest, it was all she could do not to raise her mouth the scant inches it would take for her to nuzzle his neck.

"Genna," he said, his voice rough, "I know this is compromising, and . . ." he sighed, "I wish it were more so, but without the warmth of each other's body we'll get badly chilled."

His breath was a warm stroke on her cheek. She nodded, afraid to speak for the emotions rioting in her heart. It felt so good to be held close to the long, hard muscles of his body. It would feel even better if there were no clothing between them. The idea warmed her as only one other action could.

It was an action she must not initiate or allow to happen because of her betrothal to Ricci. Unfortunately, she and Jason had the rest of the night to spend in each other's embrace.

Chapter Eight

Jason woke automatically, his senses alert, his fingers curling around the knife lying hidden in the hay by his side. Motionless, eyes closed, he listened. After several minutes had passed with no alien sounds, he opened his eyes. Only then did he release the weapon.

It was still dark outside, the moon long set, so that the inside of the barn was shades of black on gray. Consequently, he couldn't distinguish Genna's features. He felt her shift within the circle of his arms so that her head lay against his bicep, her face tipped up toward his. It would be so easy to kiss her, to experience the surge of desire she sparked that quickly became more than an urge for physical gratification.

All he had to do was move his right arm up from her waist, where he could feel the boning of her corset under the weave of her kerseymere dress. He could cup in his palm the heavy swell of her bosom that pressed with hot intensity against his chest.

But having wanted her so much and for so long, he knew that he would be unable to stop once he started down that path.

He took a deep breath to cool the blood flowing warmly and eagerly to his loins. That wasn't enough to douse his ardor when the scent of the lavender from Genna's hair and clothing mingled with the musky smell of the hay they slept in. He almost groaned aloud.

She shifted again. Her leg wedged itself between both of his, sending flashes of lightning shooting up his thigh to the portion of his anatomy he was trying to calm down. If he didn't move away from her, he would do something they would both regret.

But *would* they? He was certain Genna wanted him, and, as God was his witness, he wanted her. The only thing that had kept him from acting sooner was the fact he would have to leave her as soon as he was able in order to get his information to Wellington. Obviously that was no longer a factor. Events had overtaken him. All that was left for him to do was reach Wellington and offer his services as a staff officer in the battle he knew was coming.

So, what was keeping him from making love to Genna? Nothing. He could even marry her when they reached Brussels.

Marry her? The idea was novel and surprised him. He'd never contemplated marriage before, and here he was telling himself to marry a woman he'd only known for two weeks. But it felt right to him. She felt right in his arms, and she engaged his mind and made him laugh. That was enough for him. He'd survived too many traps by following his hunches for him to disobey them now; every ounce of his being cried out that she was the woman for him.

"Genna," he whispered, his decision made. He ran a finger lightly over her cheek. Her skin was so smooth and soft it reminded him of the finest silk. "Genna," he whispered again, "wake up. 'Tis time."

Instead of waking, she snuggled closer, sending Jason's pulse racing. She also pressed on his wound, eliciting a sharp jab of pain that he barely registered. All he wanted was to make love to her, to feel her surround his throbbing manhood and take from him all he had to give.

He gave up fighting his better inclinations and moved his right hand from her waist to cup her chin, which he lifted so that he could find her mouth with his. Slowly, he lowered his head so that his lips brushed along her brow and skimmed her eyelids, dropping then to move over the satiny warmth of her cheek until he found what he sought.

Her mouth was as sweet as he remembered and as full and plump as any ripe peach. He knew her breasts and belly would feel the same when she was finally under him, writhing with the desire he knew she was capable of.

Gently, his lips moved over hers, pressing and retreating until his mouth was fully slanted over hers. Only then did he allow his tongue to lave her with slow, long strokes. His seduction started at one corner of her mouth and progressed along the curve of her lip to the other side and then between her lips until they parted on a sigh.

Exultation swept through Jason at her unconscious response to his loving. "My fiery angel," he murmured, breathing in the moist air from her lungs just as his tongue slid into her mouth.

Genna moaned deep in her throat, sucking on Jason's tongue as delicious tremors rippled through her body. He was kissing her with a thoroughness that heated her completely, defying the damp coldness which lay all around them.

"What a delightful way to be awakened," she murmured.

"My God," he groaned, gliding his hand from her face and down her neck, over the wool of her bodice to where her waist indented.

Lost in what he was doing to her, Genna reached up and pulled his face closer so that she could insert her tongue into his mouth and run it over the smooth ridges of his teeth. When his tongue began to duel with hers, she led him back inside her warmth and gently nipped the tip of his tongue before sucking it softly in apology.

His sharp intake of breath excited her as nothing before, and her lips curved up in a secret smile. He wanted her as much as she wanted him. His desire for her made her feel feminine and sensual.

Her senses were intensified by the feel of him pressed hard against her stomach. More than she'd ever wanted anything, Genna wanted him inside her. Without conscious thought, she'd allowed him to become a part of her life. Now, experiencing his lovemaking, she realized that she didn't want to let him go. *Ever*.

"Jason," she said softly, almost desperately, "never let me go."

With an exultant chuckle, he pulled her so close that her breasts flattened against his chest. "Don't every worry that I won't keep you, Genna. You're mine."

She heard the possession in his voice and reveled in it. She had never wanted to belong body and soul to anyone before.

She ran her fingers through his thick blond hair and pulled away just enough to look at him. The sun was beginning to rise and there was just enough light for her to read the passion and the promise in the depths of his gold flecked olive eyes. It was enough for her.

More than enough, she thought as his fingers roved up the bones of her corset and his mouth moved with persuasive persistence over her neck. Then he cupped the swollen mound of her breast in his hand and his thumb began to circle around the hard nubbin of her nipple.

Little gasps of pleasure escaped her, and Jason rapidly brought his mouth back to hers, swallowing the small sounds of passion as he would drink from a flagon of the finest wine. His hand began to knead her sensitive flesh, moving in time to the plunging rhythm of his tongue in her mouth. Genna thought she would expire from the intense delight.

Instead, she pressed her breast further into his

palm, arching her back to get closer and rubbing her pelvis into his. Her hand left his hair and traveled down to his hips where it circled around to the small of his back and sought to bring him nearer.

"Gen . . . na," he groaned. "I need you."

"Good," she gasped, punctuating her words with deep kisses. "Because I'm already delirious from needing you."

It was all he wanted to hear. The hand that had been massaging her bosom went to the back of her bodice and began undoing buttons. Within seconds he had the material parted and pushed down her shoulders. Not saying a word, she helped him slide the sleeves down her arms until she was free except for her corset and chemise.

Jason gazed down at her pearly skin, feasting on her lush fullness that was pushed up by the tightness of her corset. His forefinger trailed along the edge where the fine linen of her chemise met the satin smoothness of her flesh.

"Your skin is whiter than the finest cream," he murmured. "And you probably taste richer." He lowered his head and followed his finger's path with the rough texture of his tongue, stroking her heated flesh with slick moisture. "Mmmm, I was right," he said, blowing on the track his tongue had left, "you're sweeter and smoother than any cream."

Genna's head fell backwards and her breathing increased, becoming more shallow as Jason inched his way lower. Her fingers twined in his hair, and she urged him to the thrusting point of her left breast.

"Do you want me, Genna?" he asked, his voice rough.

She laughed, the sound catching in her throat. "You know I do."

With careful deliberation, he put his mouth to her breast and sucked, his teeth closing around her nipple. She thought her world would shatter as he took her aching breast into his mouth. Even through the filmy material of her chemise, Genna could feel his tongue swirl around her flesh.

Jason seemed to loom above her. He was poised on his elbows, his chest laying on her abdomen, and one of his thighs thrown across hers. She ran her hands up and down his ribs, feeling the rough weave of his shirt under the pads of her fingers. His muscles rippled with reaction to her caresses, and his knee inserted itself between her thighs so that his groin met hers in a hot triangle of desire.

He lifted his mouth from her breasts and returned to her mouth. He shifted so that he lay completely atop her, his forearms taking his weight. His lips slanted over hers and his tongue plunged deeply, enjoying an amorous game of chase with hers. His hips wedged between her thighs and he began to move in rhythm with his pillaging tongue.

Lost to everything except the sensations Jason evoked, Genna responded, her loins rising to meet his in a dance of desire and completion.

She moaned deep in her throat, her hands clawing at his back, lowering to grab his thrusting hips and move them in time with hers. Never had she felt this wild abandon, this soaring need to unite with a man. She wanted to give everything to Jason and in return receive all he had to offer.

He drew slightly away from her, running the tip of his tongue along her lips, and laughed low and exultantly. "I want you so badly, Genna, that I'm like to burst if we don't consummate this."

She smiled up into his golden eyes. "I . . . Jason, I've never felt like this before."

The passion in his eyes flared to a white heat and he crushed his mouth back on hers, putting one hand on the nape of her neck and pulling her with him when he rolled to the side. Lying side-by-side, he kissed her until her senses reeled.

His right hand slid down her outer thigh, smoothing over the material of her dress, then his palm slid back up, taking the skirt and slip with it so that under the covers her skin was bare to his heated touch. Genna felt his fingers on her thighs like tendrils of smoke wafting and expanding, sending warmth to her womb. In the deepest part of her womanhood, she swelled and wept in preparation for his loving.

The gray light of dawn cast shadows over Jason's face as he hovered above her, tempting Genna to trace the firm line of his mouth and the arched strength of his golden brow. Struck by the tenderness in his eyes she found herself more overwhelmed by the emotions he caused in her than by the pleasure he gave her.

"Oh, Jason," she whispered, threading her fingers through his thick hair and pulling him down for her kiss, "I love you."

Even as the words left her lips, his finger penetrated her moistness, sending flames dancing along her nerves. Her hips lifted and her stomach clenched. "Oh, love," she moaned into his devouring mouth.

"Yes, Genna, yes," he said, thrusting his tongue in consonance with his plunging finger. "You're so tight and slick. I can feel you squeezing me."

His words inflamed her passions. When he inserted two fingers into her damp depths, she thought her body would explode. Trembling in every fiber of her being, she strained against him, wanting the release from tension she sensed only he could give her.

His thumb began to flick the swollen nub of nerves between her engorged netherlips, and all her perceptions soared out of control. Only this man and the pleasure they were sharing mattered.

"That's it, Genna," he murmured, taking her tongue inside himself just as she was taking him inside herself, "let me give you this gift. Let yourself go."

Her stomach knotted and her back arched. Her whole body began to shake. She was so close to experiencing something she'd never imagined possible.

"Shhh!" Jason stilled his mouth on hers, stopping everything at once.

Genna's eyes flew open, her body convulsing in frustration. "Wha—"

Jason's hand, the same one that had been pleasuring her, whipped over her mouth. She could smell the musky scent of her own excitement on his skin.

His voice barely audible, he said into her ear, "Someone is outside the door. Stay here."

He rolled away from her and out from under the covers, all in one graceful movement. Caught between her body's adjustment to the cessation of her climax before it was reached and her fear that they were discovered, Genna watched Jason grasp the nearby knife. He held it as a man who knows how to use it, loosely gripped, his elbow flexed so the weapon pointed away from him at hip level.

She wanted to burrow under the covers, to close out the scene she knew was coming. She wanted to go back in time and awaken in her bed in that dismal room in Paris. She wanted anything but the position she was in.

She couldn't even straighten out her skirts or pull her bodice up to cover her bareness. Jason had said stay still, and she knew by now to do as he said. Mortification stained her skin scarlet as she waited.

And she had told him she loved him.

The breath caught in Genna's throat, her admission of love immaterial in the threat of the barn door opening. A husky youth entered, a hat pulled low over his brow and a worn coat pulled tight around his chest. In his hand was a bucket of slops.

Genna's mound of hay was by the wall, not directly in the youth's line of sight, but she knew it would only be minutes before he became aware of her. Her muscles tensed as she prepared to jump from her bed and run. What would Jason do?

Jason silently cursed his misfortune. He'd been so close to making Genna his. To be interrupted just when he knew she was near the height of her pleasure was as frustrating to him as he knew it was to her. But he shrugged mentally. He'd been a fool to do such here. *A weak fool.*

Flipping the knife in his hand, so that the hilt was outmost, Jason advanced on the farmer. Raising his arm caused his wound to pull, but Jason blocked out the twinge of pain and concentrated on what he was doing. With one deft movement, he knocked out the farmer with the knife's brass hilt. The youth slid silently to the ground.

Not bothering to move the limp body, Jason stepped around it and fetched the horses.

Seeing the farmer hit the ground, Genna quickly straightened her clothing before leaping from the covers and rushing to help Jason. Her voice shook when she asked, "Did you kill him?"

He shot her a look that told her nothing of his feelings. "No."

His curt reply was enough to douse the last remaining flickers of fire his amorous attentions had ignited in her just minutes before. He no longer was a lover. Now he was a spy on the run and every second counted. Even his fingers on her back as he fastened her bodice were impersonal and cold.

"This is where we trade horses," Jason stated.

Genna stared at him. "Trade? Why?"

He turned hard eyes on her. "Because as much as

I appreciate your efforts to speed us on our way, 'tis more important that we pass unnoticed. This farmer is well-off enough to have several plow horses. He will be even better off when he finds these thoroughbreds." He led one of the farm horses out of its stall and began to saddle it.

Genna said no more, realizing that Jason was right. They mounted the horses and left.

On the road to Brussels, Genna remembered Ricci and her promise to Luigi. How could she have forgotten?

Facing the truth, she knew how. She was in love with Jason even though she knew nothing about him but his Christian name and the fact that he was a British spy. No, that wasn't true. She knew that he was honorable, dependable, considerate, and that he was patriotic. Those were all qualities she valued highly and made him much more admirable than Ricci would ever be.

But again, there was her promise to Luigi. And there was her own honor that wouldn't let her forsake that vow, no matter how tempted.

Just then Jason grunted and shifted in his saddle, interrupting her introspection. Chagrined at her selfishness, she realized she hadn't even asked Jason about his wound. So much had happened that morning, that his wound and her aches from riding sidesaddle for longer than she was used to had paled into insignificance.

"Jason," she caught up with him, "I need to tend your wound."

He glanced at her then back at the road. "When we stop to rest."

Before she could protest, he spurred his animal forward and it was all she could do to keep up with him. Shortly after, he slowed into a ground covering trot that jarred her spine with every hoof her horse put on the ground. She knew it must be worse on Jason, but he uttered no sound.

They stopped when the sun was high in the sky. Jason handed her some cheese and bread and they ate hurriedly in silence. Genna licked the last crumb from her fingers, relishing even the taste of the day old bread, then went to her saddle and got the bag containing her medicines.

Rising to secure the food, Jason said over his shoulder, "Not yet. We have too much ground to cover. I want to be in Brussels before the week is out."

She stifled her gasp. Ordinarily, she would have protested the hard usage that pace would subject their mounts to; one look at the resolve hardening his jaw and she knew it would do no good. He would run their horses into the ground if he must.

Jason studied Genna as she settled herself on the plow horse. This journey was as hard on her as it was on him. And when the animals trotted, he wasn't sure which pained him more . . . his side or his loins.

His only consolation was the knowledge that she wanted his lovemaking as much as he wanted to give it. But that didn't help his situation. It only made him harder and tighter. Tonight couldn't come too soon.

But when night finally fell, there was no shelter to be had. They had skirted every village and group of dwellings they'd passed and now they were in flat land with not even a tree to hide them.

Running his fingers through his hair in irritation, Jason searched the horizon. There was nothing to do but strike out away from the road and hope for something. In the end, he settled them in a depression in the otherwise flat ground, out of sight of anyone traveling the road. He gave the horses several handfuls of oats and hobbled them so they could munch on any nearby grass or plants.

After they ate, Genna was determined to take no refusal from him. She would tend his wound.

Jason sat on the ground, using the saddles to support his lower back as Genna unwound the bandage. In the meager light from the small fire Jason would allow them to have, Genna could see that the edges of the dressing were brown with dirt and perspiration. The wound however was dry; the edges of the cut a healthy pink.

Genna released the breath she'd been holding. "You're healing nicely. In a day or two it should begin to itch."

Jason chuckled. "Aye. I know that particular agony well. Another part of my anatomy already suffers it."

Her eyes flew to his. The hunger he made no effort to hide turned her insides to languid softness. Her hand shook when she dusted the wound with basilicum powder. It took all her resolve not to run her finger along the fine stitches she'd put in his skin, just to feel the texture of his flesh.

"I wish I had a clean cloth to rebind you with, but . . ." she sighed.

He stopped her busy hands with his and raised her palm to kiss it. "You've done more than needed. Were it not for you, I'd probably be dead."

Her chest constricted at the truth of what he said. The pain of just imagining losing him overwhelmed the delight of his mouth on her hand. She looked deeply into his eyes, seeing the golden flecks of desire, but also seeing more. He cared for her and made no attempt to hide it. Her heart swelled with emotion.

Emotion she'd revealed to him during their lovemaking that morning. Did he love her as she loved him? That was something she couldn't discern from his look.

Genna squeezed her eyes shut. It would be better for him not to love her. That way led only to heartache for him. If he loved her, he might wish to marry her and she couldn't wed him. She was promised to Ricci, and no amount of desire or caring or love could alter that fact.

No, it was better if her love for him remained unrequited.

Chapter Nine

Genna groaned, each muscle protesting movement of any kind. What was wrong with her? Why was her pillow hard and uncomfortable? Then one of the horses snorted and her memory returned.

She and Jason were fleeing goodness only knew who, and this had been their second night sleeping on the road, if you could call the exhaustion that had made her pass out sleep. She couldn't even remember crawling under the cocoon of capes and blankets that were keeping her warm even though she was the only one....

Where was Jason?

Bolting up, she forced her leaden eyelids to open. He had to be somewhere near by. He would never leave her.

Fully awake, she scanned the surrounding area. Both horses were still hobbled, and each had a small mound of oats to eat from, so he couldn't be far.

A sound caught her attention, but when she

looked she couldn't see anyone. She dared not speak, just in case it wasn't Jason. Her hands froze. Was there someone close by whom he was hiding from? Had the man they'd left in the wardrobe in Paris gotten free and caught up with them? Her pulse jumped.

She heard the noise again. Someone was whistling a jaunty tune low and out of tune. It couldn't be someone stalking them, it had to be Jason.

Relief melted the tension holding her stiffly erect, and she sank back onto the rapidly cooling ground.

"Genna, as much as I want to join you and finish what we started yesterday morning, I dare not," Jason said, interrupting his tune to grin suggestively at her. "We need to get on the road. The sun will be fully up by the time we get the horses saddled."

Giddy from the rapid change of emotions, fear at his disappearance and now desire at his open confession of wanting her, Genna giggled. But she sobered immediately when she levered onto her elbows and stared at him in the gray light. He didn't look dangerous, except to her peace of mind. He was too disturbing, with his hair falling roguishly across his forehead and his well-shaped lips quirking into a knowing grin.

The slash of white teeth emphasized the growth of beard on his cheeks and jaw. Unlike the golden honey of his hair, his beard was russet with smatterings of blond. She wanted to rub her palm across his cheek to see if the hairs were still short enough to be rough, or if they were now long enough to feel like fur.

She resisted the impulse to reach for him and frowned instead. "You should have told me you were leaving. Something might have happened to you, and I wouldn't have known where to look."

His smile widened into a teasing twist of lips. "We almost make love and now I can't leave your side long enough to relieve myself." His shoulders shook with suppressed mirth. "I shudder to think what it will be like after I love you completely."

A fiery blush suffused Genna from head to toe at his blunt speaking. She fully understood nature's morning call, but his statement about what to expect from her after they made love was a reminder of how close they'd come. It revived the fire in her stomach that he'd kindled so expertly.

She squeezed her eyes shut to block out the sight of his heated gaze. This had to stop. Letting Jason think any differently was dishonest and cruel.

Opening her eyes again, clenching her fists in determination to ignore the desire in his eye, she knew she had to tell him about Ricci. It was the only thing that would keep Jason from making beautiful, irrevocable love to her.

"Jason, I. . . . that is, we. . . ." She couldn't finish it. She didn't want to tell him. She didn't want to see the light of admiration in his eyes die.

Her gaze dropped from the fire in his and she fumbled with the covers, trying to stand. She knew it wasn't fair of her not to tell him about Ricci, but . . . but she was weak. Just for the remainder of their journey she wanted to bask in the warmth of his attraction that Jason made no attempt to hide. When they reached Brussels, and Jason took up his duties as a spy again, would be soon enough for her to deny their future together.

"I know," Jason said, trying to soothe her obvious nervousness. "I shouldn't have bedeviled you." He shrugged his shoulders. "No gentleman would speak so boldly to a lady. And you're right, I should have told you I was leaving, only you were sleeping so soundly and I knew you were tired beyond imagination." The expression on his face became rueful. "My apologies."

"No, that is, 'tis all right, Jason." She felt like such a hypocrite not to tell him about Ricci. She consoled herself with the knowledge that no matter what Jason felt for her, he hadn't mentioned marriage. In fact, she might very well be seeing in his eyes only the reflection of her own love for him. He hadn't said he loved her.

Appeasing her guilt with that sop, Genna took the hand he offered her.

Jason pulled her to her feet. "You're so fine and noble and brave, Genna," he murmured, taking her into his arms and enfolding her in the warmth and strength of his embrace.

Held tightly to his chest, the steady beat of his heart firm under her cheek, Genna knew herself to be the antithesis of all those qualities. She wasn't fine and noble and brave, she was deceitful and low and cowardly. She should tell him now about her promise, but she couldn't. She loved him too much and wanted him beside her too much to end it all abruptly by telling him the truth. Brussels would be time enough to deal with disillusionment.

Disillusionment was soon lost, along with any other finer emotion in Genna, as the trot Jason kept the horses to for the rest of the day made her back and thighs feel as though she'd been put on a torturer's rack and torn apart. It was all she could do to keep her spine straight and words of protest from escaping through her clenched lips.

She knew Jason must be in as much discomfort as she, particularly with his wound. That morning it had looked as though it should be itching mightily. Yet, not a murmur of complaint came from him. She could do no less.

By the time he finally called a halt for the night, somewhere in the middle of a wheat field with no trees or buildings in sight, she was numb from her shoulders down. If it was cold or if the wind was blowing, she didn't feel either. Her right leg, that had been hooked around the saddle's pommel for better than twelve hours this day alone, felt like a lead pipe that someone had taken a hammer to at the joint.

When she slid to the ground, she hit with a bone cracking jar that buckled her knees. Jason caught her as she collapsed.

"Genna!" His fingers held onto her shoulders, the only things keeping her upright. Putting an arm around her waist, he helped her to a small mound of dirt where he'd spread one of their two blankets. "Damn. I should have never allowed you to ride on that bloody contraption. At the next town we pass, I'm going to find a hostler and trade that blasted sidesaddle."

Somehow she managed to smile. "Don't be silly. You know we can't take the chance. Whoever is hunting you might have caught up with us, and if we do anything to draw attention to ourselves they'll find us. No," she shook her head, "I'll be fine after a good night's sleep."

"Yes," he said sarcastically, "and I'll be healed." He sighed and took off his hat to run his fingers through his hair, changing the compressed locks into a mass of unruly waves. "God, Genna, I wish you didn't have to endure this."

Contrition tightened Genna's chest. He was so tired that deep lines bracketed his mouth and dark shadows circled his eyes. And here she was adding worry to his burden. Smiling tenderly, she reached out and stroked back one piece of his hair that had fallen into his eye.

"'Tis all right, Jason. I must admit that I would have preferred to meet you under better circumstances, possibly at a ball or rout. And it would be more comfortable to go riding in the park to further our acquaintance, but I'm still grateful that we have this time together. I know you so much better than would've been possible under ideal conditions."

He rocked back on his heels, his face full of wonder. "To find something positive in these deplorable conditions, Genna, I couldn't find a partner like you if I searched till hell froze over. And I promise you, when we reach Brussels I'll make up for this."

Genna had to blink away the moisture his praise

caused. He was so sincere and she loved him so much. She tried to laugh over the catch in her throat. "But right now Brussels is far away and we both can barely stand."

"True." With a grunt, he rose and started settling them in for the night.

Genna got up and did her share, determined not to increase Jason's load. Even when he scowled at her and ordered her to sit back down and rest, she continued rubbing down her mount.

When they finally stopped to eat their meager supply of bread and dried beef, she could only keep her eyes open by will power. She didn't know how Jason was managing.

As they crawled under the bedding, she was thankful for the fatigue that kept her from having any kind of amorous inclinations. While she wanted Jason in the most fundamental way possible, she also knew that their union would only bring heartbreak to them both. Thusly, she mumbled good night to him and promptly passed out.

Her deep, even breathing told Jason she was asleep before he'd had a chance to do more than adjust the covers around them. He turned to his side and positioned her in the curve of his body. The sound of contentment she uttered in her sleep was more satisfying to him than any amount of sexual gratification could have been ... maybe.

When she wriggled her hips to fit her derriere more flush against his loins and thighs, he began to seriously doubt his choice of priorities. In spite of all his good intentions, his response to her increased to the point of painful deprivation.

But she was more to him than an object to slack his lust. In the few short weeks he'd known her, she'd proven that she had all the courage and loyalty of any man. More importantly, she'd roused his heart as well as his manhood.

He brushed away pieces of her hair that were tickling his nose and marveled at the way the strands clung to his fingers. Even so minor a part of her as the wisps of hair escaping her chignon was inseparable from him.

Such a small thing, but it was significant because it made him realize that he didn't just want to make love to her. He wanted to hold her and cherish her. He wanted to wake up next to her each morning for the rest of his life. He wanted to marry her and give her his babies . . . *their* babies.

And, he vowed, he would do just that.

"Damn," Jason muttered under his breath as cold water dripped onto his jaw and then down his neck. His teeth chattered and even Genna's body pressed warmly against him couldn't dispel the chill wracking him.

He didn't need to open his eyes to know that it was raining or at best drizzling. What did surprise him was the horse's nose suspended just above his own. A low whinny apprised him of the animal's dissatisfaction.

Disentangling himself from Genna's warm embrace, Jason crawled reluctantly out of their makeshift bed, and got the horse the oats he expected. After pouring each animal a ration, he stretched out the kinks in his muscles. A glance at the overcast sky told him that it was later than he'd thought. The clouds obscuring the sun had confused his internal clock and he'd overslept.

As unconventional as his alarm had been, he was glad for it. They needed to be moving.

Slapping on his hat, even though it was as soaked as the rest of his clothing, Jason strode to where Genna still slept. Her hair had loosened further from the chignon and strands lay like a fiery halo around her face. Her lashes lay like thick brown feathers on her pale cheeks, and her lips curved upward like rose petals.

She was beautiful in every way imaginable, both physically and spiritually. Luck had been with him when it had guided him to her door out of all the other possibilities.

But luck wouldn't stay with him if he wasted time. Pushing his love for Genna to the back of his mind, he roused her with an economy of words and broke camp. There would be a better place and time for him to love her.

Genna pulled herself from sleep and peered through drowsy eyes at the sky. How had the weather gone from bad to worse so quickly? Yesterday she'd decided there was nothing that could increase her discomfort. This miserable excuse for a day proved her wrong.

"Thank you," she mumbled to Jason when he handed her the last piece of cheese. They'd finished the bread the day before, just ahead of the mold ruining it. All they had left was some dried meat.

His curt nod told her more clearly than any words just how he viewed the day. And neither one of them had a change of opinion.

The only thing that brought any warmth to her was the memory of lying in Jason's arms, his mouth a hot brand on hers, his hand a moving flame on her body. And when she reached the part where his fingers entered her, it was all she could do not to squirm in the saddle.

Despite the burning need evoked by her thoughts, she was still miserable beyond words. Suddenly, instead of veering around a small cluster of buildings, Jason made directly for them. She knew he was doing this for her and she couldn't let him.

Urging her mount into a gallop, she caught him. "Jason, no. I'll be fine."

Water dripping off the brim of his hat, he angled around to look at her. "Genna, your cape is sodden so that it clings like a limpet to you. Your lips are blue with cold. We will stay this night in a warm inn."

She had to convince him that she was fine. "I may be wet and cold," she couldn't deny the obvious, "but my constitution is strong. I've withstood worse than this. We dare not take the risk."

He gave her a considering look then shrugged. "Well, you may be made of sturdier stuff, but I am not."

In the dark of evening, compounded by the

overcast sky, she hadn't been able to see him clearly. Now, in the golden glow coming from the door of a tavern that someone had just opened, she saw the thinning of Jason's lips and the paleness of his skin. He looked ready to fall from his saddle. "Oh, dear, how selfish I've been."

Without a second's hesitation, Genna slid to the ground, sinking up to her ankles in mud. The saving grace was that the muck cushioned her landing, otherwise she would have hit hard since her legs were as void of sensation as they'd been the night before.

Jason followed her example. Taking the reins of both horses, he tied them to a post when no help was forthcoming.

"Everyone is too smart to be about in this soup," he grumbled. Before entering, he took her arm and secured her by his side. "We stay together, no matter what."

Grateful for the security, and not anxious to be left alone in the cold, wet night, Genna kept close.

"My God," he muttered as water seeped between his fingers from her drenched cape, "you're wetter than I thought, and that's hard to do."

She managed to smile, but said nothing as they crossed the threshold. Heat, like a wall of flames, hit her with welcome intensity. Only then did she look around. The main room was empty except for two rough looking men, probably farmers, who huddled by the open hearth, large mugs in their fists. Still, the place smelled of unwashed bodies and soured ale.

"Isn't much," Jason said for her ears only, "but

it'll have to do."

"'Tis better than outside," she agreed.

He cast her a grateful smile just as a thin man, with a dingy gray apron tied around his waist, came from a side door. Obviously the owner, he looked them over carefully.

"How may I help you?" he finally asked in Flemish, his mouth just barely turning upwards.

"We need a room," Jason answered in the same language.

Genna suppressed her start of surprise. She hadn't realized they'd crossed into Belgium. It was good for them that Jason spoke Flemish, although not as fluently as he spoke French. The only languages she knew were English, French, and Italian.

Quick on the heels of that thought was a belated curiosity about what else Jason knew. He was remarkably well educated to be nothing more than a spy. All the time she'd spent in his company, and only now did it occur to her to wonder who he really was.

Up to this instant, she'd just assumed that he was an Englishman who was loyal to his country's cause and happened to speak fluent French. While that wasn't all that common, it wasn't impossible either. Many French emigrés had married Englishmen, and that would explain his French. But what explained his Flemish?

From the corner of her eye, she watched him haggle with the proprietor. Now that she thought of it, even dressed as deplorably as he was, Jason carried himself with an assurance that commanded acquiescence from others. Her study roved over him, from his squared shoulders to the casual grace of his hands.

"Genna," Jason said in French, "the landlord has one room he will let us have for the night. Come."

After the heavy oak door was bolted on their side, she turned to him. "Who are you that you know three languages?"

His face was inscrutable. "Why do you ask now?"

Confused and chagrined at her failure to do this sooner, her shoulders drooped. "I did ask once."

He studied her a moment longer, then shrugged out of his soaked coat. Turning from her, he went to the hearth and began igniting the small pile of kindling.

Genna stared dejectedly at his back, knowing that he wouldn't tell her anything. She consoled herself by the private admission that it didn't really matter what his past was. She knew him better than she knew anyone else in the world, including Aunt Hester, her mother, and Ricci.

Ah, Ricci. Her future. She sighed in resignation, a cry of despair from her heart.

Jason was at her side immediately, his face drawn with fatigue, but his eyes alight with concern. He took her into his arms, drenched cape and all. "I would give my life for you, Genna, but I can't tell you my identity. Not yet. If we're caught, any information you have only increases your risk. Trust me."

How could she not? She loved him with a depth

that defied all wisdom.

Resting her forehead on his chest, she slipped her arms around his waist. "I trust you, Jason." Barely above a whisper, she added, "I love you too much not to."

He lifted her chin so that their eyes met. "And I you."

Chapter Ten

He loved her! *He loved her.* In her heart, she'd known he did, but to hear him say the words was beyond wonderful. And when his lips parted in a smile of such tenderness it made her eyes ache with unshed tears, Genna knew she would find no greater happiness than now.

"Genna, love," he chided gently, "surely you knew how I feel about you. I've never hidden that from you."

She shook her head slightly. "No, you never have. It's just . . . it's just one thing to think you do and another to hear you say it."

She gazed up at him, secure in the belief that this man was worth any sacrifice. Even betrayal of her betrothal vows. She reasoned that it wouldn't matter to Ricci if she came to him from another man's bed. To deny and avoid the love Jason professed would hurt not only herself but Jason, the man she loved. And Jason hadn't asked her to marry him, only to love him.

She lifted her hands to his head and pulled him down for her kiss. No matter what the future held, she wanted this moment of fulfillment and unconditional love to keep safe in her heart. It would be all the happiness she would ever have. Just for tonight, she would forget her promise to Luigi and give herself completely and irrevocably to the only man she would ever love.

Their lips met, tentatively at first and then more fully, until their tongues were dancing in heated delight. Genna felt as though she'd come home.

Jason lifted his head, breaking the thread of longing uniting them. "Love, you're cold as ice."

Genna murmured her denial. "No, I'm hotter than yonder fire."

He chuckled deep in his throat. Instead of kissing her again, he began to undo the strings holding her cape around her neck. Then he pushed the sodden wool off her shoulders, running his palms down her arms. "If possible, you're wetter under that mess. Come," he drew her toward the fire, "I don't want you getting sick."

Smiling, she allowed him to guide her. "You're beginning to sound like me."

He gave her a quizzical look. "Am I?" Then he shrugged. "I've been told that 'tis not unusual for lovers to pick up each other's characteristics."

Genna marveled at his easy acceptance of their bonding as she sat in the chair he drew near the flames for her. "Are all spies as adaptable as you?" She meant the question to be teasing, but her need to know more about him seeped into her voice.

He knelt at her feet and took her hands into his.

"Genna, just for this evening, believe that I love you and that nothing else matters but the pleasure we give one another."

She looked into his eyes and saw in them the promise of a joy so great that all else would be dwarfed by it. Fervently, she wished it could be so.

Unable to withstand the intensity of his regard, she dropped her head. Was the love she felt for this man wrong? She didn't think so.

Jason hadn't asked her for marriage, only for a night of love. What she and Jason did now would take nothing from Ricci. Ricci didn't love her, and he didn't want love from her. He was drawn to her money, which he would receive when they wed. In the meantime, she could give her love, her body, and her soul to this man kneeling in front of her, to Jason.

She slid off the chair onto her knees so that the only thing separating them was the air they breathed.

"Genna," Jason whispered, her name a vow of love, his arms around her a band of possession.

This is where she had longed to be, Genna realized, sinking into the strength of his embrace. Her head tilted back, her eyes half closed, she offered herself to him.

"Jason, I'll always love you."

His eyes blazed with satisfaction, and his shoulders bunched under her hands. "Then let me love you. Let me complete what we started in that damn barn."

She giggled at the fierceness of his last words and ran one finger lightly down his jaw. "I have very fond memories of that 'damn barn.'"

He caught her hand and slowly kissed each finger, pausing at the last one to suck gently. It felt as though he'd pulled every nerve from the tip of her nail down to the bottom of her toes into his mouth.

"Oh!" she gasped. "I didn't know something as simple as that would feel so . . . so. . . ." She didn't know how to describe what he did to her, she only knew she never wanted it to end.

"That will teach you to mock me," he said playfully, his loins heating from the anticipation of other things he intended to teach her.

Her laugh echoed softly in the tiny room. "If that is the forfeit I pay for mockery, you may be sure that I will do it frequently."

"Saucy wench." His arms circled her waist, and his fingers began undoing her buttons from the bottom up. "You're like a block of ice, and these wet clothes don't help."

She shivered, as much from the nimble work of his fingers as from the cold. "No, and neither do yours." Just as eager to feel their skin pressed tightly together, she worked at pushing his coat off his shoulders. But the coat caught and she couldn't get it all the way off. "You're much harder to undress," she muttered.

He bent his head and kissed her pouting lips. "There, your bodice is undone, so I'll help you with my clothing."

So saying, he let his arms fall to his sides so that she could wrestle his coat sleeves down and the garment completely off of him. Her eyes widened at the way the coarse fabric of his shirt lay like a second skin over the rippling muscles and broad expanse of his chest. He was the epitome of masculine magnificence.

"You're beautiful," she murmured, running her hands over his biceps up to his neck where she began to unbutton his shirt. Her pulse quickened and her fingers began to shake.

"No," he deferred, "you're the beautiful one here." He slipped his hands inside the back of her bodice and began to loosen the strings holding her corset in place.

"Lower your arms," she commanded.

His eyes dilated with passion. "Must I? I'm so close to accomplishing my goal."

She chuckled. "Yes, you must, because I'm much nearer to my goal than you are."

With an exaggerated sigh, he did as she bade. Genna pushed the shirt off and spent long minutes reveling in the sight of his naked torso. His muscles were well-defined without being overly bulky, and his nipples stood in peaked brown circles with golden hairs circling them. Needing to feel him, she lifted one hand and tentatively rubbed it against the nipple opposite his wound.

His sharp intake of breath enervated her and made her bolder. With a smile of power, she raised her eyes to his. The green of his irises was almost gone, replaced by the black of his enlarged pupils.

He was hers and she thought that she could see into his very soul where the love he felt for her resided. It humbled her.

"Jason," she said softly, honestly meaning every

word, "take me. Please."

Triumph, primitive and fierce, lit his face. Rising, he bent and lifted her in his arms.

Anxiety stiffened Genna. "Jason, put me down. Your wound."

"Shhh," he gentled her, continuing to carry her to the small bed they would share. "I'm fine." He set her down and she reclined there only long enough for him to divest himself of boots, stockings, and breeches before levering herself up on her elbows.

The breath caught in her throat at the sight of him. Proud as any wild animal, he stood before her, hands on hips, feet spread hip width apart. Even the bandage, girdling his ribs, did nothing to diminish the blatant display of his virility.

He was everything she'd ever imagined a man could be. From the unruly thickness of his blond hair to the straight angles and planes of his face, to the broadness of his shoulders and narrowness of his hips, to the musculature of his thighs and calves, Jason was more perfect than Michelangelo's David.

And his manhood was so powerfully erect that the sight of it sent heat waves radiating throughout her body. Genna raised her arms to him in silent acceptance.

That was all Jason needed. She'd seen him fully aroused and still wanted him. He moved into her embrace. "I promise you, love, that this will be good."

She smiled gently at his masculine pride. "I never doubted it, beloved."

Jason's eagerness to possess her completely was like flames in his loins, bursting into a conflagration and spreading like wildfire through his limbs. It took every ounce of his self-control not to fall on her, push her skirts up, and bury himself so deeply inside her hot warmth that he forgot all else.

No, for her sake, he forced himself to go slowly. With her help, he took off her bodice and pushed it and her skirts down over her hips and legs. There he had to pause and regain his control as his gaze traveled back up her body.

Her long, lithe legs tempted him with the pink stockings continuing over her knees to the middle of her thighs where they were held up by blue ribbons tied in bows. She wore no slip, that having come off with her dress, and the hem of her chemise just grazed the top of the auburn-haired triangle gracing the apex of her thighs.

Jason sucked in his breath, and his manhood quivered with longing to be in that nest. He had to wrench his gaze upward or take her then.

Her corset had come loose after he'd unlaced it and now lay lightly over her ribs, no longer pushing up the tips of her breasts. Yet, her nipples lifted like pouting pink rosebuds above the white edge of her chemise. His palms itched to caress the hard nubs of her bosom, but he resisted, knowing that once he started he would be unable to stop. Before taking her, he wanted to ensure her pleasure, to see it in her eyes.

When he looked at her face, the expression there undid him. Her eyes were slumberous and her lips were ripe, both an invitation he couldn't resist. Bending over her, he took her mouth with his, pressing until her lips parted and his tongue could slip in.

She moaned, and he thought he would explode. The desire she felt for him, and made no effort to hide, was a more powerful aphrodisiac than any fantasy.

His lips still on hers, he pulled away her corset and then lifted her chemise until he had to release her mouth to pull the garment completely off. He gently inserted his fingers in the luxuriant thickness of her hair and removed the pins holding her auburn tresses in a chignon. Wrapping the length of satin around his fist, he pulled until she rose up to meet him.

Genna wrapped her arms around his neck and pressed herself to him, feeling the coarse hairs surrounding his nipples and the weave of his muslin bandage against the sensitized skin of her breasts. Excited by the tingling spreading through her like a blaze out of control, she rubbed across him, making her bosom swell.

"I like that," Jason growled, slanting his mouth over hers.

"Mmmm," she answered, meeting the demands of his tongue thrust for thrust.

Wanting him closer, she pulled until he lay beside her on the bed. Instinctively, she rubbed her leg up his and delighted in the contrast between his muscled ridges and her softer curves.

His lips left hers and he glanced down. "It seems that I've wanted to see you like this for an eternity." His palm spread out over one of her breasts and he squeezed gently.

His tongue flicked out and traced the line of her collar bone. Then he kissed back along the trail and up the side of her neck to her ear. With a touch as light as a feather, he ran his teeth along the rim of her ear, sending shivers of delight coursing through her.

"Did you like that?" His voice was rough as he continued to explore her, moving over her face in butterfly kisses that traversed her closed eyelids, the tip of her nose, and down to her chin.

"Yes," she managed to say, her fingers tangled in his hair. "I like everything you do to me."

He lifted his face to look at her. His eyes were dark with carefully banked passion, and she felt her womanhood clench in response.

He shifted so that one leg rode her thighs and he slid his body downward, dragging the erect length of his manhood across her stomach. Genna's abdomen tightened and hot moistness stirred deep inside her. She wanted him.

"Jason," she whispered urgently, transferring her hands to his shoulders and trying to pull him upward, "take me now. I want you now."

His lips parted in a wolfish grin. "Not yet, love. I want you writhing with need and so wet that I'll slip into you like a hot knife into butter."

Before she could protest, he was kneeling at her feet. Lifting on her elbows she watched him, mesmerized by the thrusting evidence of his arousal between his thighs. That alone told her he wanted her as much as she wanted him. Why was he waiting?

Perhaps she could speed him along. She ran her stockinged foot up his inner thigh, stopping just short of his manhood.

Jason gasped for air. "Ge . . . nna. Who's seducing whom?"

She grinned, very satisfied with what she'd accomplished.

He shook his head in wonder. "I was right the first time I laid eyes on you. You're a fiery angel."

Then he straddled her legs and began to untie the blue ribbon keeping her right stocking up. Slowly rolling the silk covering down, he inched down her leg rubbing himself like velvet along her quivering flesh. Next he did her left leg. When he was finished, he lifted each foot in turn and kissed her instep. Then he placed her feet so that he sat on his heels between her legs.

His fingers traced along her calves and up her inner thighs as he feasted on the sight of her femininity. "I could enter you now," he said roughly.

Still on her elbows watching him, she nodded agreement, unable to speak for the desire welling up inside her.

Jason wanted her so badly, it was torture to wait, but he didn't want to hurt her. And he didn't know if she and her late husband had ever made love. Perhaps the man had been too feeble to do so. He looked into her eyes. "I don't want to cause you pain, Genna. Are you a virgin?"

She met his look without flinching. He was her love, her life, and with him she could be herself without any maidenly modesty. "Only in my heart, Jason, and that no longer. Everything I am is yours."

"You'll never have cause to regret giving yourself to me, love." In that instant, Jason knew he would go to hell for her and never think twice about it. She was the woman he wanted, even his commitment to Britain was forgotten in the depth of his vow to Genna.

"Never," she agreed, wanting this joining of their bodies in love above all else.

Jason's gaze held hers as he lowered himself on his chest between her thighs. When he saw her startlement, he chuckled. "This will increase your pleasure, love. Relax and let me enjoy this, too."

She couldn't believe he was going to do what she imagined. At the first touch of his lips on her nether ones, her body flinched but she also understood his words about pleasure. The delight his sucking mouth and stroking tongue gave her was exquisite.

To Jason, she felt like the finest satin. As he caressed the folds of her femininity, he had to fist his hands into the covers under her to keep himself from grabbing her hips and impaling her with his staff.

"That's it, Genna," he encouraged her as she arched her back to give him better access. "Give yourself to me. You're so moist I could slip into you without hesitation."

His tongue dipped inside her, and Genna clenched his hair with fingers that shook. "Jason, what are you doing?"

"Enticing you so that you'll want more."

She heard the roguish humor in his voice, but realized it was underscored by truth. He wanted her with such a feverish pitch of desire that she opened for him willingly.

"I'll..." she gasped as he inserted a finger where his tongue had been, "always...." Her breath caught when he withdrew his finger and rapidly plunged it back in deeper, his tongue flicking the sensitive nubbin farther up. "... want you."

When he used two fingers, Genna thought she would go mad. Even what he'd done to her in the barn was nothing compared to the sensations rocketing through her now. Her stomach was quivering, and her bosom was rising rapidly with each shallow breath she took. Her head twisted from side-to-side, and her hips moved in rhythm with his penetration.

"Yes, Genna," he urged her onward. "Yes, that's the way I want you. So hot you drip with honeyed desire and you spasm around me with slick need."

His words only increased her response, making her buck. "Jason, please take me. Take me now." The words wrenched from her, barely above a whisper.

Then there was nothing. His mouth, his fingers, they were gone. Dazed, Genna lifted her head.

He was poised between her legs, his eyes dark and hungry, his shaft held in his hand to be guided into her. She spread herself wider to receive him.

With one smooth, slow motion, he entered her, stretching her and filling her until Genna's world spun out of focus. Her hands slid down his shoulders, over the ridged muscles of his back, corded now by his determination to hold himself in check. She finally fitted her palms against the swell of his buttocks and urged him deeper.

At her blatant pull, Jason released an exultant laugh from deep in his belly, and plunged into her until his hot flesh met her heated flesh with a soft slap. "You're mine!"

Genna held him prisoner as she reveled in the feel of him rubbing secret places she'd not known existed in her body. Tightening around him, she undulated beneath him.

"Genna," Jason moaned, "don't do that or I won't be able to last."

"Good," she murmured, awash in exciting sensations that made her want to thrust against him until they both lay damp and exhausted with repletion. These were experiences she'd never had before. "I can't wait any longer."

Jason heard the tension in her voice and felt it in her womb, closed like a vice around him. All he could think of was the infinite delight he knew would encompass them shortly. Then she twisted, her loins pressed against his, swallowing him completely. He was lost.

Unable to stop, he pumped into her; going deeper and quicker with each movement. Every nerve in his body throbbed with the need for release.

Genna met him, motion for motion; her breasts flattened against his chest, her womanhood dripping with anticipation of the ultimate pleasure that would soon engulf her.

Jason thrust, long and straight, and the world shattered around him. His voice erupted in a groan that was almost a shout of release.

Genna spasmed under him, her body exploding, her mouth clinging desperately to his. They were one, joined in the most elemental union two beings in love could achieve.

Chapter Eleven

They lay entwined, two halves of a greater whole. The fire Jason had started in the hearth was down to cinders. A chill lay over the room, cooling the moistness of their flushed skin.

"Brrr," Genna said, squirming from his possessive hold so that she could get the covers from the floor where they'd fallen. Settled at last, she inched back into the curve of Jason's chest, so that her back and buttocks nestled against his stomach and thighs.

"Mmmm." Jason murmured, nuzzling the nape of her neck. "You fit perfectly."

Drowsy with repletion, Genna mumbled an answer. Contentment was like Morpheus to her tired body, and she fell into sleep without further thought.

Jason lay for long minutes listening to the gentle inhale and exhale of her breath. She was warm and silky smooth in his arms. Her lush hips were pressed to his loins so that his erection nestled between rounded mounds of soft flesh. It would be so easy to take her again, entering from behind, he mused. His hands gently squeezed her full breasts, and his thumbs stroked back and forth over her nipples that were hard even though she slept. But, no. He could wait.

They had a lifetime for this.

At her body's insistence, Genna woke slowly, reluctantly leaving behind a dream where she and Jason were together with nothing and no one keeping them apart. Even as she became more aware, Jason's hands moving on her body made her realize that his ministrations were her reason for wakening.

His mouth was hot and soft on her nape, moving over her shoulders, sending showers of sparks cascading down her spine. One arm was under her head and crooked at the elbow so that his hand could cup one of her breasts which he was kneading with increasing urgency. His other hand was between her thighs, stroking slickly between the folds of her netherlips. His manhood pressed at the entrance to her womanhood, stretching her delicately, enticingly so that unconsciously she arched her back.

The air left Jason's lungs in a gush as Genna shifted so that he inched into her tight moistness. When she contracted around him, he forgot the desire to tease her and instead plunged in, his fingers rubbing her.

Genna gasped as Jason slipped deeply into her,

making her stomach clench in delighted spasms that spun outward to every limb. Slowly he withdrew, then just as slowly pushed inward again.

He whispered in her ear, "I could awaken like this every day for the rest of my life. You're so tight and wet and good."

It felt so right to her, having him inside her, his hands caressing her. "I love you, Jason."

"I know," he said softly, kissing her shoulder, continuing to stroke her with his manhood. "And I love you."

No other words could have made her desire him more. She wriggled against him, trying to take him deeper inside.

He chuckled. "I'm not a stallion, love. There's only so much of me, and in this position I can't penetrate you completely."

She laughed with him, a short, breathy release that was both amusement and embarrassment at her eagerness for him. "I'm sorry. I didn't know."

"Apology accepted. Now relax and enjoy this for the slow building delight it can be."

He continued to nibble on her shoulders and nape while his fingers strummed upon the rich smoothness of her satin skin. His shaft moved in slow, rotating glides that sent tendrils of desire curling into her womb. She wanted the final pleasure, but no matter how she tried to adjust herself for him he went no deeper and no faster.

"Ja . . . son," she moaned, unable to bear it any longer.

"Hmmm?" He continued his torturous attentions, content to take it easy until neither one of them could stand it.

"Jason," she said, biting her lip to keep from gasping with the mounting tension each thrust of his hips brought her. "I can't take this. I need you to fill me."

"Greedy," he murmured, delighted with her open avowal of desire for him. "I will fill you, when I'm sure that you're almost at your peak. The longer we play, the more intense the final release."

"I . . . I don't know," she said, doubting that anything could be more exquisitely pleasurable than what he'd done to her the night before. "I don't have any experience with this part of life."

He smiled, knowing she couldn't see him. He was immensely pleased that he was the first man to do these things to her. And he would be the *only* man to ever do this to her. He would make her crave his caresses above all else. When they were married, he would love her as thoroughly as any man could love a woman.

Each time he felt her begin to tense and her passage start to tighten rhythmically, he withdrew so that only her opening was stretched by him. When he felt her subside and her breathing slow, he pushed inside. For a while, he even withdrew and used his fingers to stimulate her, afraid that if he remained buried in her he would lose his control and finish too soon what he'd started.

Genna moaned deep in her throat, her mind incapable of rational thought. What he was doing to her was beyond anything she had ever imagined possible. How much longer could he continue this? How much more could she stand before she reached her release in spite of his withdrawal?

Finally, when her tension was so great that her legs quivered from strain, Jason left her. She gasped in protest at the surcease of pleasure. Before the sound was completely out, Jason mounted her.

His mouth slashed down on hers, forcing entry for his tongue. His staff plunged into her so that he touched and stroked her deepest part.

Their stomachs met and retreated, slapping with soft enticement as their hips moved. Genna rose to encompass him totally, her legs locked around him.

Their rhythm increased, the heat from their bodies an extension of the heat coiling inside them about to burst forth. Genna grasped his shoulders, her nails raking down the rippling muscles of his back. She sucked his tongue into her mouth and pressed upward, encouraging him to penetrate deeper.

Then, with a flash like a match struck to tinder, her body burst into waves of burning heat. She clung to him with arms weakened by her ordeal.

With a final thrust and a groan of pure pleasure, Jason spewed forth his seed. His release was so intense that his heart pounded erratically and his shoulders shook from exhaustion.

When the ripples of his release grew smaller and smaller, he still lay buried in her. He loved her and desired her equally. Spent as he was from the past weeks and the last hour's passion, he still wanted her again. He knew he would never get enough of her sweet endless surrender.

"Genna," he murmured, finding it an effort to even speak, "you're mine. Let me love you again."

She opened her eyes, heavy from passion's release, and gazed at him towering above her. His face was drawn in lines of fatigue and hunger; his mouth swollen from their kisses, yet firm with the resolve to continue loving her. Sweat beaded his forehead, and his sun bleached hair clung in damp locks to his face.

Gone from his eyes was the pain caused by his wound, and in its place was a sensuality so great that his irises were golden, the green gone. In that instant, she knew he would risk anything to possess her and that knowledge was a fierce exultation in her heart.

"Yes, Jason. Love me again."

This time their loving was rapid and violent, the crashing rush of river rapids speeding to disintegration over a precipice. Their hips thrust, their lips plundered, and their hearts pounded.

Genna no longer cared about tomorrow, or yesterday, or even the next moment. Her body strained with every motion, every breath, as she sought the ultimate expression of her love for the man who touched her secret depths.

His body already extended beyond anything he'd ever experienced, Jason pounded into her woman's caress. The blood thundered in his ears like water plunging over a waterfall, dropping with a crescendo and exploding into multitudinous water drops which spattered outward in ever widening circles.

"Yes, Genna, yes," he groaned into the warm depths of her devouring mouth. "Take me whole. Consume me. Take everything I have to give and give it back to me in your love."

Her words joined his, her body disintegrating into pure sensation. "I love you."

Genna felt as though every pore in her body was saturated with Jason's lovemaking. Her skin was surfeited with his touch. Her nostrils were flared with the musky scent of their lovemaking which clung to her skin and their sheets. He had imprinted himself on her, and she knew the brand would stay with her for life.

Jason collapsed to the side, pulling her onto her side to face him. He kissed her forehead, the tip of her nose, and her lips. His touch was passionless, but tender.

"When we reach Brussels, we'll be married." His words were soft and clear, his eyes watching for her reaction.

We'll be married . . . She had never thought he would offer marriage. If she'd thought so, she would never have let him make love to her, knowing the pain it would bring him afterwards.

The languor, the satisfaction was leached from Genna. It took all her self-control not to let her dismay show on her face or in her body's posture. What was she to say? Loving him as she did, she should be ecstatically happy that he wanted to marry her.

The irony that she couldn't have him, and realizing he wanted her as badly, was breaking her heart. Holding back the tears which misted her eyes was one of the hardest things she'd ever done.

But there was Ricci. No matter what she felt for Jason, she couldn't break her promise to Luigi. Luigi might be dead, but her sense of honor wouldn't allow her to renounce her word. No matter how that word had been coerced. Without Luigi, her mother would have died.

She felt like a broken woman, but somehow, she managed to continue smiling at her beloved. If nothing else, she would have the memories of their lovemaking and Jason's proposal to cherish throughout the remaining purgatory of her life.

With her finger, she traced the line of Jason's brows and down the straight bridge of his nose, pausing as she reached his lips. He was her lover, her love, her life and she couldn't have him.

"Let's wait until we're in Brussels to make plans."

"Genna?" His expression was worried and he put one hand on her waist to keep her from rising. "Is something the matter?"

She swallowed the lump lodged in her throat. "No, love, nothing."

He continued to frown as she slipped away from him. She could feel his eyes on her as they both began to dress. Unable to meet his look, fearing that she'd be overcome with grief, she kept her gaze averted.

Instead, she memorized the small room, from its rough walls, and sputtering fire, to the bare floors and small, lumpy bed where they'd consummated their love. It was the wrong thing to do. Genna turned her back to Jason and dashed furtively at the moisture trailing down her cheeks.

Jason saw the sorrow on her face. When her arm raised, he knew she was crying. Not able to tolerate her pain, he went to her, uncaring of the cold permeating the air and causing gooseflesh to raise on his skin.

"Genna," he murmured, taking her into his arms and holding her close to his heart. "Why are you crying if nothing is the matter?" When she refused to look at him, he lifted her chin. "Won't you tell me?"

Genna drank in his tender concern, tempted to tell him everything. Perhaps that would be best, she reasoned. If he knows, it doesn't mean we can't continue this way until we reach Brussels.

A sliver of doubt nagged at her that this wasn't the way. Once he knew about her betrothal he should, by honor, not touch her again, something she couldn't tolerate. Not yet. That estrangement would come all too soon.

As much as she craved the completeness his embrace gave her, she wanted even less to lie to him. And continuing to tell him that nothing was wrong would be lying.

"Oh, Jason," she said, hiccupping on a sob and burrowing her face into the warmth of his chest. "I love you so much it hurts."

Lifting her, Jason strode to the bed. He sat on the edge with Genna on his lap like a small child. "Genna, I don't think I understand. I never made love to you intending to give you pain. If you love me so much, why does it hurt?"

She took a deep breath. "Jason, I love you until my heart feels as though it will explode from more love than it can contain. I think I've loved you from the instant you opened your eyes when my needle was sewing you up. Instead of complaining about the pain, you joked."

He nodded, encouraging her to continue, but dread began to grow in him like an icicle that lengthens with each drop of water in a freezing winter.

Emotionally bleeding, Genna finally let her tears start. They moved down her face like tiny jewels. "Jason, I'd give everything I own, everything I am as a person, to marry you." She looked at him, her eyes beseeching him to understand and continue loving her. "But I'm betrothed to another. I can't marry you."

The words should have been a catharsis for her. But instead of easing the agony she felt, they only increased it. Now she'd put into motion the end of her dream. Now Jason would despise her and revile her for not confiding in him before they made love. He would be hurt and condemn her for not being stronger.

"What?" he said, relief flowing over him like a hot breeze, melting the ice that had begun to form in his heart. He began to lightly wipe away her tears. "Is that all?"

Bewildered, Genna clutched his sleeves with nerveless fingers. "Isn't that enough? It means we can never be together."

He shook his head, denying her statement and refusing to hear the finality in her voice. "It means nothing of the sort. You'll just have to cry off. Then we'll be married."

Stunned, she slid from his lap and stood. "Jason, I can't renege. I gave my word to Luigi on his deathbed."

Jason blocked out the meaning of her words. He stood and took her into his arms. "You love me, don't you?"

"Yes." She looked up at him, feeling the warmth of his body penetrate their clothing to heat her skin. "More than anything."

Satisfaction lit his face, curving his mouth into a triumphant smile. "That's all that matters."

"No, it isn't." she said even as her heart told her to hold her tongue. "It isn't all, Jason. I made a promise, and I can't renege on it. All my life I've respected any commitment I've made. My father raised me that when all is said and done, we have to live with ourselves. If we aren't true to what we hold important, then we aren't true to ourselves. I can't break my word."

Jason couldn't believe she was saying those things. How could she put a promise made to a dying man before the love they shared? She couldn't and he would prove it to her.

With the swiftness of a hawk, his mouth came down on hers, sending all thought of existence without him fleeing Genna's mind. All she was aware of was the feel of his lips pressing hers, his tongue dancing with hers, and his hands roving her back and hips with a possessiveness born of familiarity and love.

He was her life and nothing else mattered.

Tomorrow, or the day after, or the week after, she would deal with the rift between them that her promise to Luigi would precipitate. But for now she would live each moment as it came, loving Jason with all the hopelessness of her passion.

Within the hour, they were on the road, a plain meal of vegetables, mutton, and coarse brown bread sitting warmly in their stomach. Genna was thankful for the food and for the oilcloth protecting her from the drizzle. Jason had purchased each of them one from the innkeeper.

However, when night fell, her teeth chattered. She dreaded sleeping on the cold hard ground more than she would have if they hadn't spent the night before in an inn. They'd just passed a small town and she'd looked longingly at the sign of an inn, but hadn't been surprised when Jason rode past. She firmed her resolve and said nothing.

She was mired in her physical misery, avoiding any thought about what had occurred between her and Jason emotionally, when he raised his hand and stopped his horse.

"Quickly," he hissed, grabbing her mare's bridle. "Someone is galloping up behind us."

Before she realized what was happening, he'd guided both mounts into the ditch bordering the road. Without him saying it, she knew he wanted quiet. In the silence, she heard the sounds of hooves hitting the hardened mud of the road.

Was it the spy who'd broken into the Paris house? Had he managed to track them? Why else would someone be out on a chill, damp night like this and traveling so rapidly?

Her pulse increased and her palms sweated inside her leather gloves. Her fingers and feet felt like blocks of ice, and were becoming frostier with each strike of a hoof on dirt.

Then the traveler sped past them, his features impossible to discern in the dark. He rode like the devil incarnate were chasing him, his cloak billowing behind him and his hat pulled low over his head.

Genna shivered. She managed to keep her mount from prancing nervously as the scent of the rider's horse reached them. Then he was past.

When the racing horse's hooves were not even an echo in their ears, Jason still waited, counting silently to one thousand. Only then did he turn their horses back in the direction they'd come, but remained in the ditch which meant they moved at a turtle's pace.

Although curiosity about why they were headed back the way they'd come ate at Genna, she dared not voice her question. When Jason thought it safe he'd tell her what he was doing.

To help tolerate the fear which gnawed at her, she concentrated on the ache in her lower back as it twinged with each step her horse took. Never again would she use a sidesaddle!

She sighed deeply, her breath floating like a cloud in front of her. Her aches and pains, the fear of discovery, they were only diversions from what she truly worried about: Jason's proposal.

She knew she should make Jason understand that she could never marry him; it was an impossible dream. But, she consoled herself, she had tried. He'd refused to hear her. She knew from dealing with Luigi that when a man didn't want to change his mind, he wouldn't hear any words spoken to him; no matter how true those words might be. Only actual events would sway him.

Lost in her dismal thoughts, they arrived at the village they'd passed an hour earlier. Jason was dismounting from his horse in front of the inn before she realized it.

"Stay here," he said, drawing her back to the present. "Keep your hood pulled over your head and face. Don't speak to anyone."

He got off his mount and rummaged in the saddlebags. When he turned back to her, one of the dueling pistols was in his hand.

"Use this if you have to."

She took the weapon, but stared at it. "I don't think I could. Can't I just come in with you?"

She could barely see him in the circle of light that eked from the inn's windows, but she was attuned enough to him to feel his discomfort.

"No, Genna, I dare not take you in. I want to see what I can find out without drawing any more attention to myself than necessary. If I weren't going to ask, I'd take you in to throw them off the track since the man following probably asked only for a man. As it is, just asking questions will probably give me away should the man return."

She didn't like any of it, but he made sense once

again. So she hunched into her cape and gingerly cradled the pistol in the palms of her hands.

He was back on a gust of air, reeking of smoke and mutton and unwashed bodies. "A slight, dark-haired and dark eyed man was here, asking for a man with blond hair. Damn! I have to think this out."

He mounted, sitting for long minutes, then turned the horses back to the road. But instead of retracing their previous path, they continued heading back south toward Paris, trudging the same ground they'd spent all day traveling.

Confused, Genna pulled alongside Jason. "What are you doing?" The moon chose that instant to come out from hiding, and she could see his face clearly in the hard light. His mouth was heavily defined by deep crevices of strain.

"I hope I'm confusing our pursuer and arranging for us to sleep in a bed at the same time."

"But I don't understand how returning the way we came can do that."

He smiled, but it was only a thin stretching of his lips. "If I were chasing someone whom I thought had information his superior needed immediately, I'd never think that my quarry might retrace his steps."

Totally confused now, she asked, "Don't you have urgent news?"

His hand tightened on the reins and the horse pranced nervously. "No. If I hadn't been knifed, I might have reached Wellington with advance news of Bonaparte's escape. Then the duke might have been able to do something to stop Bonaparte's advance into France. Now, it's too late."

Comprehension brought her increased admiration for this man whom she'd thrown her lot in with, even as she sympathized with his obvious sense of failure. Much as she wanted to console him, she knew there were no words that could negate his sense of having failed.

By the time they reached the next town with an inn, the moon had set and the sun would soon be rising. Genna was maintaining her seat only with deep concentration. She knew that with his wound barely healed Jason couldn't be much better off.

In the murky gray light, Jason went in and got them a room. Genna didn't know how long he intended to stay here, and she didn't care. She didn't even care if the bed had bugs.

Not even bothering to undress, Genna collapsed on the single bed. Vaguely, she registered Jason pushing the one chair under the door handle, and then everything went black.

Jason gazed down at her, fully sympathetic with her exhaustion. Using the remainder of his energy, he pulled off her boots and then his, before crawling under the covers and curling up next to her.

When Genna next regained consciousness, Jason was fondling her breasts and kissing her face with delicate touches. All thoughts of the chase, the danger, and the dark future waiting for them receded as she responded to him in the most basic way possible.

They consummated their love until both partners were shaking from exertion. Only then did other concerns intrude.

"Jason," Genna asked, her voice slumberous with repletion, "shouldn't we get started?"

He ran one hand down her side, lingering at the swell of her hips and trailing his fingers from her hip bone to her pelvis, making her draw in her breath. "Does that feel good?"

She groaned as his fingers toyed with her sensitive skin. "You know it does, but it doesn't answer my question. I thought we were on the run because you had to reach Wellington, not so that you could make love to me constantly."

He chuckled. "You're right." But he didn't stop his fingers. "However, I figure that we have the rest of today and tonight to spend here. The man who was following us should already be in Brussels by now, or damned close. Wellington probably isn't there yet, and so there's no need for me to hurry. My contact will remain in place until Wellington tells him differently, and I haven't got any information that the duke doesn't already have."

She gasped with pleasure as he continued to massage her now swollen flesh. Somehow she forced her concentration to stay on their conversation. "Then why were we rushing?"

He grinned at her discomfiture and bent his head to take one of her breasts into his mouth. He sucked gently and rubbed the rough flat of his tongue over her nipple, sending jolts of pure delight speeding to her knotted stomach.

He took his mouth from her. "We were rushing because I feared the man was following us. I had no desire to be caught." With careful deliberation, he took her other breast into his mouth and proceeded to bring it to the same state of attention that its mate was already in. "You're beautiful, Genna," he murmured. "And now that our enemy is ahead of us, and will probably lie in wait for us in Brussels, we can linger here and enjoy ourselves."

At the last of his words, his fingers moved deeper into her aroused body and his mouth lowered over her abdomen. Running his teeth lightly over her ribs, he nipped and kissed her, making her flush with desire.

Jason felt her tremble beneath his mouth and her honeyed depths rippled around his fingers; exultation moved through him like a tidal wave. She was his and he would wash away any thoughts she had of the man she was betrothed to. He would consume her, body and soul, until she wanted no one but him.

He would possess her completely; constantly filling her with his seed until she conceived his child, tying her to him for eternity. She would be his, and he'd be damned if he would let her go to another man. No matter what she'd promised.

Chapter Twelve

Brussels, April 1815

For the rest of that day and the next, Jason and Genna had stayed at the dilapidated inn. Looking back on it from the distance of two weeks, Genna realized that both of them had been unwilling to leave the drab little room because it would mean returning to civilization and the demands of their personal lives: Jason to his spying, and she to Ricci.

Genna shifted on the settee where she sat, pulling her feet up to the cushions and her knees up to her chin. The remainder of their trip to Brussels had been quick. When they'd reached Brussels, Jason had left her in an inn bordering the city while he went alone to find out if Aunt Hester and the household had arrived. Returning for Genna, he'd told her that her aunt and servants were comfortably ensconced in a rented house on the Rue Ducale, across from the city's park.

Now, exactly fourteen days and seven hours later, Genna sat gazing out the window at that park. The trees, green with budding life and swaying in the soft breeze, spoke of springtime and happiness. People strolled the immaculate paths, their faces alight with laughter.

Fervently, Genna wished she could share in the pleasant scene, but her spirits were at their lowest point since Jason had deposited her on Hester's doorstep. Jason had kissed her and promised to return to her as soon as he was able. She hadn't seen him since and was constantly in fear that the spy they'd eluded on the road had finally caught up with Jason.

She sighed deeply and turned away from the bucolic sight being enacted in the park. Deep in her heart, she knew that if he was able, Jason would return to her. Even though she'd told him repeatedly that she couldn't marry him because of her promise to Luigi, she understood him enough to realize that he would never allow her to go to another man without a fight.

So, where was Jason? Day and night she prayed for his safety, wanting his touch even though she knew it would only bring them pain. If he should return to her, their agony when they finally separated would only be that much harder to bear.

Still, she yearned for him.

"Ahem," Michaels's voice interrupted her melancholy thoughts. "Milady, the Conte di Ponti."

Ricci was the last person she wanted to see. He'd been pestering her every day since her arrival, and she was heartily sick of him. But he'd already pushed his way past the butler. So she made the best of it. "Good morning, Ricci."

Without glancing in her direction, he told Michaels, "Out. And make sure that we are not interrupted."

Michaels glanced at Genna for her confirmation or denial of Ricci's order. Even though her spleen boiled at Ricci's presumption, she didn't have the energy to fight with him. She nodded.

Ricci pivoted on the heel of his immaculately polished boot and stalked toward Genna, stopping inches from her. "Where were you when your household fled Paris?"

His question, unprompted and unexpected, set her back. But in spite of that, she met his glare with one of her own, refusing to let him make her cower. She was not ashamed of what she'd done, and she didn't know how Ricci could have discovered what she had done. Hester had already told her that the household had managed to leave the designated rendezvous early so that Ricci hadn't traveled with them. Therefore, he was very likely bluffing for some obscure reason of his own. And it was none of his business, anyway.

Cool as an autumn day, she asked, "How do you know I wasn't with them . . . since you weren't, either?"

His dark eyes flashed and his complexion turned a mottled purple. "'Tis none of your affair how I know. Just answer my question."

She imperiously raised an eyebrow, unwilling to let him dictate to her. If she allowed him to have the upper hand now, he would be insuperable after their marriage.

"How I arrived here in Brussels is my personal business, Ricci, and I'll ask you not to pry."

His face darkened and his hands clenched into fists. "You have *no personal business*. You are betrothed to me, and what you do is subject to my approval."

The words roared at Genna, making her hackles rise. Since Jason left her, she'd been existing in a state of nervous anxiety over her feelings for him. And now, listening to Ricci rant and rave at her, her tolerance snapped.

"You're my betrothed, not my keeper, Ricci. Best you remember that."

The redness of his face deepened. His hands shot out, grabbing her upper arms, and he yanked her up against him. "I will shortly be your master, Genna, Contessa di Ponti. Best *you* remember that."

His fingers bit into her skin as he kept her so tightly bound to him that she could feel the rapid rise and fall of his chest. She was so close that she could see the pores of his face and the dark stubble that, even this early in the morning, was beginning to dot his jaw. He was nothing like Jason. The knowledge that this was the man she had committed herself to marry was bile in her throat.

"Release me immediately," she said, drawing her face as far away from his as possible, not wanting this physical contact between them.

"When it is my pleasure to do so." His mouth

curved into a snide smile. "I wager you were with another man, *cara mia*. And I wager even more that you gave to him that which you should have saved for me."

She started at his accurate assessment and tried to pull away. How had he guessed she had been with a man? Logically, it wasn't such an astounding deduction. A woman alone would have never made the trip.

She had to keep him from learning any more than that for Jason's sake. A British spy, no matter how brave and wonderful, didn't stand a chance against a nobleman who wanted revenge. Therefore, she must refuse to answer any of his questions and insure that the servants and Aunt Hester said nothing. Things were becoming more complicated than she knew how to handle adequately. For the first time in her life, she began to understand the saying about deception and tangled webs.

"You've an active imagination, and you would bet on anything."

"Slut," he hissed, his hands digging into her flesh. "Your reaction betrays you. Not that it signifies. I knew before. Several times I called here and was told that you were indisposed. Hah!" His eyes glittered dangerously. "And to think that I must marry you in order to get the wealth that should have been mine. Well, I will take now what you have already given another."

Horrified by his meaning, she stared into his eyes and saw in their brown glitter the truth of his words. He intended to take her by force, with no regard to anything but his own desires. Her stomach curdled.

"Let me—"

His mouth slashed down on hers and his body bent over hers, forcing her to flex backwards. She twisted in his grip, but slim as he was, his determination lent him the strength to overpower her. She kicked at him, but her slippered feet were ineffective against the thick leather of his boots.

Deep in his throat Ricci laughed, a guttural sound that turned Genna's palms to ice. A cold sweat broke out over her body. She couldn't let him do this to her.

He lifted his mouth from hers. "Perhaps you would care to tell me about the man you fornicated with when you should have been with your people?"

Genna took a deep breath to try and still her clanging nerves. She had to think about his words. For some reason, he wanted very badly to know about Jason. Why? To challenge Jason to a duel? She hadn't thought that was something Ricci would do.

Carefully controlling her anxiety, she met his demand with a raised chin and haughty bearing, no small feat when his arms still held her like a vise. "You've no right to speak such crudity to me. I demand that you leave. *Now*."

His answer was to throw back his head and laugh. "You are in no position to dictate to me." Then his face hardened and his eyes narrowed to sly slits. "Since you will not answer, I see that I must show you who is master. I do not intend to tolerate your insolence now or after our marriage."

His hands tightened painfully on her arms, and she had to close her eyes to keep from showing him that he was hurting her. At least he was momentarily diverted from Jason.

His voice was a hiss. "On the floor, whore. Spread your legs for me like you did that other man."

Fear that he truly intended to force her gave her the determination to defy him. She'd be damned if she would cower to this bully, no matter what his hold on her was. "You can't do this. Let me go."

The sneer on his face increased, turning his countenance into a mask of hate. "I can do anything I want with you, and I intend to prove it."

Gripping both her hands in one of his, he used his free hand to raise her skirts. Genna struggled to keep him from reaching her, thrashing her legs and trying to avoid him. Nothing worked. His fingers were between her thighs like cold iron.

"Stop it, stop it," she gasped, kicking futilely at him. She wouldn't let him do this.

A scream rose to her lips, but she bit herself to stifle it. If she called for help, it would be Michaels who came. She couldn't subject her butler to the wrath Ricci's anger would take later. Ricci was vengeful, particularly to anyone who'd thwarted him.

He knocked her legs out from under her so that she hit the floor with a thud with him on top of her. Her skirts rode her hips, and his knee pressed between her thighs, forcing her open.

His breath was hot and fetid in her face. The stench of stale liquor from his mouth made her gag. His body was a weight pressing her into the carpet, and his hands were shackles keeping her from fighting him.

This couldn't be happening to her. Surely, she would wake up and discover this was only a nightmare, a creation of her loathing for Ricci. Surely, she would open her eyes and this would all disappear. Surely...

Ricci's fingers at her innermost portal shocked her, wiping away thoughts of unreality and sending shivers of revulsion pulsing through her abdomen. His wet, slobbering mouth covered hers, cutting off her ability to breathe. This horror was all too real.

He lifted his lips to ask, "Are you enjoying yourself, Genna?"

His voice, deep and guttural, mocked her. She twisted her head to the side, trying to avoid his kiss. He released her so that he could use his hands to force her face back to his.

Her hands were free! In the same instant that fact registered, she knew she either stopped him now or he would rape her.

Desperately, she raked her nails across his cheek. And while his face contorted with rage and his mind focused on the pain, she thrust him off her.

She scrambled away from him and got to her knees. Before she could stand, his fist slashed out and caught her on the jaw. She reeled from the blow, seeing points of light in place of the room.

"Rutting bitch. I will teach you a lesson you

will not forget."

Genna swallowed the blood coming from where she'd bitten her tongue, determined not to give Ricci the satisfaction of seeing just how much he'd hurt her. Even so, she couldn't stand let alone dodge his next blow. Realizing that, she strengthened her resolve and met him face-to-face.

Ricci paused, his eyes locked with hers, his mouth a snarl. Then he pulled back his arm.

Her gaze flicked to his movement, but she kept her face defiant, even though she dreaded the anticipated pain. Instinctively, she knew that if she showed fear to him now, the rest of her life would be worse than anything that could happen in this room today.

The door banged open, slamming against the wall. She heard men's voices arguing.

"Damn it, I'm going in and nothing you can do will stop me!"

It was Jason! He was alive and safe. Relief moved through Genna like a warm rush of heat after the freeze of winter. Her legs gave completely out, leaving her sprawled on the floor. Everything would be all right.

"You can't go in there." She heard Michaels's distraught voice in the background.

Jason came anyway. He might have been conjured from the magic yearnings of her heart. She didn't know why he'd come at this moment, but she was eternally grateful.

Only for an instant did he pause, but it was enough for Genna to feast on the sight of him. Gone were the rags of a servant; his tatters were replaced by the somber, but costly, dress of a gentleman. A blue, tight fitting jacket, buff pantaloons tucked into gleaming Hessians, a white vest and immaculate cravat. But it was his face that caught and held her attention.

His eyes blazed with wrath. His mouth was a thin line of menace. His hands bunched into fists as he stalked Ricci.

"What the hell?" Jason thundered upon seeing Genna collapsed on the floor. Her lovely face was blotched from a blow; her disheveled skirts raised around her hips. A dark man towered over her, his arm raised to strike her again.

"Damn you to hell!"

Rage, such as he'd never known, propelled Jason forward. Instead of seeing a human being, he saw an animal mauling his woman. Everything turned to shades of angry red for Jason as energy flowed to his muscles, making them harden into pulverizing weapons.

He grabbed the man from behind and twirled him around. Then his right fist slammed into the man's face, then his left, then his right.

All Jason could see was Genna's beautiful, caring face whitened by pain and her exquisite legs exposed to this scum's evil lusts. When Genna's attacker sank to the floor, Jason reached down and wrapped his fingers around the bastard's throat and pulled him up. He shook the man like he would a cloth doll.

"Jason," Genna pleaded. Then louder, "Jason!"

In a blood thirst that demanded slaking, Jason belatedly registered Genna's voice. He turned eyes dazed by violent passion toward his love.

"Jason," she said firmly, "you have to stop or you'll kill him. He's not worth it."

The calm conviction of her words worked on Jason's taut nerves. Marginally less furious, he focused his attention on the man hanging limply between his fingers. For the first time since starting, he comprehended what he'd done. The man's face was a bloody pulp, his nose certainly broken; both eyes already swelling shut, and his full mouth bleeding.

Slowly, Jason came back to rational thought. The intensity of his fury lessened and with that came the glimmerings of disgust at himself for what he'd done. His grip slackened, allowing the man to slide to the floor. But before Genna's attacker even lay on the ground, Jason knew that he'd do it again if he ever found the bastard touching Genna.

Jason's breath came in jagged drags as he looked at the cringing thing by his feet. "I'll beat you to within an inch of your life if I ever see you with her again. But if you ever lay a finger on her again, *I will kill you.*"

Stepping over the heap on the floor, Jason went to Genna.

Genna had pulled herself up before stopping Jason's rampage. She stood with one hand on the settee to support her weight. When Jason reached her, she fell into his outstretched arms, no longer caring whether or not Ricci knew about Jason.

She felt so good and so safe to be held by her love.

Genna doubted if she would ever feel completely protected without him beside her. And she couldn't have Jason. No matter what Ricci had done, she would still marry him. She'd given her word. The tears started falling.

Genna's shoulders shook within Jason's tender embrace, and he cursed anew the man who'd done this to her. Without a word, he scooped her up and headed for the door. Before leaving, he glanced back at the man.

Did he see a flicker of recognition in the bloody bastard's eyes? Jason shook his head. That was ridiculous. He didn't know the man, so that excuse for a human being couldn't know him. He was reacting to what the bastard had done to Genna, nothing more.

Turning his back on the pitiful figure, Jason strode up the stairs, an anxious Michaels in his wake. "Send for the housekeeper," Jason said over his shoulder.

"Will she be all right, sir?" the butler asked, a new tone of respect for Jason in his voice.

Jason stopped long enough to give Michaels an exasperated look. "She will be if you'll get your wife here to help me. Or go get the other lady." He took another step. "Or better yet, get Alphonse."

"Yes, sir," Michaels said, adding under his breath, "Best to leave Lady Hester out of this until everything is settled." With that, he hurried down the stairs.

Only after the butler left, did Jason remember that he didn't know where Genna's bedroom was in this house. He would have to ask her, but he was loath to do so because she was continuing to sob quietly. Only the shivering of her shoulders and an occasional soft sniff told him her terror hadn't subsided.

"Genna," he said softly, "love, where's your room?"

His voice drew her back from the hell she'd allowed herself to sink into. Ricci had tried to rape her, and very nearly succeeded. Then he'd beaten her. And she had promised to marry him. Could there be any worse fate? God, why did things have to go this way?

Jason promised her happiness and love for the rest of her years. And she loved him with a fierceness to match what he felt for her. But she was committed to marriage with Ricci, and there was no calling back the words of agreement. She had promised. From some reservoir of strength she wasn't sure she possessed, she would have to draw power and endure her fate. Self-pity wasn't going to make the situation change.

Pulling her torn emotions under control, she swallowed the last sob. "Turn right. It's the third door on the left."

While Jason carried her, she wiped away the final drop of moisture from her face and longed heartily for a handkerchief. She was almost composed when Jason kicked open her door.

"You can put me down now," she said when they were inside, the door closed behind them.

Instead of releasing her, he sat down in a chair and kept her on his lap. One arm circled her waist, and the other stroked her hair that had come down and now flowed over her shoulders and back in a rich copper cascade.

Compassion for her pain contorted his features. "Genna, I wish I'd been able to come sooner. I'd do anything to erase what you just went through. I can't. But I vow by all I hold sacred that it won't happen again. I won't let it."

"Shhh," she said, putting her finger to his lips. "I know that if you could have, you'd never have left me when we arrived. Please don't torture yourself with *what ifs.*" She sighed, and rubbed her forehead wearily. "I wish it hadn't occurred, but 'tis over now and, really, nothing happened."

His brows met in a straight bar over his flashing eyes. "Nothing happened? That bastard almost raped you and then he hit you. I meant what I said to him. If he lays another hand on you, I'll kill him."

She longed to give him the right to protect her, but she couldn't. Ricci would touch her again, and the law would protect him when he did. Knowing this, she became frightened for Jason. His obstinacy would cause him trouble. She had to protect her love from the consequences of his love for her. She had to tell him again that they could never wed.

Her heart began to break into tiny pieces. She twisted away from him, her fingers clenched in the folds of her dress, unable to watch his face when she told him.

Her throat swelled shut, and she had to force the words out. "Jason, I can't give you the right to protect me from that man."

The hand that had been stroking her hair stilled. "What do you mean?"

Her pain was a palpable constriction of her heart. "I can't marry you..."

Suspicion narrowed his eyes and his lips became a thin line. "Who was that bastard I just beat the hell out of?"

She didn't want to tell him. Jason was so angry right now that he might very likely go down and finish what he'd already started.

"Oh, Jason, I love you. I love you so much that life is nothing without you. But I can't marry you. You know I can't." Her head dropped in weary resignation, no longer able to withstand the furious intensity he radiated.

His arms tightened around her waist. "You're not answering my question."

Before she could reply, the door slammed open.

"Genna," Aunt Hester's high, scandalized voice penetrated Genna's despair. "Michaels said you were hurt."

"Hester!" Genna pushed at Jason's chest, trying to get him to release her so she could stand up. He held her firmly until she subsided. She put the best face on as possible under the compromising circumstances.

Jason was put out by this interruption when he sensed Genna was keeping something important from him. He couldn't keep the irritation out of his voice. "Aunt Hester, I presume?"

Hester stopped in her tracks, her plump mouth a plump 'O' of amazement. Then her gaze ran over the pair of them, Genna still held immobile on *his* lap. "Well, I never. You are bold as brass with your fashionable clothes, but they do not hide the scoundrel in you. And Genna, how you can sit in that man's lap . . ." She looked to heaven for help then back at the two. "I told you he would ravish us in our beds."

Pushing futilely at Jason's chest one last time, Genna sighed and relaxed. There was nothing she could do to change this situation, she might as well make the best of it. Hester would be Hester, and Jason would be obstinate. "Yes, dear, but at least you're spared. I'm the one he was ravishing."

Hester glared at her. "Such levity." Then she pointed her finger at them and began to shake it. "You being seduced by this brigand . . . and that is probably a polite term . . . while your betrothed is downstairs barely able to stand. Genna, I am ashamed of you." She put a hand to her brow. "I knew no good would come of your staying behind in Paris to nurse this scoundrel. And I was right."

The damning words were barely out of Hester's mouth before the atmosphere in the room chilled. Genna knew before Jason turned to look at her that he comprehended everything. She hadn't wanted him to ever know that the man he'd saved her from was the man keeping them apart.

She put her hand on his chest in an unconscious plea for understanding. "Jason."

His voice was as soft and as cold as the first snow of winter, and his lips were white from strain. "I just beat the hell out of the man you insist on marrying."

She nodded, unable to speak past the constriction in her throat. The hurt emanating from his eyes was a knife in her heart. She wanted to tell him she'd changed her mind, and that she'd marry him. But she couldn't. She'd promised.

Abruptly, Jason set her from him and stood. He paced to the window, his hands fisted at his side. When he turned back to her, his face was twisted with incredulity, anger, and pain. "That groveling animal is the man you insist on marrying? That foul excuse for a human being is the reason you refuse my love?"

Her eyes never leaving his, her heart pounding heavily in her breast, she nodded.

"He tried to rape you, Genna. He hit you."

The sobs caught in her throat, and she buried her face in her hands. "God, I know."

Aunt Hester's gasp was the only sound. Then she started babbling. "Ricci hurt you? Oh, dear. What does this mean, Genna? If that is true, you cannot marry him. Even Luigi, in his pride, would not wish that on you."

Unable to take any more, Jason twisted around and roared at Hester, "Get out!"

Eyes wide with surprise and not a little fear, Hester hesitated, her glance going to Genna. "Child?"

Genna raised her tear-stained face. "Please, dear, leave. Jason and I have much to settle."

At her niece's reassurance, Hester cast one last searching look at Jason and then fled the room.

Genna wasn't aware of Hester leaving, all her concentration was on Jason. "Jason, please, you have to understand. Luigi made me promise, and I can't go back on it now. But 'tis more than that one promise. All my life, my father raised me to honor my word. I married Luigi, a man old enough to be my father, because it was what my mother wanted and I couldn't in all good conscience refuse. I have always done as I've said I would. I can't stop now. I can't stop being me, no matter how much I love you and how much it hurts to deny the glimpse of heaven that marriage to you would be."

Silence reigned for indeterminable minutes as Jason studied Genna. He knew she loved him, she would have never given herself to him otherwise. She must value her honor greatly to put it before their happiness. While he couldn't understand it, he had to admire it. The anger began to drain from him and his muscles began to loosen.

Genna watched her love. She saw his shoulders relax. He would forgive her. It was all she could hope for, and she was grateful for it.

In several strides, Jason was in front of Genna where he knelt. He took her hands in his and kissed them. "Genna, I don't understand why you're doing this, but I can't hurt you further by berating you. I love you too much to want to harm you."

He reached up and gently brushed her cheek, checking the fresh anger that swelled in him at the sight of the bruise beginning to show on her fair complexion. "I just wish I understood why you insist on marrying him? If he treated you with respect and care, I would accept your wish to fulfill your promise." A rueful grin curved his lips. "I might not like it, but I know how broken honor can ruin a life. But that man is a bastard."

The truth of his words was a fresh blow, and the tears that she'd striven so valiantly to suppress welled to her eyes.

Jason caught one tear on the tip of his finger and brought it to his tongue. The taste of salt caused by Genna's agony was more than he could stand. "Please, love, don't cry. I won't press you any more today."

Genna smiled tremulously at him. "You're too good to me, Jason. I don't deserve your concern after what I'm doing to you."

He chuckled, a poignant sound. "You're no angel, love, but I'm no saint either."

In proof of his words, he took her lips with his. It was a gentle kiss, a light melding of flesh that bound them in their agony as no harsh demand could have. When he pulled away, both were breathing faster, but their hearts were lighter.

"You're mine, Genna. I won't let you go."

"I'll always be yours in my heart, Jason. But I will marry Ricci." She put a finger to his parted lips to stop him from speaking. "I know it isn't the best thing for us and that Ricci will treat me abominably, but I owe it to Luigi. He married me when I had nowhere else to go and was in desperate need of funds to care for my mother. Because of Luigi, my mother is safe and well in a Swiss sanatorium for consumptives. Without him, she would have died years ago. I can't fail him now."

Wonder and admiration at her loyalty and strength swelled Jason's chest with pride and love for this woman he intended to wed no matter what she said. "Genna, you're the most noble person I know, but be warned. I said I won't badger you further today, but neither will I stop pursuing you until you are mine. I won't let you sacrifice the rest of your life because of a debt you think you owe a dead man."

She sighed and drew away from the warmth and security of his arms, unconsciously shivering at the loss. "I must, Jason. Otherwise, I wouldn't be able to live with myself, knowing that I let Luigi down, knowing that I didn't keep faith."

"You *will* be mine, Genna. No woman as self-sacrificing and generous as you should have to live the life that bastard will grant you. I won't let you destroy yourself, or me, by marrying him."

How she wanted to believe him, to let him take her into his arms again and never let her go. She had to be stronger than this. Even as she sought strength, a small voice insisted. Is it truly so bad a thing to break a promise when keeping it would mean the misery of two people so that one person could live a life of leisure? Immediately, Genna banished the insidious thought. It was too alluring to contemplate at length.

Jason saw the tension in the way her shoulders were squared and the clasping of her hands. He loved her too much to remain when his presence caused her this much turmoil. Going to the door, he looked back at her one last time.

"I'll return for you."

* * *

Even as he left, Jason vowed within his heart not to let her go. He would pursue her until he finally wore down her determination. He would hound her until she finally admitted that the love they felt for one another was more honorable than fulfilling any promise extracted under duress.

So absorbed was he in these thoughts that he didn't realize he'd reached Wellington's headquarters until one of the duke's attaches spoke to him, saying Wellington was waiting for him. The duke had requested a meeting with him even though Jason had already told his superior everything he knew.

A tiny qualm nagged at Jason. Wellington never wasted time, so the duke wanted something. Jason hoped it wouldn't keep him away from Genna again as his superior had already done for over a week.

Jason didn't have long to wait. Entering Wellington's office, Jason quickly took stock of his surroundings. Austerely decorated with only the finest furniture and accessories, the room was impressive like the man standing behind the desk. Wellington dressed neatly as befitted his station, but he never strove to impress. Jason admired that.

Moving easily, Jason approached the desk where the Duke of Wellington stood. He stopped several feet away and waited for the duke to speak.

"Everly," Wellington said, extending his hand.

For an instant, Jason wondered who Wellington was addressing. It had been almost a year since anyone had called him by his title. Then, wits back, Jason took Wellington's hand in his and said, "Your Grace."

Wellington motioned to a chair pulled up in front of his desk. Jason sat down and crossed one ankle over his knee, a casual pose that belied his alertness. He noted that Wellington looked no more grim than normal. But he had to concede that with the duke, the expression on his face meant nothing.

"Thank you for coming so promptly, Everly. I heard that you just arrived a week ago and have been busy passing on gleaned information."

Jason nodded. His superior had hinted that Wellington wanted something done that was of the utmost urgency.

Wellington steepled his fingers. "I asked you here because I have documents that must reach London as quickly as possible. They must be carried by someone in whom I have the utmost confidence. That person is you."

"Your Grace?" Jason managed to say in place of the words he wanted to use. Damnation! He didn't have the time to travel to England. Genna was here in Brussels, and he was determined to convince her to call off her engagement, something he couldn't bloody do if he were across the Channel.

He must have done a superb job of covering his chagrin because Wellington continued as though Jason had already agreed to do the mission. "I understand that your cover has been blown and that you were seriously injured while trying to leave Paris with vital news of Napoleon. I was also told that you traveled here in disguise and in the company of a widow, the Contessa di Ponti to be precise."

Jason nodded warily, unsure where all this was leading.

Wellington continued with a brief history of Genna's past, then said, "I ask that you not contact the woman again until this particular errand is accomplished. We have reason to believe that someone with well-placed connections is leaking information to Napoleon about our troop movements and strength. We cannot take the chance that word of your pending trip will spread and the person who is responsible for this leak might know that you have spied for us. No one must know you have left, or at least no one must know when you leave and where you are going."

Bloody hell! Now he was being instructed to disappear without a word. What would Genna think after he'd vowed to come back to her? Every muscle in Jason's body was bunched into rock hardness by his longing to refuse this mission.

He couldn't leave Brussels now. He had to woo Genna. He had to win her before she made the mistake of his and her lifetime by marrying that bastard.

Wellington continued on. "Therefore, all the arrangements have been made, even to having a portmanteau packed with your clothes. You leave as soon as our talk is concluded. There is a sealed letter amongst the packets for London. You will find further instructions in it. Open it when you reach your ship, then burn it. Any questions?"

Jason looked at Wellington who was now

standing. It was obvious that the duke didn't expect him to refuse. And how could he? Left unchecked, Napoleon would ravage the world, bringing hardship and suffering to too many people. Jason couldn't live with himself if he didn't do his best to stop the French domination.

Resigned to his fate, Jason rose. "No, Your Grace, I haven't any questions."

"Good." Wellington reached out once more to shake hands. "Take care and remember, someone knows too much and is passing that information on. Trust no one."

"Yes, sir."

Jason pivoted on his heel and exited, all his plans for pursuing Genna crashing down around him. Disappointment was a tight vise in his throat, and he was thankful no one met him outside the duke's office. He needed to do some fast walking to work off the anger and disappointment clouding his thoughts.

He'd entertained such high hopes of being able to convince Genna to leave the man she was engaged to. Now he had to leave without even explaining why to her. His sole hope and consolation was the knowledge that Genna loved him.

Chapter Thirteen

Genna gazed desultorily around the coach house that the Duchess of Richmond had turned into a ballroom. Groups of people milled about, dressed in their finest evening clothes and bent on enjoying themselves. The women were like plumaged birds in rich iridescent colors, the men perfect foils in their more somber attire.

Standing off to the side, reluctant to participate in the hectic gaiety, Genna caught sight of Ricci flitting from beautiful woman to beautiful woman like a bee collecting pollen.

In the past months since Jason had beaten him, he'd been sullen and even more temperamental than was his wont. And she was heartily sick of him. Before she'd felt aversion and disgust at his compulsive pursuit of pleasure at the expense of everyone else, but lately she'd begun to actively dislike him. She almost hated him.

But to follow that line of emotions would destroy her, and she wouldn't allow Ricci to do that to her.

With a smile pasted on her face, she took a glass of champagne from the silver tray a footman was holding toward her.

The light, effervescent taste went to her head just as the bubbles did to her nose. It tickled, and she giggled. But her thoughts sobered immediately as a man separated from a nearby group and bowed to her. "May I have this dance?"

She managed to smile at him. "Thank you, but I'm very tired."

She didn't really feel tired. What she felt was distaste for the touch of any man who wasn't Jason. Hurriedly, she moved away to a quiet corner where she could be alone with the misery that ate constantly at her.

Where was Jason? When he'd left her, promising to return, she'd known that for both their sakes he should stay away. Yet, as she went about in Brussels society, she realized that he was nowhere to be found.

It was now June and the last time she'd seen Jason had been April. In April, he'd vowed to return. And in her heart, she knew that he would never stay away from her of his own volition.

Something had taken him out of the city . . . or he was once more disguised as a lower class denizen and spying for the Duke of Wellington. She prayed that wasn't the case. The French knew about him and to disguise himself again would be suicide. Just the idea made her chest tighten and small, sharp points of worry stabbed through her.

The band struck up another waltz and still another man sought her out for a dance. She managed to refuse him without giving him the cut direct, but the incident convinced her that it was time for her to leave. She'd found out what she came for. Napoleon was steadily advancing on Brussels and everyone expected Wellington to shortly set forth to meet the Emperor Bonaparte.

There was no further reason for her to subject her raw nerves to this display of forced unconcern. Couples crowded the dance floor. Their swirling and dipping, the high brittle laughter of the women and the deep rasping chuckles of the men, grated on her.

Genna briefly closed her eyes to give herself a respite from the glittering array of people. When she once more looked on the frenetic scene, she was moving in the direction she knew led to the exit.

Just then, a commotion ensued at the door and the music stopped. Genna, curiosity overcoming nervous tension, stood on tiptoe to see what was going on. Wellington and a group of men whom she took to be his staff officers had just arrived.

People flocked to them, deserting the dance floor and the tables laden with food. The buzz of human voices, raised in questions, lowered in answers, hummed everywhere. Almost immediately, the music began again and the men with Wellington fanned out to claim friends, parents, lovers.

Genna didn't want to be caught up in the emotional fervor permeating the room. The talk would center on war and death. She waved down a rapidly moving footman and told him to inform Hester that she was leaving, but would send the coach back to await Hester's pleasure. Just because she was exhausted was no reason to cut short her aunt's enjoyment.

Genna hadn't taken two steps when a woman addressed her.

"Contessa di Ponti?"

Not recognizing the voice, Genna turned to see the Duchess of Richmond dressed as though she were in a London ballroom entertaining the Regent. Jewels dripped from the woman's ears and circled her throat.

"Yes, Your Grace?" Genna dropped into a curtsy.

"Tut, tut. No need for such formality. I merely wish to introduce you to someone. Genna, Contessa di Ponti, may I make known to you Jason Robert McClenna, Viscount Everly?"

Genna stared at Jason. Lost in wonder at his return, she was barely aware of the duchess melting into the crowd. He was Viscount Everly? It didn't surprise her to learn that he was an aristocrat. His bearing and manner had always struck her as being too self-assured for the poor man his spying had forced him to portray.

"Contessa," he murmured, making a perfect leg.

"Jason? Viscount Everly?"

He rose back up, contrition putting a deep line between his brows. "Both."

She smiled up at him, still not sure whether to believe her eyes. "But if you're English aristocracy, where did you learn to speak such fluent French?"

He grinned. "My mother was a French emigré."

Such a simple answer, she marvelled that she hadn't thought of it before. Now all the mystery about him was clear.

Before she could speak, Jason asked, "Will you ever forgive me for my deception?"

She nodded, drinking in his dear features as the first flowers of spring drink in the sun's life-giving warmth. All thought of his previous deception was gone. Love shone from the depths of his long, olive green eyes, shadowed by lashes as thick as a beaver's fur. And a stray lock of golden hair strayed over his forehead. She reached up to push it back.

Letting her hand drop, an embarrassed blush turned her cheeks warm. "I don't care what you call yourself, Jason. I know who you really are."

A slow, tender smile transformed Jason's features as he caught her hand and brought it to his lips. "I've missed you."

"And I you." The feel of his skin on hers sent hot tremors rushing up her arm.

He turned her hand over and kissed her palm. "Then will you forgive my leaving without word? I would have sent a message, but I was instructed to tell no one."

Glad just to have him near her, she didn't care. "I thought as much."

A weight he'd been conscious of carrying for the last two months fell from Jason's mind at her words. She trusted him enough to know he would never willingly leave her and would come back to her as soon as possible.

He put the hand he'd been kissing on his arm and guided her to a quiet alcove. Once there, he took her into his arms without a thought for who might stumble upon them. All that mattered to him was having her next to him again.

"I've waited too long for this, Genna. I can't wait longer." He brought his head down to hers.

She went to him, wanting the heat of his embrace more than she'd ever wanted anything in her life. When their lips met, she knew that her world, so confused just minutes before, was put right.

"So," Ricci's high tenor impinged on them. "A bit public to be flaunting your lover, Genna."

With a small gasp, Genna tore her lips from Jason's and pushed against his chest. She didn't want to prompt a scene that could harm Jason. But Jason refused to release her, keeping his arm around her waist and pressing her close to his side.

"Fresh from some new adventure?" Ricci asked Jason, a sneer twisting his mouth. "However, your current adventure of pawing my betrothed is not to be borne." With that, Ricci reached out and slapped his gloves across Jason's cheek. "I demand satisfaction."

Jason studied the effete man in front of him, seeing the sly cunning in the dark eyes and the weakness in the receding chin. This man would cheat in any duel of honor.

Genna, terrified of Jason being harmed, hissed, "Go away, Ricci. What I do is no concern of yours. Just as what you do is none of mine."

"You are wrong, *cara mia*."

The endearment grated on Jason's nerves. He would tolerate no more from this slimy excuse of a man. In a dangerously low voice, he said, "I warned you once, di Ponti."

Eyes suddenly leery, Ricci took a step back. Then he seemed to regain his bravado and his chest puffed out. "My seconds will call on yours." Without waiting for a reply, Ricci retreated into the crowd with a nervous glance back over his shoulder at Jason and Genna.

Fear lent Genna urgency. "Jason, you can't meet him. He'll kill you. He'll trick you and kill you."

Jason gazed into Genna's distraught eyes and knew himself to be the luckiest man alive. He'd disappeared from her life for months with no explanation, and she still cared enough for him to worry about his life. He had to reassure her.

His gaze held hers. "He'll try, but nothing will come of it. Neither will I kill him. Only prick him." He paused and a frown darkened his countenance. "Unless that bastard has done something in my absence to make him deserve death."

Fright at the sudden fierceness in Jason lent speed to her denial. "No! Nothing! But I still worry for you. You don't know Ricci. He's cunning and totally amoral."

Jason chuckled, but it was a derisive sound that didn't change the hardness of his eyes. "Di Ponti is a coward who has no intentions of meeting me. And by tomorrow, no one will even remember so flimsy a thing. We're about to go into a battle that will change the face of history."

Genna shuddered at the truth he spoke, terror

stiffened her body. In an attempt to warm herself, she tucked her hands around the lapels of Jason's black evening jacket and snuggled closer into the curve of his arm.

"Are you chilled?" Gone from his face was the anger of seconds before, replaced by concern for her.

"No," she said softly. "Not physically."

His concern was replaced by incredulity. "Surely, you're not worried about di Ponti. The only harm that will come to that worm is if he touches you again."

Genna gulped at the fierceness Jason made no effort to disguise. "Only partly. You're right about Ricci, but he could make trouble for you. However," she paused, striving to lighten the heavy pall of doom that had come over them, "since you're a viscount, he'll have a much harder time of doing so."

Jason grinned, dispelling the rigidness of his features. "So true. Rank has its privileges. But right now, all that matters to me is you. I can do nothing about it while we stay at this ball."

The desire for her that he'd managed to tame over the interminable weeks flared again. He had to get her away from here; get her to a place where he could worship her with his body as she deserved.

"Come, Genna, we're leaving." He guided her through the crowded room.

Genna went eagerly. It would be better if they left before any further threats were made. And she wanted Jason to herself. Just for a little while she wanted to find happiness in the arms of the only man she would ever love.

They were almost at the door when Wellington beckoned. With a groan of frustrated ardor, Jason knew he had to respond to the duke's summons.

Jason turned to Genna, his olive eyes dilated to near black and flecked with gold from the heat of his passion. "Don't move. I must speak with Wellington and then we're leaving. I need you too badly to linger."

The breath caught in Genna's throat at the naked longing Jason made no effort to hide. Her body warmed as memories of their lovemaking played through her mind, making her knees weak.

To curb her reaction before she melted onto the floor, she turned her attention to the group of men surrounding Wellington. Even in such a distinguished crowd, Jason stood out. He was taller than most, and he held his head with a regal authority that sent shivers chasing down her spine. Pride and love for him swelled her heart to near bursting.

Then he was beside her again and whisking her outside to the warm evening air where he instructed a footman to call his carriage. They waited, their hands clasped together like two children. Overhead the stars were like brilliants and the moon resembled a silver orb, delicately chased with engravings. Not a cloud marred the perfection.

"I only have a few hours, Genna," he whispered, his breath moving warmly over her ear. "Our intelligence indicates that Napoleon is rapidly moving this way."

She gasped, squeezing his fingers in dread. "Surely you aren't going to fight. You've already risked your life by spying. You've already come close to dying for England."

Just then the carriage arrived and before Genna could protest further, Jason hastened her into the interior of the vehicle. He seated her on the cushions beside him, his arm around her shoulders holding her to his heart.

"Oh, love," he said, "you don't know how good it feels to hear your concern. But, yes, I'll fight." He rubbed her cold hand, still in his. "A lot of good men will die tomorrow. If I don't fight and do my best to help us win, possibly saving others' lives by being there, I won't be able to live with myself." Then he shrugged, a gesture very Gallic in its insouciance. "More importantly, I believe that sometimes you have to risk everything for what you believe in . . . even death."

"Jason!" She burrowed her face into the hollow of his shoulder, wanting to be as close to him as humanly possible.

Jason groaned. "Hush, Genna. I shouldn't have gotten carried away. I didn't mean to. When I'm with you, I feel free to speak and do what I wish." He laughed ruefully. "Sometimes I've been very foolhardy with you."

"As in telling me your name and asking if I spoke English when I was nursing you? You didn't even know me then."

He nodded.

She chuckled with him, but was unconvinced of

his attempt at lightness. War was never free from danger.

"And besides," he added, "I don't intend to be killed. I'm too lucky for that, and we have too many good men on our side." What he kept from her was the most recent intelligence indicating that Napoleon had at least twenty-five thousand more men than Wellington.

Genna sensed he wasn't telling her everything, and apprehension tightened her chest until it was difficult to breathe. The only way to control her fear for him was to focus on him.

The light from the single lantern made his features hard and demonic. She could almost believe him when he said he was too lucky to die. *Almost*. But she'd heard the rumors about not enough soldiers and not enough skill because too many of the men who'd fought with Wellington in the Peninsular Wars were still in America.

"Jason, I love you. Please be careful."

Genna's words and the face she turned up to him were so full of love and concern for him that Jason couldn't keep from taking her into his arms and covering her mouth with his. It was a kiss born of love and respect for her as a person.

When Jason felt her lips move under his, a spark of desire shot through him like lightning. He wanted her so badly that his need was a fire in his belly and an ache in his loins. She would be his, but . . .

He lifted his head and gazed down adoringly at her. "We can't make love in the coach."

"Why not?" She didn't care where they loved.

He chuckled. "Because I want this to be perfect."

She raised a finger to caress his mouth. "'Tis always perfect with you, beloved."

"Genna, Genna." He pulled her onto his lap, his arms going inside her cloak and wrapping around her waist.

She smiled down at him, reveling in the possessive strength of his embrace. When he smiled up at her, she kissed him fully upon the lips, drinking in his fresh taste. Pulling a fraction away from him, she murmured against his lips, "Almost . . . I miss the scent of basilicum powder. 'Tis a smell I always associate with you."

He nipped her lips playfully. "Vixen."

Laughter gurgled up in her. "How I've missed you."

For answer, he caught her mouth with his, plunging his tongue deep into her moist warmth. Amusement fled Genna to be replaced by desire, so poignant and so encompassing that it took her breath away.

When she thought she could stand his kiss no longer without having more of him in her, his mouth left hers and trailed down her neck. Shivers of delight shook her as his tongue glided over her heated skin and his teeth rubbed at her collarbone.

But that reaction was nothing compared to the shock of pleasure that flashed through her when his lips nuzzled the swollen flesh of her bosom just above the decolletage of her gown. Her neck arched back and the breath left her lungs in a long sigh of satisfaction. Her fingers curled in his thick hair and held him prisoner against her sensitized skin.

Jason gave to her willingly, wanting her to enjoy their coming together as much as he did. Their reunion must be a culmination of all the wonderful pleasures they gave to each other.

Gently, so as not to tear or wrinkle the fine silk of her bodice, Jason eased the material off her breasts, revealing the almost transparent linen of her chemise with its fine white lace that lay like froth on her porcelain skin. Through the fine material, he could discern the darker outline of her nipples, and the raised points that indicated her arousal.

"Genna," he murmured, lowering his head to the tempting morsel, "you were made to be loved."

Even through the delicate linen, Genna could feel the rough texture of Jason's tongue as he laved her aching bosom. Then he took her nipple into his mouth and suckled her. Genna arched as spasms of pure delight sped from his ministrations to the knotted tension in her stomach.

"Do you like what I do to you?" Jason raised his head to look at her dilated pupils and flushed face.

Her words were breathy. "You know I do."

A smile of such rakish satisfaction curved his lips that Genna couldn't help the warmth of love that suffused her heart. He cared so much for her own enjoyment that knowing he could excite her filled him with delight. Many men didn't care about their partner's responses. She was doubly blessed to have Jason.

Jason, immensely pleased with Genna's reaction to his skills, brought his mouth down on hers again. He would love her until the carriage reached her house.

The vehicle hit a hole and Genna bounced against him, breaking their contact. "'Tis a most eventful ride," he said, settling her back on his lap where he had easy access to her charms.

Giggling over their interruption, Genna started to undo Jason's cravat. He caught her hand. "No, love."

She was puzzled, but willing to hear his reason before continuing the pleasant line of action again. "Why ever not? I've no intentions of being the only one to enjoy this ride."

He grinned at her huffy rejoinder. "And I've no intention of denying myself, but I've also no intention of shouting to the world what we've been doing in here."

Understanding dawned on her.

"That's right. There's no way I could tie my cravat again without a mirror and complete stillness, and I'm sure that Michaels would be scandalized if he knew what we've been up to."

"True. However, I've already disarrayed your hair and Michaels is observant enough to notice that. But I concede that you are correct. 'Tis one thing to know we've been kissing and quite another to know that there were clothes involved." She smiled provocatively up at him.

He groaned. "If you continue to look at me that way, I won't give a damn what your butler thinks."

Having gotten the reaction she wanted, Genna dropped her head demurely. She didn't want to wait to have all Jason could give. But for right now, she was content to stay on his lap, her cheek against his chest where she could hear his heart beating strongly.

"But," Jason said, his fingers raising to dally with her still exposed breasts, "you'll be easy to set to rights as long as we don't mess your hair."

"Jason!" She was caught between scandalous amusement and wanton curiosity at what he intended. "What happened to rectitude?"

He laughed. "I'll be the only one having to practice it."

"Jason, I don't want this to be something that only one of us enjoys."

He cupped her breast in one hand and began to gently squeeze, his thumb flicking over her pointed nipple. "Never worry. We'll both enjoy this."

Genna had her doubts when she was the only one to be fondled. When Jason's mouth met hers, she forgot everything but the joy of being loved by him. His kiss was long and drugging, sending her rational mind into limbo as his tongue delved deeper. He exerted pressure until her head was leaning back against his supporting arm so that her chest rose upward.

Jason's lips left hers and he gazed longingly at her exposed bosom. The flickering light from the carriage's lantern lent a golden cast to her creamy skin and emphasized the deep hollow between the ripe mounds he longed to taste.

Just before he took one in his mouth, he whispered, "You have such firm, full breasts."

Then he was suckling her inflamed flesh and small gasps of delight escaped Genna. One of his hands massaged her swollen breast as the rough tip of his tongue swirled around the darker areola of her nipple. His tongue spiraled inward until he was flicking the hard bud in rapid succession that made darts of pleasure shoot through her.

"Savor this, my fiery angel."

Genna could do nothing else but take her satisfaction as his touch on her became progressively intimate.

Before she knew what he was doing, she was lying across his lap, her back bowed over his thighs and her head cushioned by the velvet squabs. Her legs were bent at the knees so that her feet rested on the seat to keep her from rolling off him.

He had both her breasts in his two hands and was kneading and kissing them, sending jolts of lightning down her spine. Just when Genna parted her lips to plead with him to stop until they were at her house, one of his hands left its place.

Genna dragged in a relieved breath. He would stop now, and she could pull herself back together. Surely, they were near the park and her house by now.

But he drew her breast deeper into the hot vortex of his mouth, and the hand that had released her bosom traveled over her ribs and down her hips.

"This silk feels like your skin," Jason murmured, "only not as warm and soft."

His hand glided up and down as he delighted in the texture of the material, lulling Genna's apprehension about making herself presentable.

She was even able to catch her breath and raise up on her elbows.

Feeling her movement, Jason lifted his head and his eyes locked with hers as his palm slid down her thigh to her calf and then under her skirt. Slowly, his gaze never leaving hers, Jason moved his hand back up her calf to her outer thigh. When her eyes widened with understanding, he slipped his fingers around so that they caressed her inner leg.

"Jason," she gasped, "not here. You said—"

"Hush. No one will know. Your skirts won't wrinkle."

She gasped again as his fingers met her portal. It was exquisite torture and she wanted him to experience it with her. "Then . . . oh!" One digit slid inside her. "Then . . ." she gulped, "undo your breeches. Let us both enjoy this."

He grinned. "I think not. Next time." He pulled out and thrust back with two fingers. "You're so slick. Like warm honey."

His eyes held hers, and Genna found she couldn't break the connection. Heat suffused her cheeks as he withdrew and plunged back, sending twinges of reaction shooting to her clenched stomach.

"You're beautiful, Genna. I want to watch you explode."

The blunt desire in his voice acted like an aphrodisiac, making her legs quiver and her mouth go dry with longing. Then he moved slowly out, drawing the pleasure to breaking point before inserting three fingers as slowly as possible. He glided into her.

"That's it," he encouraged her. "Feel me stretching you. You're so tight and slick."

Under her back, she could feel his hard shaft pressing into the small of her back, telling her as effectively as his husky words that he wanted her as badly as she wanted him. She wanted to give him pleasure as he was so ably giving her.

Somehow, even with his ministrations to her womanhood, she managed to rub against his manhood. The look of heated desire that darkened his complexion was her reward.

"Don't tempt me, love. 'Tis hard enough to deny myself the comfort of your tight sheath as it is." His throat was tight with sensual tension, and his shaft throbbed with an almost painful intensity. "I don't want to take you here, and I don't want to lose control either."

Then he increased the rhythm and it was all Genna could do to gasp, "But I want you . . ."

His thumb flicked over her swollen outer lips even as he plumbed the depths of her moist core until Genna could stand no more. Ripples of release began deep inside her womb and quickly spread until her very abdomen shook with them.

Jason never took his gaze from her. He saw her eyes widen just as her body began to explode around his buried flesh. Small moans of pleasure came from her lips even though she bit them to stifle the screams he knew she wanted to release.

The sight of her was enough to draw his flesh up into an aching ball of frustration. His manhood stood rigid, pressing urgently against the confining material of his evening breeches. It would be so easy to release himself and insert his shaft into her still pulsing depths. So easy, that his spare hand moved to do just that.

He squeezed his eyes shut to block out the sight of her sensual beauty. No, he wouldn't take her here. This night was too important for him to cheapen it by loving her completely in a moving carriage. What he'd just given her was only the beginning of the love he wanted to share with her before following Wellington into battle.

Genna clung to Jason as her reeling senses righted themselves and she began to remember where they were. Self-conscious that he watched every emotion mirrored on her features, she buried her face into the folds of his jacket.

Tenderly, Jason smoothed the fabric down over Genna's legs and up over her bosom. Then he adjusted her so that she sat beside him on the seat.

Putting a finger under her chin, he raised her face so that he could see her reactions. "There should be no embarrassment between us. We're two adults in love and what we choose to do together can only be good and right."

Genna looked at him, seeing the love and desire in his eyes that he made no effort to hide. She was a thousand times blessed to have a man such as he.

Just then the carriage pulled to a stop, and the footman was opening the door and lowering the step. "Thank you," she said to the young man who helped her down while she waited for Jason.

With athletic grace, Jason exited the vehicle and took Genna's hand which he put on his forearm.

Together, they went to the door Michaels was opening.

The butler's eyes widened, but he managed to cover his surprise. "Milady and, ahem, sir."

Genna swept past Michaels, her lips twitching. Jason removed her cape and handed it to the butler who eyed him with misgiving.

"Michaels," Genna said, enjoying her butler's confusion, "Viscount Everly and I will be in the parlor. Please see that we're not disturbed."

Michaels's eyebrows rose. "Yes, milady."

"Now, Genna," Jason interposed, taking pity on the poor servant, "you should tell Michaels that I was only pretending to be a ragamuffin." He turned and smiled hugely at the butler. "I want to thank you for all the help you gave me in Paris. I don't believe I've had the opportunity to do so before. And, if you don't mind, please convey my thanks to Alphonse."

Taken aback, but with a gratified smile on his countenance, Michaels bowed. "Yes, milord."

Grinning in unison, Genna and Jason passed through the door Michaels held open for them. A fire was going in the grate and a cut glass decanter of brandy sat on a pier table, two glasses reposing in shining majesty beside it. Genna led Jason to it and bade him sit down.

Jason cocked an eyebrow at her. "Only if you'll enjoy the comfort of my lap."

She tsked at him, but sat across his thighs as requested. "Although," she said with a sly grin, "I doubt it will be comfortable. More likely I shall be pricked by some insistent demand of yours."

His lips curved in pleasure at her wit. "Never a dull moment with you, love."

She chuckled as she reclined against the broad expanse of his chest. The fire was a warm caress against her side and face. Her eyes met Jason's and her lips were suddenly dry. She ran her tongue over her mouth.

Jason groaned. "You're too tempting." Before she could reply, he pressed his mouth to hers.

They sank to the floor and within minutes both were divested of clothing, their fevered flesh pressed so tightly that none might separate them. Their lips clung as two persons thirsting for something only the other can provide, and their hands roved like raging rivers over one another's body.

Jason's fingers skipped down her ribs, circling her hip bones with deft flicks that sent rivulets of delight shimmering along her nerves to pool in her womb. When she was weak with need for him, he rubbed his palms down the ridged muscles of her back until the friction of his caress made her skin electric with response.

"Genna," he murmured, kissing her with sweet abandon, "I wanted to love you as never before, to have you writhing under me as I took you higher than either of us has ever been. But I can't wait longer. I need you now."

Completely satisfied that he should want her this quickly and totally, she opened to him. He came into her like a raging tidal wave into a calm bay.

She shook with desire for him.

A whirlwind of emotions flooded Genna as Jason loved her. She clutched him to her, striving for a joining of their bodies to transcend and magnify the love she felt for him. Her breasts pressed to his chest, her hips pressed to his loins, and her lips pressed to his mouth, she drank in the wonder of his love and gave him her soul.

Jason devoured her. As no other time during their loving, he rode the primordial urge to plant his seed in her. The need to confirm life through his love for her was so immense that he felt himself exploding outward before he realized how close to completion he was. Throwing his head back, he released all inhibitions.

Instantly, the outward spiral of their lovemaking took them simultaneously, rushing them both over the precipice of emotions that had carried them to this peak.

For only a while they lay entwined, their flesh slick with repletion and warm from the dying embers of the fire. Then Jason gently pulled away. Before rising, he dropped a butterfly kiss on Genna's lips.

Through eyes heavy with satisfaction and exhaustion, Genna watched him dress. He was beautiful; his hair burnished bronze from the orange glow of the flames, his skin shining hotly from the perspiration of their lovemaking, his eyes still golden with desire that truly could never be slaked.

He noticed her studying him and knelt down beside her. "I wish it didn't have to be this quick." He smoothed back a strand of her copper hair. "I wanted this moment to be special. Genna, keep me in your mind and heart until I return. I'm sorry it was so rapid."

She caught his hand and kissed his palm. "Stop, Jason. 'Twas perfect. Any slower and I would have thought you didn't want me as badly as I wanted you."

He pulled her hand to him and kissed her in turn. His eyes filled with all the emotions she aroused in him: possessiveness, hunger, desire, the need to have her by his side every day of his life.

"My fiery angel. I love you more than I can ever express. Wait for me."

Chapter Fourteen

Before Genna could answer, Jason was gone and she was alone in the rapidly cooling room. The dread clutching at her heart made her whole body shudder.

"Please, God," she prayed, "bring him back to me."

A worried frown puckered her forehead. What if he didn't come back to her? What if he were killed? What would she do then? How would she continue to exist? She didn't know, it was all too awful to contemplate.

And what if she had his baby? Instinctively, her hand went to her flat abdomen. Even after all their lovemaking on the journey from Paris to here, she hadn't once considered that possibility. She'd been too caught up in her own private hell of being promised to Ricci while in love with Jason to consider the consequences of having loved Jason.

She could have conceived tonight. It wasn't beyond the realm of possibility. A little boy with hair as blond as his father's and eyes as green. A smaller version of Jason to cherish. The idea brought a smile to her lips.

The skirl of a bagpipe interrupted her happy fantasy. Right after the pipes, came the sound of drums and then the marching of men.

Grabbing her dress and hurriedly donning it, she rushed to the window that overlooked the park. She pulled back the curtain and peered outside.

The sun was just beginning to rise, casting its pure morning light on multitudes of marching soldiers. Just passing out of her sight were the Scottish Highlanders, the high, piercing melancholy of their bagpipes fading on the wind. Following them, were British regiments, the Union Jack flown proudly in front of them as their drummers set the pace.

It was all Genna could do to keep the tears from flowing as she watched the hundreds of men and boys setting out to meet Napoleon. Many of them wouldn't return. That much she knew, even though Jason had tried to keep from her just how seriously undermanned Wellington was.

And what of Jason? she asked herself again. Surely, he would return to her. He always had before, she couldn't begin to doubt it now.

Jason would return to her.

That afternoon, Genna was still telling herself Jason would return to her as she listened to the sounds of battle coming from the confrontation.

Couriers reporting back from Wellington were saying that Wellington's troops had finally encountered the emperor's men at Waterloo.

Several hours before, the sounds of cannon shot and the rumble of wagons over cobbles had been ominous and threatening indications of the battle. Now they were both normal. Even the cries of the wounded as they were trundled by in open carts, no longer wrung dry sobs from her.

Instead, determined to help all she could, Genna rapidly tore into strips the sheets Mrs. Michaels had scrounged from every bed and cupboard in the house. Beside her, the housekeeper folded the new bandages.

That done, Genna gathered up her needles and thread, tinder box, and any basilicum powder left from tending Jason. Picking up the half empty box of powder, she paused.

The smell reminded her so forcefully of Jason that for a moment she thought she could see him standing beside her. If she reached out her hand, she would touch him.

Alphonse's voice intruded. "My lady, I've ordered the carriage brought around. We can't carry all these supplies by ourselves."

"Wha . . . ?" Turning, she saw Alphonse and realized that her longing for Jason had made her imagine what wasn't there. She had to stop this. Right this moment there were dying and hurt men who needed her. She couldn't stand here lost in day dreams. Taking herself in hand, she said briskly, "Very practical, Alphonse. We'll need Mrs. Michaels, too. She's a very able nurse."

Into this orderly confusion, Aunt Hester stepped. "Genna, what in goodness name are you doing?"

Genna paused in picking up a pile of makeshift bandages. "Exactly what it looks like, dear."

"Genna, really," Hester expostulated, her plump hands beginning to flutter in agitation. "You can't go out into those streets and care for those men. It isn't seemly."

The small thread of restraint that Genna had managed to maintain snapped. "I can and I will, Aunt. And I'll thank you to stop this caterwauling and whining. If you had any sense of humanity, you'd come with me."

Hester's round face crumpled. Sobs squeezed from her pinched mouth and tears fell from her hurt eyes. "Oh dear, oh dear," she mumbled, pivoting on her feet and scurrying to the door.

Aghast at what she'd done, Genna rushed after her aunt. She caught Hester just outside the room. Circling the distraught older woman with her arms, Genna forced Hester to remain with her.

"Oh, dearest, I'm sorry." She'd hurt Hester who had only spoken out of concern for her. It was too much for Genna. All the pent up emotions and fears that had ridden her since Jason's departure burst out. She began to cry softly, the moisture trailing down her cheeks to leave the bitter taste of salt in her mouth. "I'm so sorry, Hester. I don't know how to explain."

The tears that had fallen in earnest from Hester's face began to abate. She sniffed audibly one last time. "There, there, now Genna. I know you did not mean to insult me. You are merely wrought up over this battle and over that *man* being in it. I assume that he is."

Accustomed as she was to Hester's emotional storms, Genna was still taken aback at how quickly her aunt had done a turn about. And because she felt Hester should know, Genna said, "You're right. Jason is in that fight."

"Tut, tut, child. He will probably be all right." She pulled herself out of Genna's embrace and steered the younger woman back into the room they'd just left. "Men such as he always land on their feet. Of course after the things Ricci has done lately, that Jason fellow is probably not such a bad sort."

Genna choked on a watery chuckle. "Aunt, you are always saying the most enlightening things."

Hester beamed, all her hurt gone. "Yes, I do, don't I?" Just then she noticed Alphonse, Mrs. Michaels and Michaels staring at her in condemnation. "Do not let me hear a word from any of you. I am a lady, and ladies do not tend strangers in the street," she cast a sideways glance at Genna, "unless they choose to. I shall stay here and continue to prepare bandages."

Genna knew that Hester considered herself to be doing more than enough. "Thank you, dear." She kissed her aunt on the cheek before turning to her people and saying, "We'd best be on our way."

It was many hours later, as dawn once more bronzed the sky, that Genna finally allowed herself to rest. Standing, she stretched her back which hurt abominably from constant bending. Even her eyes ached. They were gritty with exhaustion and blurry from too many hours spent on close work as she sewed up the wounds the military surgeons were too busy to tend.

Alphonse, who'd stayed by her the whole day and night, said, "Milady, we had best get home. You need to rest."

She looked at him and shook her head. "You go on. I have business still."

Stubbornness hardened his jaw. "I will stay."

Genna sighed. "Have it as you wish."

She turned away and began to weave her way between the wounded men who were strewn across the streets like so much garbage. Groans of pain or wracking coughs made her stomach knot with the futility of knowing she couldn't help them.

Stifling the sobs she wanted to release, she continued walking, pausing every now and then. She didn't want to find what she was searching for, but she had to assure herself that Jason wasn't here. If he was, she would be with him.

A man grunted to her left, catching her attention. In the glow of the rising sun, the soldier's hair glinted like gold. Her breath caught in her throat. It was Jason! On wings, her feet took her forward.

She reached the man and looked down, prepared to call Alphonse and have Jason lifted up and carried back to her house. The man's arm fell away from his face. He wasn't Jason.

Genna stared down at him, uncertain of what she felt. On the one hand she was disappointed that this man wasn't Jason; this man was alive and, while he had a gash on his forehead that needed tending, otherwise appeared intact. On the other hand, she was glad he wasn't Jason because until she knew differently, there was always the chance that Jason would return perfectly healthy.

"Miss?"

The hoarse request stopped her musing as nothing else could. He needed help.

Stooping, she examined his wound. It wasn't deep, but had bled profusely as all head wounds. Quickly, she sewed it up and bandaged it. Before leaving, she gave him water to drink.

With a last smile of encouragement, she picked up the basin of water, now pink from blood, and shuffled to a place where she could safely dump the contaminated water.

She continued searching until she no longer knew where she was. All the time, carriages continued to rumble in, filled with the grisly reminders that war was no game.

One wagon trundled past her, close enough that she could distinctly see an arm hanging out the back, blood coating the remnants of a coat sleeve. She didn't have to see more to realize the man didn't feel anything. He was either unconscious from shock or dead.

After all the gore and suffering she'd endured, this last was too much. Bile rose from Genna's stomach, burning her throat. She gagged to keep from vomiting.

Alphonse was by her immediately. "Best we leave," he said, his voice full of compassion.

Although she wanted to stay, to continue her search, Genna was too weak to resist when Alphonse led her away. She'd look again later. A grim smile twisted her lips. It wasn't as if any of this was going to disappear in the next few hours.

Genna only allowed herself to sleep until dinner, then she was back on the streets. Walking with a purposeful stride, she moved toward the area where the bulk of the wounded had been placed earlier. To her horror, she encountered soldiers blocks away from where they'd been just hours earlier.

Her hand went to her throat in despair. If she weren't seeing it with her own eyes, she wouldn't believe the carnage. Under her breath, she muttered, "Instead of fighting, they must be butchering each other."

Her eyes widened and her knees began to buckle. To steady herself, she took a deep breath. Immediately, she regretted it. The air was stale and heavy with the stink of blood and death. It wasn't helped by the humid heat that seemed to sit like a pall over the carnage.

Tears came to her eyes, tears she couldn't stop even though she'd thought herself beyond them. This was horrible.

"Dear Lord," she murmured, "please bring him back to me."

"My lady?" Alphonse said from directly behind her.

His voice was like a splash of ice water, and Genna was able to gather up the shreds of her composure. Losing control of her emotions was no help to these poor men. She had to be strong so that she could tend to them. Anything else would be a sacrilege.

In a voice hoarse with pain and desolation, she said, "Don't worry, Alphonse. I'm not going to faint."

She moved away before he could say anything sympathetic. If he spoke gently to her or even suggested that her tears were understandable, she would dissolve.

Throughout the day, she moved like a zombie, helping anyone who needed it without consciously thinking about the suffering going on all around her. It was the only way she could tolerate the destruction surrounding her.

As the sun set on her second day of nursing, she once more straightened up and stretched the tight muscles of her back. There wasn't a part of her that didn't scream abuse. She shrugged, knowing that tomorrow she would do the same.

Trudging among the increased numbers of hurt and maimed bodies, she carefully looked for a flash of golden hair. Again, the gleam of gold caught her eyes and again she rushed toward it, only to pause when the man rolled onto his back and she could see his face. No Jason.

The breath left her lungs in a sigh so torn with mingled gladness and regret that it was all she could do not to sink down and wallow in sorrow. But she didn't. There were still the wagons of dead to be studied, their bodies held in one pile until they were either identified or buried. She intended to search them before leaving tonight.

Fetid waves of gagging air choked her as she methodically examined the dead bodies. None of them were her beloved Jason.

"Dear God," she murmured, "thank you."

Instantly, she felt ashamed for wanting her own happiness at the cost to another. It was an added burden she couldn't shoulder.

Turning from the wagon, she stumbled, the tears falling unheeded from her eyes. Alphonse caught her.

And the next day Alphonse followed her through a routine that both were learning to tolerate. They split up and each gave succor where they could, but never going too far from each other since they shared the same supplies.

Genna was mindlessly wrapping another broken arm when a faint, hoarse "Miss" caught her attention.

Finishing up, she rose and went toward the man whose request she'd heard. She bent down to hear the soft rasping of his voice and blanched. His legs were so mangled, she wondered he was coherent.

"Yes?" She laid a hand on his brow which was burning with fever.

"Water? Please."

"Of course," she managed. His hair was bleached by the sun, much like Jason's. Even his eyes were green. The tears she'd thought herself to be beyond threatened to spill anew.

To save herself, she turned away and searched until she found him some lukewarm water. He gulped the liquid, then his head fell back and his eyes shut. Genna started, sure he must have died, but his chest was rising and falling.

He was beyond her help. His legs would have to come off. Standing, she went to look for the surgeon, whom she finally found in a nearby building. "Sir, you must come quickly to help this man. Both his legs are ruined."

The surgeon looked up from the arm he was setting and frowned at her. "Miss, can't you see I'm busy?"

"Yes, yes, I can see that, but this man will die if he isn't attended to." She stopped and took a deep breath, willing herself to be calm. It was a mistake because the air was heavy with the heat and the stink. Fighting through her nausea, she said slowly, "I think his legs must come off."

The surgeon shook his head and resumed wrapping the bandage around the arm he was tending. Then he stood and followed Genna. When they reached the wounded soldier, his chest was still, but there was a smile on his lips.

For some reason, Genna had convinced herself that this man would live. Even knowing the severity of his wounds, she'd deluded herself into thinking that he could be saved because his blond hair and green eyes had reminded her of Jason. She'd been a fool.

In her agony, the dead man became Jason. It was Jason lying in the mud at her feet, his legs a tangled mess of blood and flesh. It was Jason whose eyes would never look at her again and whose mouth would never move in words of love spoken to her.

"Oh God," she moaned.

The death and dying, the pain and agony, went beyond anything Genna could have ever imagined, and this was the summit. It was the end of her endurance. No sleep for thirty-six hours, the strain of watching men suffering and dying, and the knowledge that Jason was in danger finally overcame her.

Turning blindly, she stumbled away. "'Tis too much . . . too much," she mumbled, gut wrenching sobs wracking her body.

She came to rest against the wall of a building, the sounds of suffering filtering through the brick to her ears.

"Please, dear God, please bring Jason back to me." She shook her head, denying to herself any possibility that her love might not return. "I'll do anything to have him safely back."

The words were out before she consciously considered them. Then she realized that she meant them, more than she'd ever meant anything in her life. Her promise to Luigi was nothing when compared to this horror. No agony of failed honor could be worse than this fear gnawing at her gut night and day like maggots burrowing into rotton flesh.

She choked on a harsh laugh. It took all this carnage, this blood and gore and flies, to make her realize that the love she felt for Jason was more important than any promise. Love affirmed life, and life was the antithesis of the death all around her.

She'd be damned before she would deny Jason

again, for she could be no more damned than thinking him dead and beyond the reach of her love.

Alphonse finally found her. He took one look at the dirt smearing her face and the defeated slump of her shoulders and called for Michaels to fetch the carriage.

Two days later, on June nineteenth, as she sewed up the wound in a soldier's thigh, she heard of Wellington's victory. For a fleeting instant, exultation swept her. It quickly passed, though, as another load of wounded clattered by her on the cobblestone street.

That day, too, she looked for Jason to no avail. And the next. When she finally found him, she would tell him of her decision. She would marry him before another day was out.

She never found him.

At last, she gave up and sought Wellington in the quarters he had resumed occupying after the battle. Everyone was toadying to the conquering commander, and it had taken several days of persistence to get an audience with him.

Waiting outside the duke's office for permission to enter, Genna smoothed the brown muslin of her morning dress with nervous hands. After an eternity, she rose and began to pace back and forth in front of the door, her slippers making no sound on the carpet. When would he see her? The composure she'd forced on herself was fast fading.

Just when she decided to knock and enter, Wellington's voice bade her to come in. Torn between relief at finally getting to speak with him and fear for what he might tell her, Genna paused with her gloved fingers hovering over the doorknob.

"Come in," Wellington said again, beginning to sound impatient.

It was enough to galvanize Genna out of her indecision. Head high and shoulders back, she entered. "Your Grace." She dropped into a curtsy.

"Please, Contessa, no formality. We have all been through too much for such things just yet."

Genna rose and her gaze met his thoughtful one. With his patrician nose and hooded eyes, he had the look of an eagle. Before she could speak, he motioned her to a chair in front of his desk.

"What may I do for you, Contessa?"

She'd been told he was a man of few words, but his direct question still took her aback. She'd expected to have to speak of his triumph and allow him to wax eloquent about how he'd accomplished it.

She moistened her lips to give herself time to phrase her question and had to stop the wringing of her hands as they sat in her lap. "Your Grace, I . . . I know I'm no relative of Viscount Everly, but . . . but . . ."

Wellington, his eyes never leaving Genna's troubled countenance, took pity on her. "You wish to know about his fate."

Genna nodded numbly. Now that her quest was in the open, she couldn't bring herself to voice her fears or anything that might lead to having those fears confirmed.

Wellington looked away from the suffering in her eyes and shuffled a pile of papers that lay under his hands. The movements caused dread to form in the pit of Genna's stomach, like a massive rock weighing her down. She knew without him uttering a word that his information was bad.

The duke brought his gaze back to her, and his voice was soft and almost gentle. "Everly fought bravely. He was a fine man and we are proud of him."

He was a fine man.... Genna heard the words as from far away. Her chest squeezed until she couldn't breathe. The fingers that had twisted in her lap became still as death and just as cold. All meaning went out of her life.

Rising, unable to listen to more, Genna murmured, "Thank you for your time."

She turned on the ball of her foot and moved to the closed door. Her hand reached out of its own volition and turned the knob. Her legs carried her out of the room without her consciously willing them to do so. Once outside, she turned to the left and began to walk down the hall to where the exit was. She made it down the steps to the street and walked by Alphonse and the carriage without seeing them, her eyes focused inward.

She had never told Jason she would marry him. She had let him go to war thinking she intended to become another man's wife. Now she would never get to right that wrong.

Tears formed in her eyes but wouldn't fall. She'd already cried enough to last her an eternity. And this pain, such as she'd never experienced in her life, was too deep for tears to ease.

Blindly, she stumbled over a rock and fell to her knees. Rising was too much of an effort for her grieving mind and body. Instead, she buried her face in her hands.

How could she continue to live without Jason?

Chapter Fifteen

New Orleans, January 1816

Why had she let Ricci coerce her into coming to New Orleans, Genna asked herself as her desultory glance took in the crowded condition of the ballroom on Condé Street? On every wall were several rows of boxes filled with Creole ladies and their daughters who weren't allowed to dance. Those who did intend to dance sat on chairs positioned at the edges of the floor. Genna sat with the ones who would not dance.

She brought her gaze back to her neatly folded hands laying in her lap. She should have never let Ricci talk her into bringing her household to New Orleans, but at the time she'd agreed to come nothing had mattered. There was a void where her heart should have been. Jason was dead.

After leaving Wellington's office, and it seemed years ago instead of only six months, she had lain in bed for a week fighting the depression that caused an inflammation of the lungs. As soon as she recovered, Ricci had begun pestering her to marry him. Even though the carnage and despair of Waterloo had convinced her to marry Jason, with the viscount gone, her reason for not wedding Ricci no longer seemed sufficient. But she couldn't bring herself to marry Ricci. Not yet. She needed time to grieve for Jason.

So, she'd finally told Ricci that she would accompany him to New Orleans if he would stop badgering her about marriage. He must be patient and wait until they returned to Italy, and then she would marry him. Now, she regretted even doing that.

"Genna," Aunt Hester said, interrupting Genna's melancholy thoughts, "let us go back to the house. 'Tis too hot here and the tempers of the Creole men are too irascible for my comfort." She wielded her fan with vigor. "I still do not know why you allowed Ricci to talk you into coming to this barbarian part of the world anyway."

Genna didn't bother to suppress a ladylike snort at Hester's verbalization of what she'd just been pondering herself. But when she replied, her voice was reasonable and tinged with resignation. "Dear, we came to New Orleans with Ricci because he is my betrothed. We came to this ball because Ricci kept at us until it was easier to do what he wanted. We both know that he is like a spoiled child when thwarted."

Otherwise, she would have never set foot here, no matter how fashionable Creole society found this place. She hated balls. They brought back memories of the Duchess of Richmond's ball; memories that tore at her heart, opening anew the wound that would never heal.

Hester interrupted Genna's thoughts again by sighing, a huge movement that inflated her already ample bosom. "Ricci is not worth the inconvenience he causes. If it were up to me, we would be on the next ship back to Europe." She shuddered. "These Creoles are more volatile than the French and the weather here is abominable. 'Tis cold and damp, the streets nothing more than rivers of mud." She stopped long enough to get air. "Even Paris is preferable to this."

Hester continued waving her finely painted fan with energy, moving the air in swirls that lifted the gray frizzed curls framing her round face. "And furthermore, I do not understand why Ricci would even wish to come to this place. Albeit, there is plenty of gambling and loose females, but he could have gotten those in Paris."

Another time, Genna would have been amused by Hester's blunt speaking, but not now. Nothing was of consequence anymore.

She was almost grateful to see Ricci coming up the steps to the dais where they sat. At least she wouldn't have to respond to Hester's continual complaints.

Ricci wore a colorful coat and waistcoat and a swordcane or *colchemarde*. The *colchemarde*, which he wore in imitation of the hot-blooded Creole bucks, was a French sword, wide near the hilt and tapering suddenly to a rapier-like blade. Sardonically, Genna wondered why he bothered.

He lacked the courage to ever use the weapon.

"Genna," Ricci said, his dark eyes flashing dangerously and his sensual mouth turned down at the corners, "why are you sitting up here with the dowagers and untried maidens? I told you to dance with the men and make yourself agreeable."

He reached for her upper arm and wrapped his fingers tightly around her flesh before she could move out of his range. His cruel grip was the first physically aggressive move he'd made toward her since Jason laid him low. For the first time since Jason's death, Genna felt an emotion that wasn't grief. Anger danced along her nerves.

She looked pointedly at his hold which was crushing the lavender muslin sleeve of her half-mourning gown, a color she secretly wore for Jason. Her teeth showed in a grimace. "Take your hand off me, Ricci. I won't tolerate your insolent, demeaning treatment."

For a second, she thought he would persist, possibly even drag her out of her seat, but he didn't. With a flourish and an exaggerated bow, he released her and stepped back.

"Of course, *cara mia*. Your command is my action." He rose and his gaze turned sly. "I only wished to ensure that you enjoy yourself. You have not been yourself since Waterloo."

Genna drew herself up. "Waterloo was a horrible experience, nursing all those men who died no matter what was done for them."

"I have not forgotten, *cara mia*, I only wonder sometimes if that is the true answer."

She met his bold eyes without hesitation. "'Tis the only one you need to concern yourself with."

He bristled at her open rebuke, his mouth thinning. With a curt bow he pivoted on his heel and stalked toward the line of young men waiting their turn to dance.

Genna watched him leave, satisfaction curving her lips. Her reasons for what she did were none of his affair. But her spurt of fury, the first strong emotion she'd allowed herself to feel since Brussels, had opened her to an onslaught of debilitating pain.

Her mouth drooped and her eyes gazed sightlessly as the loneliness of desolation swept her body and heart. No one, not even her dearest Hester, knew of the agony that made her days seem never-ending and her nights the darkest hours of her soul.

Was she being punished for not telling Jason she would marry him no matter what? Was she fated to be eternally damned because she realized too late that a love as pure and good as hers and Jason's was truly as honorable as keeping a promise, let alone one made under duress?

Why else had Jason died? Why else had her flux started within days of her learning his fate? There could be no doubt in her mind and heart that she would never be blessed with his child.

It was this despair that had led her to agree to Ricci's demands to come to New Orleans. After Waterloo, she hadn't cared if she lived or died, so where her body went was immaterial.

Her hands clenched until the knuckles were

white. God, how could she go on living without Jason?

"Genna," Hester prodded Genna with her closed fan, "I would like to leave."

Tears hesitated on the brink of her lashes as Genna absorbed Hester's demand. In her complete despondency, she'd forgotten they were in a ballroom crowded with people. As long as Jason was dead and she lived, her surrounding would never be important again.

Belatedly, Genna focused on the activity around her and rose, pulling herself almost physically from the brink of total misery. She gave Hester her hand, and the two moved to the stairs that would lead them to the dance floor where they could make their way to the door.

To reach the door they had to pass the line of bachelors waiting their turn to ask a Creole lady to dance. All the men were dressed elaborately and wore *colchemardes*. Genna had heard that the weapons were used nightly by more than one volatile young man in a duel of honor.

The idea of such violence made her shudder and she looked away. They were almost out of the room when the noise of jostling and shuffling feet, followed by imprecations, caught her attention. Another fight was starting, and the only question was whether it would be fought in here or if the two parties would go outside.

Glancing at the line of men where the scuffle had originated, one man held her gaze. He was taller than most, his shoulders broad and his hips narrow. He was dressed in more subdued black evening dress, and he wore no sword.

But his clothing wasn't what held her interest. It was his face. His hair was golden, worn casually and slightly long, and his complexion was tanned from exposure to the outdoors. His one eye was moss green, long and almond in shape, and framed by lashes as lustrous and thick as a beaver's pelt. A black patch covered the left eye.

Hester prodded her niece. Genna, realizing she was staring, made to move on. But something wouldn't let her go. She looked back at the man.

He resembled Jason. Or was longing making her conjure him out of any man with blond hair and green eyes? Was she so heartsick that she would do anything to bring her love back, if only for a fleeting instant of time?

"Come along, Genna," Hester said, putting a hand on Genna's arm and trying to urge her on.

Genna pulled from Hester's clasp, her concentration never wavering from the man. He looked just as Jason would if he had only one eye. Against every reason, she wanted him to be her love.

"Please," she murmured the word as a prayer.

He had to be Jason. There was gray in the hair at his temples, and the face was thinner than she remembered, with the lines around the mouth deeper. But the angle of cheek and jaw were the same, only more pronounced. Even the shape and color of the eye were the same. The only difference was the weariness gazing out of the one good eye. But those were minor changes.

He was her love.

A gasp escaped Genna. Her fingers went to her

throat, pressing the rapid, painful beat of her pulse, trying to still it.

Her hand went out to the man, to Jason, and she took a halting step forward. Everything seemed to rush in on her, the sounds, the sights . . . and then nothing.

Jason saw Genna reach for him and not reaching back was the hardest thing he'd ever done, harder than not returning to her after Waterloo. Having Wellington tell her he was dead had been like having the living, beating heart in his chest torn from him.

Even now, six months after their last time together in her house in Brussels, she still had the power to twist his guts in knots. He couldn't help the longing for her that made his palms break into a cold sweat.

When she fell to the floor, folding like a limp doll, he clenched his fists and twisted away to keep from rushing to her. She was his only love, and it was tearing him apart not to help her. But she was better off without him.

Waterloo had cost him an eye. While it no longer mattered to him, he knew it would make a difference to Genna. Now she would agree to marry him for pity, and he couldn't survive that. He wanted her because she loved him beyond all else, but he knew that was an impossibility. She'd turned him down when he was whole because of her promise; he wouldn't use her sympathy for him now to make her break that promise.

She would be repulsed by him; she would never admit it, but he would know. She was so beautiful and perfect that his deformity couldn't help but give her pause. No, he would never burden her with his presence.

His teeth clenched. So, he must allow her Aunt Hester to take care of her. He had to stand by and allow someone else to pick Genna up and take her home, even though all he wanted to do was take her into his arms and carry her away to a place where no one else existed but the two of them. It was a fantasy, and he knew it.

"Damnation to bloody hell!" he growled under his breath as a new thought took him.

She wasn't supposed to be in New Orleans. With her nearby he would be constantly tempted to seek her out, to court her, instead of concentrating on his efforts to find out how the Creoles planned to free Napoleon from St. Helena. But even worse could happen. She might inadvertently betray him. A slip of her tongue and his true identity could be exposed.

He would have to seek her out.

It was a thought so tempting that he understood how Adam must have felt before eating the apple. Lost in thought, he paid no attention to what he was doing. His shoulder caught one of the young Creole bucks off balance and the youth stumbled into one of the chairs holding a woman waiting to be asked to dance.

"Monsieur," the youth exploded, "I demand satisfaction."

Pushing the allure of being with Genna again to the very back of his awareness, Jason focused on the situation he now found himself in. To act in any way that might be misconstrued as conciliatory would brand him as a coward in the eyes of the very Creoles he was trying to infiltrate. Such an event would ruin his chances of being accepted by them.

Against his better judgment, because a spy never called attention to himself by acting out of the ordinary, he hardened his features and sneered. "What satisfaction can a whelp such as you gain?"

The young man flushed to the roots of his glossy black hair. "I can kill you in a fair fight."

Jason laughed to cover his disgust at the boy's eagerness to spill blood. Obviously, this young man had never been in battle, or he would be less willing to risk his life so foolishly.

Thus, it was with barely covered distaste that Jason immediately left the ball to meet the Creole in St. Anthony's Square, the site of most duels in New Orleans. Upon arriving, Jason took off his jacket and folded it neatly before turning to the man who'd agreed to be his second and taking the *colchemarde* he had offered to let him use.

Jason hefted the sword, feeling the balance of the finely made blade. It was made as well as the knife secreted inside his boot. There should be no problem with the weapon.

A bitter smile twisted Jason's lips. He would be the only threat to his own safety. Even though he'd practiced every day since recovering from his battle wounds, he was still not fully adjusted to the limited sight and distorted depth perception that his loss of one eye created. Dueling in the dark, with only the silver light of the moon, wouldn't help.

Running his fingers through his hair, Jason studied his opponent, who stood directly across from him. The young man had good form and well muscled shoulders.

At the second's word to start, Jason went onto the balls of his feet and began to warily circle his opponent. The Creole, hotter of blood and eager to avenge the slight done him, attacked.

For the first few minutes, Jason spent his energies fending off the youth. He was glad he'd spent so many hours after Waterloo regaining his proficiency with the sword. While his opponent soon became winded and the youth's lunges went wide of their mark, Jason was able to parry each succeeding blow more easily than the last.

The youth, realizing that he was losing, tried to switch hands. Jason, his eye working rapidly in unison with his highly trained reflexes, made his move. With a flick of his wrist, Jason caught his opponent's sword tip with his and flipped the Creole's weapon high into the air. The *colchemarde* buried itself, hilt up, in the moist dark earth.

Jason stepped back and allowed his sword to point downward. Quickly, the boy's second came forward and agreed that the duel was over. Jason readily accepted that decision.

There was a light film of sweat on his upper lip and he was in no mood to fight the youth again. Every time he dueled, he took the chance that he might misjudge the distances or fail to see the slight flicker of an opponent's eye that said louder than words what the next move would be.

And besides that, he had an appointment at Maspero's Exchange ostensibly to drink coffee with Nicholas Girod, the leader of the Creole faction planning to free Napoleon. It was a meeting he didn't want to miss.

The sooner he found what he came to New Orleans for, the sooner he would be gone. However, to insure that his identity wasn't revealed, he must seek Genna out quickly. While he trusted her not to expose him intentionally, she didn't know he was in disguise and might reveal his real name in passing.

As it was, the only reason he'd fallen into this dueling situation was his clumsy reaction over seeing Genna again. He should have asked Wellington to keep him informed of her whereabouts instead of trying to put her completely out of his mind.

But how could he have anticipated her showing up in the Americas? She should be in Italy.

Even as Jason dueled, Genna regained consciousness. At first, she didn't remember where she was, then slowly her memory returned. She was in her bedroom in the house Ricci had rented on Levee Street in New Orleans.

With the comprehension of her location, came the picture of the man standing in line at the Condé Street ballroom. He had to have been Jason. But how?

Wellington himself had told her Jason was dead. She'd heard his words spoken not two feet distant from her: "Everly was a fine man. He fought bravely and we are proud of him."

It was the first time since hearing Wellington's words that she'd allowed herself to decipher them one by one. He hadn't come out and said Jason was dead, she'd put that interpretation on what he said.

Therefore, Jason could be alive. The man she'd seen last night with the eye patch could very well be her beloved.

Her mouth formed an 'O' and the blood rushed from her head leaving her faint. She had to lean back against the pillows. Jason could be alive!

The emotional void that had held her in its merciful grip since leaving Wellington's office began to dissipate like fog on a river under the hot blaze of the rising sun. But it wasn't only love that animated her.

If the man was Jason, then why had he never returned to her? Could he have decided that he didn't truly love her as he had once professed? Why else would Wellington phrase his reply to her in such a way as to make her think Jason was dead? Why else would Jason have left her to suffer the agonies of believing him dead?

She couldn't accept that Jason was capable of such cruelty. Not her Jason. He was brave and honorable and true. He would never leave her in the hell created by his death. Yet, there was no denying that the man she saw last night was Jason. In her heart she knew he was, and he had condemned her to hell on earth.

Uncertainty clouded her sight. There was much here to learn, and it couldn't be too soon for her peace of mind. She had to know urgently, before she drove herself crazy with doubts.

And she had to see Jason again, talk with him, touch him, love him. Without him, her existence was worthless.

She would seek him out.

That determined, she found herself no longer weak. One quick motion and the bed covers were flung from her. Rushing to the window, she pulled back the curtains to gaze down at the still dark garden tucked like a jewel within the safe confines of the brick house. The sun hadn't risen yet, but soon the servants would be out buying the day's produce. She would send Alphonse to the French Market to seek out news of a newcomer to the city who spoke impeccable French and wore an eye patch.

It was considerably later that morning, just as Genna and Aunt Hester were sitting down to breakfast that Alphonse returned.

Alphonse's face was drawn in sharp lines of dislike as he relayed his findings. "A man named Gaston Everly fits our description." He lives several houses down from us on Levee Street." He stopped and his bearing tensed as though he prepared himself for an onslaught. "Milady, perhaps this man does not intend to contact you. He did nothing to help you last night after you fainted."

Aunt Hester, liberally spreading her toast with

marmalade, added her opinion. "'Tis true, Genna. In fact, the scoundrel turned away without a second glance."

Genna put down her morning chocolate and frowned. What they said coincided with her own doubts. But now that life had returned to her through seeing this man, she couldn't rest until she knew for certain that this Gaston was really Jason. And that he no longer wanted her.

The possibility that his love for her had been nothing but a sham... she stopped herself. She wouldn't doubt the love that he'd demonstrated repeatedly to her. But it was possible that Waterloo and her refusal to marry him had killed that love. And if that were so, she had no one to blame but herself. Cold comfort at best.

She lifted her chin defiantly and spoke firmly. "I know that both of you are only concerned about my well-being, but this is something I must pursue."

Without giving them a chance to add to their arguments, she rose and left, determined to go to the address Alphonse had given her. Genna donned a woolen cape against the damp breeze blowing from the Mississippi River across Levee Street, much as she donned the courage to go unescorted to a single man's dwelling. She hadn't been in New Orleans long, but she knew it was much like Europe in this respect. A maid or Aunt Hester should accompany her, but she wanted no one along. This was too personal and too critical a meeting for witnesses.

Genna walked down the narrow, muddy street.

"This Gaston has to be Jason. There is no other person he might be." She repeated the words to herself as her courage faltered. What if he weren't?

Stopping in front of the house Alphonse had named, she took a deep breath and rubbed her frozen hands together hoping to bring some warmth to them. Before her courage could falter, she knocked loudly and imperiously.

She hadn't even counted to ten and the door was opened by a Negro butler, his bearing impeccable and very similar to Michaels's. He looked down his nose at her.

"Madam?"

The inflection of his voice implied many things, none of which were complimentary to Genna. It put her back up. "I am the Contessa di Ponti here to see your master."

A flicker of respect lit his dark eyes, only to be replaced by a very knowing look. "Monsieur Everly is not at home."

Genna knew enough about servants to read the stiffening of his back and the flick of his eyes to the side. Monsieur Everly most definitely was home, but she also knew the butler would never admit her.

Drawing herself up proudly, she handed him her visiting card. "In that case, please give this to him when he returns."

The butler took her card, and Genna hoped fervently that it would reach Jason. She had done all she could at the moment, and it didn't seem that it would accomplish anything.

Turning away, she retraced her steps, her

shoulders slumped. She'd had such great expectations and all for naught. She'd been foolish. If she were meant to be with Jason, he would have returned to her after Waterloo.

Doubts assailed her as she stopped and gazed in the direction where she knew the muddy Mississippi waters flowed. Perhaps this Gaston wasn't her Jason, but she sensed in her heart that he was. Jason was here in New Orleans, had survived Waterloo, and hadn't returned for her.

She had to face reality. He no longer loved her. He couldn't love her and do this to her.

Her heart, that battered organ that had been through so much, contracted painfully at the realization that Jason's love for her was over. It hurt so badly that she wanted to curl up into a ball, but she didn't. She took herself in hand.

Jason might no longer care for her, but at least he was alive and well. He would never be hers, but thankfully he wasn't dead. Loving him as totally as she did, she was glad for his sake. It was enough. It would have to be, it was all she had left.

Unable to endure the biting cold of the weather and the emptiness of her loss, Genna trudged the remaining distance to her house. Tomorrow, she would tell Ricci she would be returning to Italy.

No matter how Ricci ranted and raved, she couldn't stay here and take the chance that she would run into Jason again. Her heart, her very sanity, wouldn't survive that.

With leaden feet, she went through the door Michaels was solicitously holding open. She gave him her cape and mounted the stairs to the second story where the parlor was located. Perhaps if she rested by the window that looked down on the enclosed patio, she would feel better.

Chin in hand, eyes staring sightlessly at the enclosed garden, Genna was caught unaware when Michaels announced Ricci. With a small start at the interruption, Genna focused on her betrothed's arrival. She noted that once more he wore a *colchemarde*. Ricci strode toward her, a smile twisting his full lips. "I see that you are fully recovered from your little episode last night." He stopped several feet from her and scowled. "I should have known that you would disgrace me in front of all my friends."

She gaped at him before managing to compose her features. It never did to let Ricci think he had her at a disadvantage, even if it was caused by surprise. "Don't be ridiculous. Why would I faint to cause you embarrassment?" She waved her hand in dismissal of his comment. "You're too much a narcissist."

His complexion darkened and he took a step toward her. "That is not how you should speak to your future husband."

She sighed in exasperation. He was such a child, and her patience with his nonsense was gone. It had evaporated in Brussels, but her grief over Jason's supposed death had kept her from realizing it.

Rising, she moved away from Ricci, wary of his hot temper that she'd already seen ample proof of. "Ricci, don't be so tiresome. I don't feel well and would appreciate it if you would leave."

He scowled and followed her. "Be sure that you are feeling better tonight. Or have you forgotten about the masquerade you agreed to attend?"

Wearily, she sighed. She had forgotten. In light of everything that had happened since yesterday, the masquerade meant nothing. But having felt the brunt of his temper in Brussels, she wasn't willing to defy him in this. She would go.

In fact, since he was already incensed, it would be best to wait until the masquerade to tell him about her decision to leave New Orleans. His mood was bound to be better when he was at a party and getting his own way.

"Hester and I will be ready." She faced him calmly, but with a finality in her posture that told him that her tolerance was at an end.

Glowering, Ricci stalked through the door and slammed it behind himself. At least he hadn't begged her for money.

Genna shook her head, but within minutes he was no longer in her thoughts. Instead, she moved to sit near the window facing down on Levee Street.

There was still time for Jason to seek her out today.

A dejected curve to her mouth, Genna watched the crowd at the masquerade and berated herself for waiting all afternoon for Jason to come to her.

No matter how she had told herself differently, her heart had hoped that he would show. She'd wanted more than life itself for him to come to her and tell her that his love was still strong. It hadn't happened, and now she had to get through this evening without arousing Ricci's ire which wasn't going to be easy. Particularly, since she definitely intended to tell him of her plans to return to Italy.

It didn't matter to her that the gaiety in the room should have been contagious as the revelers milled around in their elaborate costumes, their identities hidden so that they could behave more outrageously than normal. She didn't want to be here. There was too much of a chance that Jason, or Gaston as he was calling himself here, would be one of the guests. He seemed to be as involved with the Creoles as Ricci was.

Her brows drew together in consideration. It was very strange that Jason was in New Orleans, probably in the capacity of a spy. But why would Jason be spying here? There was nothing in New Orleans that could be a threat to England.

Could there be a connection between Ricci being here and Jason coming here? Both men were heavily involved with the Creole society that dominated New Orleans or Jason wouldn't have been at the Condé street ball.

Surely, that was a ridiculous assumption. True, Jason was probably spying for England, for whatever reason. But Ricci was too cowardly to be involved in anything that remotely smacked of danger.

So her betrothed must be here for the reasons he gave her. He claimed he wanted to travel before marriage, and he liked the continental ambience of New Orleans and the very Frenchness of the

Creoles. He had no real purpose in life, and dissolute pleasure seeker that he was, he needed none. She was just sorry that she'd allowed herself to be forced into accompanying him.

She was distracted from her mental perambulations by a movement that focused into a tall, lithe man whose broad shoulders were covered by a black domino. She didn't need to see his face to know he was Jason. She could tell by the way he carried himself and the proud angle of his head. The black band that ran horizontally along the back of his head confirmed it. It was his eye patch.

Her shoulders tensed and her stomach knotted; even her knees began to weaken. It hurt so much to see him and know that he didn't care for her.

Her heart ached just knowing he was in the same room and she couldn't go to him. And her spine hurt from the strain of keeping it straight to hide her agony. She refused to show anyone the despair she felt knowing that Jason didn't want her anymore.

A sigh escaped her. She should leave. It would be easier than staying here, following him constantly with her eyes, wondering when he would ask one of the numerous ladies to dance. Possibly even dance more than once with a lucky woman.

Twisting from side-to-side, Genna looked for the closest means of escape. Sighting the door, she pivoted on the ball of her foot and wove her way through the shifting mass of people. Escape was only a few steps away when a hand descended on her arm.

A gasp took her breath away as the warm

strength of long fingers held her immobilized. She didn't have to look to know it was Jason who pinioned her with only a light clasp.

Shivers pervaded her body. Had he gotten her visiting card and decided to see her after all? But this was an odd place to do so.

Ah, she decided, he might not know who she was since she had on a mask. But her hair was uncovered, and in this crowd of dark-haired people her red tresses stood out. So perhaps he did know her identity. Perhaps he intended to explain to her why he had let her believe him dead. Perhaps, she squeezed her eyes shut in silent prayer, he would tell her that he still loved her.

"Genna, I need to speak to you." He drew his breath in harshly. "Alone."

The shivers that had wracked her body just seconds before returned with a vengeance. It seemed that her dream of a reconciliation might come true. Why else would he wish to speak to her where no one could hear?

Hope flared in her heart, so strong that it was a bright fire. She dared not look at him, afraid that she would see denial in his face. She didn't want the dream blossoming within her bosom to be crushed and thwarted.

Still not looking at him, she focused her eyes on the door and nodded. "As you wish. Where?"

Jason saw her nod in agreement even though she refused to look at him and see the patch over his eye. He'd felt the shudders of revulsion that shook her whole body when he'd put his hand on her. Even though he'd expected her to be revolted by his lack of one eye, her revulsion was still a tormenting pain. The only way he could deal with it was to become furious with her callousness.

Silently, every muscle in his body stiff with restraint and unable to speak lest he betray his mounting wrath, he steered her out the door and toward the Place d'Armes. He kept them moving rapidly, almost running so that neither had the breath to speak.

She stumbled once, and he pulled her up and against his side to keep her from falling. He regretted it immediately. The feel of her lush curves pressed against his starved flesh was almost more than he could resist. With a curse, he put her from him and withdrew the support of his hand on her arm.

Genna swallowed a cry of pain when Jason thrust her from him and released her. If he couldn't bear to touch her, how could she continue to delude herself that he was still in love with her? She couldn't.

Her step faltered as the agony of knowing all was finally lost swept over her. Why had she been so bound by her word to Luigi when she'd had the chance to marry Jason? Love, not misguided promises, is the cement that gives people the strength to do what is right. Now Jason didn't want her.

"Come along," Jason said.

His flat voice stopped the tears caused by her hopeless situation from welling up in her eyes. She drew herself up straighter. She would be strong.

Quickly, they turned into the Place d'Armes and Jason threaded them surreptitiously through the paths. This, as much as his taking her from the masquerade, told her that he needed something from her. He wouldn't have sought her out otherwise.

Well, if he needed her, then she had to help him. Even though he no longer loved her, she loved him. Whatever she could give to him or do for him, she would.

Her resolve firmed when Jason stopped and took a thorough look around. No one appeared to be nearby, so he ushered her under the heavy branches of a weeping willow tree, where even the moonlight couldn't penetrate.

She turned expectantly toward him. Being under the branches of the tree was as private as being in a room by themselves, so that she couldn't help the sense of imtimacy that engulfed her.

She couldn't help the longing that flowed through her veins. She loved him so much and it had been so long since she'd been alone with him like this. Until yesterday, she'd thought she would never experience this bliss again. And now that the opportunity was hers, it was a mockery of what she'd dreamed of. She'd forfeited his love by refusing it.

"Genna."

She started at his use of her name. It was ecstasy to hear him say it, even though his voice was strained and cold. If only he were saying her name in love. When he cleared his throat, she forced herself to concentrate on his words.

"Genna," Jason repeated. Then paused and grimaced at the way her Christian name came from his lips, feeling so right and so natural, as though the months of separation and her refusal to marry weren't between them. He was ten thousand times a fool for this weakness. He should address her as Contessa di Ponti, but it was too late to call back her given name.

He continued, "There's no sense in mincing words with you. I'm here as a spy," he ignored her start, "and I'm asking you not to reveal my true identity."

Where before her pain had been bittersweet, now it was piercing. How could he doubt her? The agony he'd inflicted by ignoring her last night and this afternoon was nothing compared to this. She lashed out at him. "How dare you call into question my loyalty? Why should I tell anyone who you are? I haven't even been introduced to you here. Until yesterday, when you left me collapsed on the floor at Hester's feet, I had no idea that you were even alive, let alone in New Orleans."

Jason took a step backwards, surprised by her vehemence. However, he quickly understood that she was irate over his implication that she might give him away. He was doubting her honor, that virtue she put before all else, and she wouldn't stand for it. He was torn between anger and understanding. Considering what her honor had cost him emotionally, he wasn't sure he wanted to feel anything but fury.

Still, he spoke calmly, knowing that to give into his wrath would only make matters worse between them than they already were. "I never doubted your discretion or thought that you'd maliciously expose me, but I couldn't take the chance that you might let something slip out or call me Jason."

Now Genna truly sneered and wished she could see Jason's features in the dark. But with the overhanging branches she couldn't. She wanted to evaluate his emotions as he uttered each word, but it was impossible. All she had to go by was the cold indifference in his voice, and that was enough to turn her blood to ice water.

"If you're so afraid that I'll call you Jason, then you'd better tell me *what* name you're calling yourself these days. I can assure you that once properly informed, I shall endeavor never to call you by any other. As far as I'm concerned, the Jason McClenna I loved is dead."

Jason's hands clenched involuntarily at the sarcastic whiplash of her statement. "That's right. The man you claimed to love, but refused to marry, is gone. In his place is Gaston Everly, a one-eyed Frenchman who sympathizes with the Creole plan to free Napoleon Bonaparte from St. Helena."

All Genna registered was *refused to marry.* Could that simple utterance be the key to the frigid dislike he made no effort to hide? Would it change the situation between them if she told him she wanted to marry him more than she wanted to continue living? Was it possible?

She had to risk it. With just that glimmer of insight into his emotions to go on, she had to take the chance that there was more to his desertion than she comprehended. She had to assume that he was hurting and thusly avoiding her out of self-defense.

For her own eternal happiness, and for the agony that may have hardened Jason's heart, she had to tell him how she felt. She had to put her own hurt aside and concentrate on the furious and possibly hurting man in front of her. She had to try.

Genna took a step toward him, pushing back the hood of her cape and removing her small mask. Even though he couldn't see her, she wanted nothing between Jason and herself as she bared her soul to him.

Only inches separated her from Jason. She could feel the heat emanating from his body and smell the faint tang of lemons wafting from his lotion.

Memories, unbidden and bittersweet, assailed her: Jason kissing her with all the passion she herself felt for him; Jason pulling her to his heart and holding her safe and secure within the confines of his embrace; Jason loving her with not just his body, but his entire being.

What she was about to do was right. She knew it as a wild creature knows spring is coming.

"Jason, I love you and I want to marry you. I knew after Waterloo. The carnage and death. The fragility of life and the strength love gave those dying men. It finally made me comprehend that our love is more worthy of honor than any promise. Especially, one made so that a weak fool can keep his wealth." Her voice caught on a sob. "I thought I'd be able to tell you when you returned for me. But you never came back. Why? Why did Wellington lead me to believe you dead?"

She held her breath, waiting for him to react. Her whole future depended on what he said next. For what seemed an eternity, he didn't speak.

Jason wanted to believe her. She was offering him the heaven on earth he'd told himself would never be his. If only he could see her face to read the emotions between her words; he couldn't

And how could she love a man with only one eye? He knew from the shudders that had wracked her body at the masquerade that she couldn't bear to be touched by him. Her offer of marriage now was only because she felt sorry for him. Exactly what he'd dreaded. He wouldn't take her pity. But what bliss if she loved him and truly had decided to marry him after Waterloo and before she saw his disfigurement.

He laughed harshly at his folly. "You wouldn't agree to marry me before, and now that I've lost an eye you do. This is why I asked Wellington to tell you I'd died. I don't want your pity."

"Pity? I don't pity you. There's nothing about you to be pitied. So what if you've lost one eye. You're the only one who cares. I don't."

She had to convince him of her sincerity. And there was only one way to do so. She must love him until no shadow darkened his heart. She must prove to him that he was the same man she'd fallen in love with in Paris.

Standing on tiptoe, Genna reached up and pulled Jason's head down for her kiss. His skin was cold and damp from the night air before slowly heating under the insistence of her lips.

He bent to her willingly, but when their flesh

met, he began to shake and tried to move away. Genna held on tighter, sensing that this would be the only chance she had to convince him that their love was still strong within the deep core of their souls.

Jason only knew that he had to break her embrace before he crushed her to him and forgot everything but the feel of her pressed to him. But she clung to him with a determination that precluded any attempt to separate them unless he used violence; something he could never do to her.

As each second passed, it became harder for him to concentrate on anything but Genna kissing him with such abandon that all else paled into insignificance. He inhaled the scent of her, remembering the other times when the smell of her had driven him wild. He could feel the ripe contours of her breasts pressed against him, even through his coat and domino. And he could feel her hips snugged up to his loins, causing the blood in his body to pool in an aching need for her that would never be assuaged no matter how hard he tried to deny it.

She was the other part of his soul. He could spend the rest of his life running from the love he felt for her and he would never be able to run far enough. He was lost and he knew it.

For these few precious moments, he would allow himself to accept that she meant what her body was telling him. For only a small instant in time, he would allow himself to love her with all the depth of his being. With a groan of passion and defeat, he wrapped his arms around her and molded her pliant figure to him.

Genna exulted in Jason's surrender. She threaded her fingers into his hair and ran her tongue along his lips, asking for admission. As his mouth opened, she thrust forward, tasting a hint of brandy that he must have drank earlier. It was a heady sensation that tensed her stomach.

Moving a breath away from him, she murmured, "Let me love you, Jason."

Chapter Sixteen

Jason reeled under the impact of Genna's words. She couldn't mean what he thought she did. To kiss him in the dark was one thing, but to actually make love to him . . . a man who couldn't even see her properly . . . certainly wasn't what she truly wished.

But if it was, it must be because she was a passionate woman, as he knew so well. She must have been overwhelmed by the physical sensations of what they were sharing. That was the only reason she would say such a thing to him. But even being logical couldn't stave off the hurt her words brought him. He'd been crazed to allow himself to respond so completely to her.

He tore his lips from hers. "Don't tempt me. You don't really know what you're saying."

Genna, nonplused by his severance of their contact, put her palms on his chest to steady herself. She felt the rise and fall of his deep breathing, and under her left hand she felt the rapid beating of his heart.

"But I do, Jason. I want to love you, as you've done so many times to me."

He groaned and pushed her away, his hands on her shoulders keeping her from returning to his embrace. It was impossible for them to do what she suggested. He wouldn't allow her to offer her body to him in pity, and that was what it would end up being. His pride wouldn't be able to live with it.

Fear knifed through Genna as he continued to hold her away from him. He was going to leave her. She had to keep him with her. She knew he loved her, or he couldn't have responded so completely to her kiss. Desperation drove her.

She gripped the folds of his domino with one hand and wound her other hand around his neck, forcing him to bend his elbows or push her onto the ground. She forged herself to him.

A slight breeze wafted by them, rustling the dense leaves and allowing a glint of moonlight to filter in. She stared into his eye, seeing only the hard reflection of her face in the scant luminescence. She almost lost her resolve, but then his mouth twisted into a bitter smile and she knew the truth. He loved her, but didn't want to.

"I love you, Jason McClenna. I want to make love to you." She said the words distinctly, watching every change of his countenance.

He laughed, a harsh agonized sound that was guttural in his throat. "Don't perjure yourself by lying to me. I felt you shudder when I touched you at the masquerade. You love the man I was before Waterloo, and even then you wouldn't marry me. Now that I'm maimed you love me from pity."

She gasped at his self-loathing, but then a smile lit her eyes, and the hope that was never far from her heart unfurled in radiant bloom. He was afraid that she would find him repulsive. That was all. Well, she would show him differently. Before this night was much further along, she would make love to him until he knew beyond the shadow of a doubt that he was the man she loved: body and soul.

With a smile so tender it made Jason's breath catch, Genna reached up and traced the arch of his brow, skirted around the blank patch over his left eye, and down his high cheekbone to his firm mouth. Her finger ringed the defining lines of his lips, and she placed her finger across them.

"Don't ever let me hear you denigrate yourself again. I shuddered because I thought you didn't care for me, and that I would have to endure your touch but never experience your love again. You're the *only* one who's bothered by your lost eye. To me, you're more man than anyone I know."

He snorted, but a tiny part of his heart began to thaw. If only he could believe she truly meant it and wasn't just feeling sorry for him. He didn't want her pity. He wouldn't take it. He'd leave New Orleans, his mission unaccomplished, before he would use her pity to bind her to him.

Genna saw the skepticism rioting across his features. Well, she had all night to convince him that she spoke the truth.

Rising up, she pressed her lips to his. When he didn't respond, standing like a statue under the touch of her mouth, she pressed harder. Still he didn't react.

She bit him; not hard, but enough that he opened his mouth and her tongue could surge in. She didn't think that even in this state of mind that he'd bite her back. He would never callously hurt her.

Slowly, knowing that she must tread carefully, she rimmed his teeth with the tip of her tongue. Her arms circled around his waist, and her hands began to move up and down the ridged muscles of his back. Her fingers kneaded him, then skipped down his spine, touching each vertebrae until they reached the small of his back. With a sigh of contentment, she spread her hands apart and cupped his buttocks, massaging him firmly.

Jason's eyes widened in surprise. She was so aggressive that his loins were tightening until they ached. But his heart ached more. He wanted her to want him so badly that he was afraid to hope. This onslaught of feeling was more than he could take. He had to try one last time to convince her to leave him alone. He put his hands on her shoulders and pushed her away.

Confused by his rejection at this point, Genna gasped for breath. Why had he separated them? She knew he wanted her.

"I've had enough of your physical pleasures, Genna. They mean nothing when your heart doesn't accompany them."

Pain at his pain formed tears in her eyes. She'd

made so many mistakes with him. She had to correct them now because she knew he would never give her another chance.

"I love you, Jason. I always have."

Jason stared at her, his face ravaged with emotions he couldn't control. He couldn't accept her protestations of love so easily. It would be more than he could survive when she told him again that love wasn't enough. "But you loved honor more."

She couldn't deny it. It was the truth. "Once. No more. I love you more than honor. More than life."

"I wish I could believe you."

The words, harsh and unyielding, seared into Genna. Running her shaking hands down her skirts under cover of her cape, she strove not to let her apprehension show. She reached up and took his hands in hers and moved them to cover her breasts.

"I want to marry you." She would convince him even though the rigid way his hands remained motionless on her breast told her clearly that he still doubted.

Genna knew he wanted her in spite of his reluctance. She could feel it in the way his fingers on her breast trembled even though he did nothing to arouse her. If she couldn't convince him, then she would seduce him. She would leave him no outlet but to make love to her.

"Touch me," she ordered in a voice low and piercing. "I want to make love to you." She gulped, not sure she could say the next words, but determined to do so. Nothing was more important than breaking through the barrier he'd erected between them. "I want to feel you deep inside me. I love you, Jason McClenna."

Blood, hot and fierce, rushed through Jason's veins, his body reacting with a will of its own. She was saying things to him that he would have never thought possible. And where she'd put his hands was more suggestive than her words.

"Genna, don't do this," he groaned, wanting to massage the full breasts she was pressing into his palms but resisting the urge. She would leave him when this was finished. She would wed her count, regardless of saying she would marry him instead.

Genna closed his hands against her and moved in such a way that his fingers rubbed against her full bosom. "That's it, love," she crooned.

When she sensed his resistance was at its weakest, she inched toward him. His elbows bent, allowing her to close the distance between them until her body was flush to his, his hands trapped around her swollen flesh.

"You feel so good, Jason."

Jason's mind reeled under the impact of her words. How could he continue to resist her when his stomach was a mass of knots and his loins were hot and pulsing with the need to bury himself so deep in her that he might never emerge again?

"Stop it, Genna. You don't need to prove anything to me. You don't owe me anything."

Why was he so stubborn? She didn't know if she could continue this blatant pursuit when he gave her no encouragement. Her face was already flushed with embarrassment at her bold actions, and someone might come upon them any minute.

She looked up at his face just as a rare beam of moonlight broke through an opening in the leaves above. His features were a mask of tormented desire and longing and, she'd stake her life on it, love. It was the impetus she needed to continue. She would do whatever it took to destroy the barrier; seduce him where they stood if necessary.

"Jason," she murmured, nuzzling his neck, "I intend to have you tonight, so please stop fighting me. We'll both be much happier for it."

He groaned. She was driving him crazy with her lips on his hot skin and her hands fondling him under his domino. Perhaps he should take what she so pointedly offered. Maybe then she'd realize that she no longer wanted him for a lover and would leave him alone. He might even be able to get her out of his system.

He laughed, a tortured sound in the stillness of the night. He'd never be over her, no matter how he tried to delude himself. But he could have her one last time; feel her pressed close to his heart one last time. And, above all else, he could pretend that she loved him.

It was a heady fantasy.

Genna circled her hands from his back to the front. She cupped his engorged manhood.

The breath left his chest in a rush that was more forceful than if he'd been punched in the gut. "Damn!" he gasped.

A moan escaped him as her fingers ran the length of his shaft. When she began to undo the buttons of his pantaloons, it was such sweet suffering that it was all he could do not to brush her aside and release himself.

Genna felt him spring forth and knew it was now or never. She fell to her knees and took him into her mouth.

Jason bit his lip to keep from shouting, his shock and pleasure were so great. He couldn't allow her to do this. Not here. Not where anyone might stumble upon them.

"Stop," he managed to say in spite of a tongue that seemed not to want to work. "Stop, Genna. Someone might see us."

When she continued to suck him, taking him deeper into her mouth, he fought the urge to buck. Instead, he grabbed her by the shoulders and gently, resolutely disengaged her and pulled her up.

His heart was pounding and his pulse was throbbing painfully in his neck and loins. He clasped her to him, his manhood pressed into the soft mound of her stomach, his forehead resting on the top of her head while he strove to regain control of his body.

Genna wriggled against him, feeling his shaft hard and long against her sensitized belly.

"Stop it," he commanded, his voice strained. "Stop twisting against me, or I can't be responsible for what will happen."

"Good," she said triumphantly. "I don't want you to be able to think of anything but what I'm doing to you."

His features contorted. This wasn't anything like what he'd expected from her when he'd come to his wits after Waterloo. He'd believed that she would never want him with this abandon and intensity again. Had he been wrong? Could he have misjudged her? Could he have made the last eight months of his life a living hell for no reason?

She undulated against him, sending his pulse soaring. Rational thought ceased as he strove to calm himself sufficiently not to throw her onto the grass and bury himself in her hot tunnel. But he was near his breaking point, and he was coherent enough to realize it.

This was sex, pure and elemental. She didn't have to love him. He had enough love for them both. For tonight, her lust would be enough. He would make it enough.

"Jason," she murmured, twisting her head out from under his forehead and placing her lips on his, tickling him with her tongue, "I want to make love to you. Come home with me."

He heard her words as though from a distance, his body too caught up in the stimulation she wrought on him. Why continue to fight her? She wanted him, or made a good show of seeming to.

He made his choice. Tearing his mouth from hers, he fastened himself back into his pantaloons. "We're going to my house. My servants have gone for the night."

Taking her by the arm, he steered her toward the river and Levee Street. He kept them to a brisk pace.

Genna, her heart lightening with joy that she'd finally convinced him of her sincerity, hurried to keep up with his long strides. "We can go to my house. 'Tis closer."

He slanted a look at her she couldn't read. "Greedy wench. I'll see you satisfied if it takes me all night and into tomorrow."

She smiled, thinking that things were returning to how she remembered them. "I've no doubt of your skills, I only want to speed their application."

This time he grinned, barely a quirking of his mouth. As wary as he was of the feelings she made him experience, he found himself glad that she still retained her ready wit. "We go to my home because I don't want to risk your reputation and because I know that Michaels won't go to bed until he knows that you're safely at home."

He glanced at her, and was taken aback by the radiance on her face. To cover his surprise, he added, "Put your mask back on. That way if anyone sees us, they won't recognize you."

By the time she got her mask and hood on, they were at his front door and mounting the stairs to the second floor. He turned them left at the top and guided her to a door which he opened with a bang.

He swooped her up into his arms and crossed to the large mahogany bed that dominated the room. He laid her on the top and in his eagerness started taking off her mask and then her cloak.

"You're more beautiful than I remembered."

She smiled, recognizing his sincerity. "My love," she whispered, her throat tight with suppressed emotion. She reached up to him, an invitation for him to lay beside her.

Jason shook his head and moved to close the door and turn the key in the lock. That done, he went to the large fireplace and stoked the wood until flames illuminated every corner of the room.

Only then did he look again at Genna, who was now sitting up on the bed. In the fire's flickering light, she appeared to recede and come closer. And though he'd expected his impaired perception to make it difficult, he found that every angle and curve of her face, every minute expression, was clear to him.

Genna watched Jason as he studied her. He was standing as though he wasn't sure whether or not to proceed. She couldn't allow him to pull back now. They were too close. She'd felt the barrier between them begin to erode.

Rising, her eyes never leaving his, she went to him. When she was so close that her breasts grazed his chest, she stopped. She loved him more than any words or any act of physical love could ever convey, but those were the only mediums she had.

She took a deep breath and began to untie the domino. When he raised his arms to take it off, she stepped closer and helped him ease it over his head. This close, their mouths only inches apart, she took his lips with hers.

At the touch of his flesh on hers, her insides melted and she wanted to flow around him, claim him as hers. Instead, she edged far enough away so that she could unbutton his coat. That done, she slipped her hands inside and ran her palms up his chest and onto his shoulders where she started to ease the coat off him. She ran her hands down his arms, pushing the garment as she went.

Under her fingertips, she felt tiny tremors begin to shake Jason's body. Exultation rose in her. He wanted her. It was a beginning.

Her mouth clung to his, becoming more insistent. With her tongue, she probed for admittance. He moaned and she surged inward. She flicked her tongue with his, becoming more excited as he responded. The liquid warmth that had started with his touch spread to every part of her body, and she had to fight her body's inclination to dissolve at his feet.

She was seducing him, not the other way around! With a smile at her own weakness, she forced her fingers to begin unbuttoning his shirt. Lightly, she raked her nails up his flesh, feeling the gooseflesh that rose at her touch.

"You want me," she murmured against his lips. "I can feel it."

Jason couldn't refute her. The hardness of his nipples and the thrust of his manhood would tell he lied.

When he made no answer, Genna rubbed her thumbs on his pointed nipples, enjoying the tactile contrast of his flesh with the wiry hairs that circled the dark areolae. Pushing open his shirt, she took her mouth from his and placed it on one of his raised nubbins.

Jason sucked in, fighting the fire that threatened to consume him as she claimed his flesh. Her teeth nuzzled the hard peak, and his hips moved reflexively. As she pulled harder, increasing the pleasure to a threshold just below pain, his hips moved again. It was as though his nipples were directly connected to his shaft.

"Genna," he said, his voice raspy from the effort to control himself, "I can't take much more of your ministrations. It's . . . it has been too long."

"Good." Genna refused to stop what she was doing; it was too enjoyable. She wanted him to writhe with desire for her, she wanted him so aroused that at the point of his climax he would call out her name and his love for her.

Transferring her attention to the other nipple, she used her hands to push his shirt completely off until it hung from his waistband. Then she began on his pantaloons. The act of having her hands so intimate with his loins was so erotic that waves of heat washed over her, making her skin warm and flushed.

She leaned into him and rubbed her swollen breasts against his torso, feeling his hard nipples through the material of her gown and chemise. Her bosom swelled in sympathy, and she wanted his thumbs to massage her as she'd done him.

Reaching for his hands, she placed them on herself. "Please, Jason."

Jason, his pupil dilated, could feel the pointed nubbins pressing demandingly against his palms. Slowly, he began to caress her, but quickly found that it wasn't enough with her clothing preventing him from feeling the silken smoothness of her skin.

He slipped one hand around her back and released the buttons until her bodice slid off her shoulders. He pushed the garment the rest of the way so that it fell to pool at her feet in a shimmering puddle of green silk.

He feasted on the sight of her. Her ripe breasts mounded above the top of her stays and the fine lace of her chemise gathered in the valley. He couldn't resist tasting her.

"Oh!" Genna gasped as Jason's tongue made a warm, moist path along her flesh while his hands continued to knead her breasts gently. Shivers of pleasure intensified to sparks of lightning that shot through her body to center in her womb.

She swayed closer to him, her fingers moving rapidly to finish his undressing. She was at the point where finesse was in the way of her satisfaction.

Careful to free his erection before pushing the pantaloons down his hips and thighs, she paused to caress the thick shaft. The velvet smoothness only made it harder for her to restrain herself long enough to finish divesting him of his clothing.

Jason, his eye closed in ecstasy as her hands stroked him, moaned deep in his throat. She was driving him to the brink of madness.

"Genna, I have to have you. I want to be buried deep in your honeyed warmth."

He kicked off his shoes, swooped her into his arms and carried her back to the bed. Laying her down, his mouth slashed over hers, demanding entrance for his tongue. He invaded her sweet depths with plunging intensity that increased the feverish need in him.

Genna sensed that he was near the breaking point and she reveled in her power to do this to him. He'd resisted her to the best of his ability and lost. He was hers. Nothing would separate them again.

Quickly, with hands that shook from the urgency of his passion, Jason released her corset and pulled her chemise over her head. The beauty of her released breasts humbled him.

Pulling himself back from the precipice of desire, he paused. His eye met hers. "Genna, unless you stop me now, I'm going to make love to you. I'm going to bury myself so deeply in your silken flesh that there will be no turning back from what we are doing."

She smiled up at him, her face radiant with love and flushed with ardor. "I want you so deep in me that you'll never leave again."

Could it be true? Jason thought. Could she truly love him scarred as he was? He wanted to believe so, but an inaccessible core still doubted her intentions. Still, his need for her was too great for him to deny them the ultimate pleasure they were both anticipating.

"I hope you never regret this." He laid down beside her.

"Never, love," Genna answered him as her arms went around him and she pulled him to her.

She kissed him with an abandon that flamed his blood, and Jason more than met her with his own response. When her leg stroked his outer thigh, he stroked her back.

Genna shivered in delight as Jason reciprocated

every caress she bestowed on him. But she wanted to love him this time. She wanted to use her body to show him that his body was precious to her, no matter how scarred he might be from Waterloo.

Breaking away from his mouth, she inched lower so that she could kiss along the white line of the chest wound that had first brought them together. It was completely healed, but he would carry the mark forever.

She lifted her head and met his gaze. "You have a beautiful body, Jason. You're broad chested and narrow hipped, full muscled and finely honed. And your battle wounds lend it interest." She ran a finger along a new scar on his hip. "Where did this come from?"

Jason drew his breath in as her path led her closer to his throbbing shaft. All she had to do was move an inch to the right and she'd be touching him. "A bayonet."

Genna smiled at the strain in his voice. She knew he was trying to fight the enjoyment her proximity to his manhood brought. "At Waterloo?"

"Yes."

His answer was curt and infinitely delightful. Feeling wicked and wanton, she traced back up the scar and away from the center of Jason's manliness.

Just when Jason relaxed, thinking she would stay clear of his most aroused area, she scooted further down, and his pulse soared again. Her lips and tongue skimmed over the flat planes of his stomach, pausing long enough to twirl in the thick brown hairs that arrowed down to his loins.

Genna felt herself getting moist from the knowledge that she could arouse Jason to this height. It increased her longing to have him inside her.

"Jason," she murmured, slipping lower, "I'm hot and wet for you."

Jason gulped. She was saying all the things to him that he'd once said to her. Her words were more precious than any gold and they heated his blood.

Need, fierce and urgent, pounded in Genna's veins as she rejoiced in her effect on Jason. She flicked her tongue out and touched the tip of his shaft.

"Damn!"

Jason's exclamation startled her and she jolted back. Surely, she hadn't hurt him. "Jason?" His eye was squeezed shut and his jaw was clenched. "Jason, have I hurt you?"

Jason forced the words out through teeth that ground together. "No, Genna. I . . . I'm not in pain."

Then it dawned on her. She'd given him a bolt of pleasure so intense that his reaction simulated agony.

She smiled, supremely confident. He was hers.

Gently, she ran her tongue down the hard length that throbbed as she stroked it. It was like iron covered with velvet. Simultaneously, she ran her hand up his thigh and over his hips before coming forward to cup him. Tenderly, she began to squeeze him in rhythm with her mouth.

"Oh, Lord, Genna, that . . . feels . . . so. . . ."

His voice trailed off as she sucked deeply, taking him inside. His labored breathing was loud in Genna's ears; it was all she could do not to mount him and seek her own pleasure. But she had to be sure of him before satisfying herself.

"Genna, you have to stop. . . ." He paused to try and end the shaking that was wracking his entire body. "I can't hold out much longer."

Delighted at his lack of control, Genna continued until his hands tangled in her hair. "Don't stop me now," she pleaded.

Jason wrapped her long tresses around his fingers and pulled her off him. An uncontrollable moan escaped him as she took one last taste of him with her tongue.

"Enough, Genna. You must have your own recompense."

She laughed, breathy and excited. Before he could prevent her, she straddled him, her inner thighs meeting his outer. She poised above him, her eyes daring him to stop her.

Jason understood what she intended and his manhood stood straighter as though reaching for the tender entrance to her silken sheath. Anticipation tensed his whole body and his muscles hardened into cords of strength.

Genna saw the effort his restraint cost him as his neck bulged. Sweat glistened on his brow and she knew it wasn't from the heat of the room.

Reaching down, she positioned him for her descent. He slid into her and it was as though he'd never left. He was meant to fill her and her alone.

A long sigh of contentment parted her lips and her eyes closed in bliss. It felt so wonderful, so complete to have him in her once more.

"This is where you belong, Jason."

Agreement was on the tip of his tongue, but he bit it off. He couldn't give himself, body and soul, to her. Not yet. His disillusionment was still too deep. But he loved her and his body cleaved to her as though she truly had been taken from his rib.

When there was no aswer, Genna opened her eyes. He was looking at her, his mouth a grim line and his one eye half shut. If he hadn't been thick and hard inside her, she would have doubted his desire for her. But he was buried in her, and she could feel the movements his shaft was making as she closed on it.

Unable to answer her, Jason thrust his hips upward, impaling her completely. She responded by bending at the waist so that her breasts met his chest, the hard tips of her nipples grazing him. He was ready to burst.

"That's it, Jason," she crooned, stroking her breasts across his while she lifted then thrust her hips in rhythm with his. "Love me, Jason. Fill me with your seed."

Her words were incredibly arousing and Jason felt himself poised on the brink of destruction. In seconds, he knew he would explode into myriad particles of pure physical pleasure.

Genna realized that he was close to his peak, and she increased her pace accordingly. She undulated and reached down to caress any part of him she could reach.

"Genna," Jason gasped as her fingers closed around the twin sacks between his legs.

"Yes, love," she encouraged, riding out his passion like she would a runaway stallion. "Fill me."

Jason's mind blanked, only his body existed. Genna was so tight and hot and slick around him and her fingers were doing unimaginable things to him. The release was so intense that for a second he thought he was passing out.

Exhausted beyond imagining, Jason lay quiescent under her. His emotions were submerged in the glow of his climax.

Genna watched every change moving over his face. The taut lines around his mouth had eased and his jaw was no longer clenched tight. Gladness that she was able to do this for him filled her heart.

He was still large inside her and she could very easily continue her own activity until she reached her own release. But she didn't.

As much as her body ached for the pleasure only Jason could give her, as much as she throbbed with the need to release the tension he'd built in her womb, she didn't. Her purpose hadn't been to satisfy herself, it had been to love Jason.

Before he could fathom what she was doing, she reached up and removed the patch from his left eye. Underneath was scar tissue, but no worse than that which crossed his chest.

His one eye flew open and his hand caught her wrist before she could get the patch completely off his head. "What are you doing?"

The harsh pain in his voice brought tears to her eyes. He was hurting so much . . . and for nothing. Leaning forward, she softly pressed her lips to the scar he mistakenly thought made him less than a man.

"I love you, Jason."

Chapter Seventeen

Jason stared at the note his butler had just brought him. It was from Genna. She wanted him to call on her at his convenience. A very innocuous request, but he knew better. She must have intuited that he would avoid her after last night.

For him, their lovemaking had been perfect, a small piece of heaven, an affirmation that life without her would be hell. And then she'd removed his eye patch and kissed his scar.

He crushed the letter as his hands fisted. Even now, the morning after, he still couldn't exorcise from his heart the impact of that action. When her lips had touched his skin, she seemed to draw from him all the hurt and doubt the loss of his eye had caused. He finally felt healed, not just physically, but deep within his soul.

And he loved her. There was no sense in denying it, it wasn't something he could carve out of his heart because to do so would be to leave him only half alive.

He sighed heavily and rose from his seat at the breakfast table, running his fingers through his hair. Still, there remained a kernel of uncertainty that once more she would honor her promise to marry di Ponti over her love for him. But, as God was his witness, he wanted her no matter what.

He paced to the end of the room and back. He had to make a decision. He couldn't continue to live like this any longer. Either he trusted her word, or he didn't. His heart said to believe her, his brain said to run in the opposite direction. Until now, he'd always done as his logic ordered.

"Damnation!" He ground the word out, frustration making him grit his teeth.

Returning to the table, he took a deep breath and opened his clenched fingers. Carefully, he smoothed out the paper and reread the message.

It was the first time he'd ever seen Genna's handwriting, which was rather bemusing considering the intimacies they'd shared. She wrote with a strong hand, making elegant, well-formed letters in dark ink. A very confident style. Much like her. Too much like her.

Once more, he crushed the paper, his knuckles white. Throwing it into the fire, he reached his decision.

Last night had shown him how much a part of him she was. She might feel more pity for him than she did love and she might once more refute him for her vow to Luigi, but he would take the chance. He would risk his future on the belief that she meant what she said.

There was nothing else he could do. Living

without her had been like living without his soul. To let her go now would be to condemn himself to eternal hell.

Even as Jason reached his decision, Genna paced the parlor floor, her heart beating like a triphammer. It had taken all her love and determination to write Jason asking him to come to her. She had swallowed every ounce of remaining pride and literally begged him to come.

But would he? He had to. Or she would go to him.

A smile lit her face. That was the answer. She would go to Jason one more time. After last night, he couldn't refuse to see her. He was too decent for that.

Twirling around, she headed for the door. It opened before she got there.

Jason was here! Her beloved had come for her. Her heart felt as though a shroud had been lifted from it and her feet were suddenly light.

Only it was Michaels in the doorway. "Ahem," he said, his face blank, "the Conte di Ponti."

Genna's face fell, and her limbs became heavy with disappointment. The hope that had flared sputtered out.

Ricci. Very likely he intended to berate her for leaving last night's masquerade early. Well, he was in for a rude awakening. She had no time for his childish antics today or any day for the rest of her life.

But what if Jason were to arrive now? It

wouldn't do for the two men to meet. They were like oil and water and, her fingers clenched in the folds of her purple muslin dress, Ricci would know that Jason wasn't who he claimed to be. She had to get rid of Ricci.

Her voice as cold as the wind-driven rain outside, she said, "What do you want, Ricci?"

"What I want . . ." he paused until the door was closed, "is an explanation." His countenance underwent a transformation. His eyes took on a feral gleam, and his lips pulled back in a snarl. "I have had all I intend to take from you, Genna. Where did you disappear to last night? I told you to become friends with the Creoles, and I meant it. You cannot do so if you are not there."

Immediately, she sensed that he was dangerous. All thoughts of brushing him off so that she could go to Jason flew from her mind. As volatile as she knew Ricci to be, she'd never seen him change this abruptly. Genna took a step backwards.

Even when he'd attacked her in Brussels, there had been some warning. Now she began to wonder if there was something more sinister in his insistence to be accepted into Creole society. Was it more than the mere needs of a rank conscious youth to have the entree into the dominant group of people? But what exactly did Ricci hope to achieve? And what did he expect from her participation?

"I asked you a question, Genna. Where were you?"

He spoke with a soft sibilance that sent shivers of apprehension racing up her spine. She stepped back again to counter his forward motion toward her.

This intensity was very peculiar, even for Ricci. And she definitely had no intention of answering his question. She dared not tell him about Jason.

Moving so that a chair was between them, she asked carefully, feigning lightness, "Why is it so important to you that I mingle with the Creoles and become accepted?"

He stopped his advance and his eyes narrowed. Before Genna's critical gaze, he became once more a languid dandy, his full lips parting in a smile, his hair shining in impeccable waves, and his attire perfectly tailored. Only a sharp light in his dark eyes belied the facade. Genna blinked, wondering if she were losing her mind.

Ricci struck a casual pose, one leg flexed and one hand on his hip. But he spoke quietly and distinctly. "You are reading too much into my words, *cara mia*. I only insist that you mingle because I worry about your happiness, and you cannot make friends if you leave every party before the fun has begun." His gaze pierced her. "You have not been yourself since Brussels."

Genna's shoulders tensed. She would swear there was more to Ricci's solicitude than met the eye. He was as selfish and self-centered as a snake, so she knew his answer was a diversion to avoid answering her real question. Just as she'd avoided answering his. But she also knew he wouldn't tell her the reason behind his persistence. They were stalemated.

Before she could think of a way to make Ricci

leave, since they both knew neither was going to gratify the other's curiosity, there was a knock on the door.

"Yes," she said.

Michaels opened the door. "Mr. Gaston Everly, madam."

Michaels had not completed the introduction before Jason was through the door.

Ricci pivoted gracefully on his heel. "You!" The accusation leapt from his mouth.

"In the flesh," Jason said sardonically, making an elaborate bow. When he rose, his lips were a thin line and his brown brows were a harsh bar. "I thought I told you to stay away from the contessa."

Ricci sneered, one hand going to the hilt of his *colchemarde*. "I do as I please, and it pleases me to spend time with my betrothed."

Jason's attention sped to Genna.

Desperately, she shook her head in denial, but she knew better than to say anything right now. Ricci's temper had already been exacerbated by her questions; it only needed a little more and he would become openly vicious.

Jason didn't know whether he believed Genna's silent denial or not, but it didn't keep him from seeing shades of red. Even though he'd been willing to release Genna so that she could find a man with no deformities, he wasn't willing to give her to this bastard.

One corner of Jason's mouth curled in derision as his gaze rested pointedly on Ricci's hand holding the sword hilt. "You fondle that weapon as though you know how to use it. Are you considering honoring the challenge you made at the Duchess of Richmond's ball?"

A cruel gleam entered Ricci's eyes. "I do not duel with cripples."

Jason flushed an angry crimson. "Coward."

Ricci took offense. His shoulders hunched and his hand on the hilt of his sword turned white. "Take it back."

Jason laughed out loud, a sound so insulting that Ricci would have had to be a consummate coward to have kept from renewing his challenge. But Jason goaded him further. "You're afraid."

Genna listened in horror. Why was Jason baiting Ricci? Surely, he realized that even someone with Ricci's cravenness would not continue to take such abuse without recourse. She took a step forward, half between the two furious men. "Please—"

"Well, di Ponti? Is there a yellow streak where your back is?" Jason demanded, cutting Genna off before she could say more.

Genna gasped, but before she could interject, Ricci fairly shouted, "Enough. I will kill you at any time and with any weapon you choose, cur."

"Swords. Tomorrow at dawn." Jason replied readily. "My second will call on yours."

"Done." Ricci clicked his heels together and cast a venomous glance at Genna. "I shall return to continue our discussion." Then he stalked past Jason, slowing down to say with insinuating emphasis, "As for you, I will silence you once and for all."

Genna's fears were true. Ricci was going to meet

Jason in a duel, and she knew that Ricci would do anything to win . . . even cheat.

Dread made her stomach churn, and the bile rose in her throat. She'd thought Jason was lost to her once before; she couldn't live through another ordeal like that. She glanced at him, expecting to see chagrin reflected on his face, but instead saw satisfaction.

She rushed to him. "How can you be so cavalier about this? Ricci will kill you."

Jason scowled. She might love him as she professed, but she didn't think him capable of meeting a worm like di Ponti. Her doubt leached away his earlier gratification. "You don't have much faith in my abilities."

Grabbing the lapels of his coat, she said, "'Tis not you. No matter how well you fight, Ricci will do something to undermine it. He's like that. You can't trust him."

He looked down into her brown eyes, at the anguish she made no effort to hide. It took one more block out of the emotional wall he'd built between them. She might very well love him enough to renounce her promise to Luigi once and for all.

Gently, he loosened her crushing grip on his coat. "Genna, the only way di Ponti can hurt me is if he arranges for someone else to attack me while we're fighting or immediately after. If he does that, he sacrifices his reputation. I'll be safe."

"Oh, Jason, you're so honest you don't understand that to Ricci ambushing you would be nothing. He has no integrity."

He held her hands in his, close to his heart. She was truly frightened for him and while he didn't want to cause her pain, the knowledge that it mattered to her reached his soul. "For your sake, Genna, I wish I could take back the words that impelled him to reissue his challenge, but I can't. Neither will I renege. I couldn't do so and live with myself."

She stared up at him, noting the determined line of his brows and the hardening of his jaw. There would be no changing his mind. She pulled her hands from the warmth of his, and a mirthless laugh escaped her trembling lips.

"You're as determined to meet your fate with Ricci as I was. And who's to say which of us is the bigger fool for putting honor above all else?"

The truth of her words struck Jason like a bolt of lightning. Until this instant, he'd never understood why she had been so determined to marry di Ponti. Now, as she so succinctly pointed out the similarity in their decisions, he was forced to reevaluate his stand when he'd told her that her vow to Luigi should be broken.

In honesty, he'd assumed that as a woman she would put love before keeping her word. And right now, she was asking him to put his personal safety and her love before his reputation which would be ruined if he didn't meet di Ponti. If he took it a step further, he had to admit to himself that she was asking nothing more of him than he'd asked of her.

"Who's to say," he echoed her softly. "All I can ask is that you accept my need to keep my promise better than I accepted yours." He reached out and caressed her cheek lightly. "If I thought there was any way di Ponti really could hurt me, I wouldn't meet him. But I believe I'm better than he with swords for all he brandishes his as boldly as the Creoles do." A deprecating smile curved his lips and lit his eye. "Call me overconfident if you wish. I don't think I am."

Genna turned her head just enough to press a kiss into the palm of his hand that still lingered on her face. She knew she would have to be satisfied with the answer he'd given her. Just as he'd had to settle for the one she'd given him before Waterloo.

"Never forget, Jason, that I love you."

Genna's avowal of love ran through Jason's thoughts as he took a sip of the brandy his host had given him. Jason was almost inclined not to meet di Ponti at dawn. It wasn't as though what he did here in New Orleans would have any impact on his real identity. And not to fight the bastard would be a gift he could give Genna.

"Gaston," Nicholas Girod said, interrupting Jason's train of reasoning, "do you not think it an excellent location?"

Jason jerked himself up mentally. This was no time to be thinking about Genna and the duel. He focused his attention on the man who'd spoken. Nicholas Girod was a wealthy and philanthropic Creole who had been mayor of New Orleans several years ago. Now, he was the financier and primary power behind a small group of Creoles bent upon freeing Napoleon from St. Helena. They'd been discussing where Girod planned to locate Bonaparte.

"Pardon, Nicholas. I didn't catch the last part. I was savoring the rich smoothness of your excellent brandy."

Girod sat up straighter in his large leather chair and laughed. "'Tis, of course, French brandy."

Appreciative of the wit, Jason murmured, "What else?"

Both men chuckled. Jason stretched his legs toward the fire situated in front of his chair.

"As I was saying," Girod continued, "I intend to build a house for Napoleon across the street from this one. Number 124 Chartres Street will go down in history as the last residence of the emperor."

"Very fitting." Jason raised his glass for a toast. "To Napoleon and success."

They both drank. Jason set his glass casually on the mahogany round table between them. He was on the brink of learning when and how Girod would free Napoleon from St. Helena, and he had to be careful not to seem too anxious.

"I suppose you have sufficient time to build the house."

Satisfaction curved Girod's lips. "Yes, Captain Dominique You, whom even Andrew Jackson admires for his fighting, will select a small group of men and they will break the emperor free. By the time they return here, the house will be finished." He shrugged. "Or the emperor can stay with me until it is done. I would be honored to have him under my roof."

At last, the final piece of information he needed. Exultation sped through Jason like the heat from a good liquor, but he had to continue playing his part. "Nicholas, you're a genius."

"I am a rich man who believes in what Napoleon stood for. And we are in even greater luck, my friend."

Jason raised an eyebrow, doubting that there was much more needed to complete his mission. Still, one never knew when another piece of information would be valuable. "More?"

"The Conte di Ponti is due here soon. I want you to meet him. He is a trusted agent of Napoleon's and will be invaluable in our effort. At first, we doubted him for he is recently arrived and with his fiancée. But he has explained that she is along to provide him with an excuse to be here. Although her reluctance to participate socially does not lend credence to his words. That is the reason it has taken us so long to accept him. However," he shrugged and took another drink of his liquor, "he is one of us now."

Shock turned Jason's blood to ice. Di Ponti? Napoleon's agent? It was almost impossible to believe, but the pieces began to fall together: the look of recognition in Brussels; di Ponti being here. However, it was also something he couldn't linger here to ponder. At worst, di Ponti would know he wasn't a French agent. At best the count would doubt Jason's credentials, something he didn't want to put to the test.

He'd best be gone before di Ponti arrived, but first. . . .

This was the part that Jason was loath to do, bringing Genna into this sordid mess. However, he wouldn't speak her name, and he needed to cover his trail. A duel over a woman would be the perfect thing. It would cast doubt on di Ponti when he came forward and told what he knew about Jason's past. For Jason had no illusions that the count wouldn't do so, and that information would be damning. Di Ponti very likely knew who he was from the Duchess of Richmond's ball.

And it was crucial that the Creole faction planning to free Napoleon not begin to doubt his validity. They must not become aware that their plot was known by the British Home Office. Otherwise, they would alter it and his mission would be for naught. He had to prevent that at any cost.

Assuming a regretful expression, Jason said, "I wish I could stay, Nicholas. It would be an honor to meet one of Napoleon's handpicked people, but I've a previous engagement. When I made it, I assumed our meeting would only take a short time."

Girod nodded. "Another time?"

Now was the time. "I hope so. I'm to fight a duel at first light, and hope I don't have to flee New Orleans."

"Eh?" Girod sat up straighter and his direct gaze held Jason. "How is this? I thought you did not like fights."

"I don't. But I like a man slurring the name of the woman I love even less."

"Ahhh . . . perfectly reasonable."

Jason took a sip of his brandy and smiled grimly. "I thought so."

"You will need a second, or do you already have one?"

That was the problem, Jason didn't particularly want a second, but he knew that the code of duello required both him and di Ponti to have one. "I don't have one."

Girod reached across the small mahogany table separating them and struck Jason a companionable blow on the shoulder. "I will second you. After all, we want you alive to help us."

"And I intend to live long enough to do so." But he didn't want Girod to know who his duel was with right now. Di Ponti was due here any minute, and he couldn't take the chance that once he was gone, as he must be when the count arrived, Girod would discuss the fight with di Ponti. "As for being my second, I thank you and accept. Tomorrow, when I've not had so much of your fine brandy, I'll return and discuss the details with you."

Jason knew his excuse was weak, but he'd carried off weaker ones. To emphasize his lack of time, Jason pulled out his gold pocket watch and checked the time. "I must go, or I will be late." He smiled knowingly, inviting Girod to share in what he was about to say. "And we all know how a woman will carry on."

"Ahh, yes." Girod nodded in understanding. "They are delightful creatures, but frequently demanding."

Relief flooded Jason at Girod's ready acceptance

of his excuse. He wasted no time making his farewells.

Striding down Chartres Street toward Levee Street, Jason whistled off-key. With luck, everything should work out perfectly. Even having Girod for a second could work to his advantage. The Creole would see for himself the animosity that neither he nor di Ponti could hide.

While Jason was meeting with Nicholas Girod, Genna was telling Alphonse exactly why he had to reveal where Jason and Ricci's duel would be fought.

"Alphonse," Genna said in her most authoritative voice, "I don't care what you think. You're my servant. As such, you will do what I say, and I say that you will tell me where the Creoles fight their duels."

Stubborn as only Alphonse could be, he reiterated, "Milady, I cannot tell you that. I know you too well. You will go to the place." He shook his head for the fourth time and pressed his lips firmly together.

Genna would have been amused if Jason's life weren't at stake. What she was about to say would hurt her greatly, but the man she loved beyond all else was in danger.

Slowly and distinctly, she said, "You will tell me, Alphonse, or I will have to release you from your position."

"My lady!" Disbelief warred with anguish on the lackey's face.

It was Genna's undoing. She took an impulsive step forward and laid her hand beseechingly on Alphonse's sleeve. "Forgive me, please. But I know Ricci will do something to endanger Jason. I must be there."

The misery in Genna's eyes was Alphonse's downfall. He bowed his grizzled head. "St. Anthony's Square, just behind the cathedral."

Genna breathed a sigh of relief. "Thank you."

Then before Alphonse could protest, she left the room. Hurriedly, she changed into a dark brown dress and picked up a black cloak. While she intended to be present during the duel, she didn't want to draw attention to herself.

Not more than fifteen minutes had passed when she left her room and went down the stairs, drawing her hood up around her head to hide her hair. She was just taking the last step down when Alphonse materialized in front of her.

"Oh!" she gasped, not expecting anyone to be around. Hands on hips, she said, "What do you think you're doing?"

Looking grim, he replied, "I am going with you, milady. 'Tis not a good time of night for a lady to be about on her own."

She frowned at him, but knew he was right. The small hours of the morning weren't safe for a single man, let alone a woman by herself. "All right." Then relaxing a little, she added, "I'll be glad of your support."

"Yes, milady," was all he said, but Genna knew he was satisfied.

They decided not to take the coach. And dared

not ride horses either. If they were discovered, the duel would be canceled until another night. They might not be so lucky in finding out where the next challenge would take place.

The sun was just a pale glow on the Eastern horizon when they reached St. Anthony's Square. A quick search around showed them a spot behind a group of shrubs that would be safe from detection.

They were just settled in, when two men on horses cantered up to the area.

Chapter Eighteen

Jason shivered in the cold, damp predawn air as he dismounted. Underfoot, the grass was dewed and slippery to walk on. It wasn't a good omen.

Neither was the absence of his opponent. While he knew di Ponti to be a coward, he'd still expected the man to show up for a duel of his own makings.

"My friend," Nicholas Girod said, looping the reins of both horses around a convenient tree limb, "this match between you and di Ponti is not good. Napoleon needs both of you to work together, not to fight one another."

Jason assumed a look of rueful agreement, even though the present circumstances suited his needs perfectly. This way, when di Ponti made accusations about Jason possibly being a British agent, there would be in Girod's mind a thorn of misgiving about di Ponti's veracity. Two men who fought a duel over a woman could be expected to further expunge one another's name in any manner available.

Jason shrugged to further emphasize his regret over the inevitability of the conflict. "I agree with you, Nicholas. But what was I to do? Di Ponti challenged me, and he insulted the lady who holds my heart."

Girod nodded in resigned agreement. "Nothing, my friend. You did as you had to."

Jason felt a relief his features didn't reflect. Things were going as he'd planned. In point, things were going more perfectly than he had a right to expect. It took an effort of will for him not to look over his shoulder for an unforeseen adversary who would turn the tide of his luck.

However, when Girod handed him the *colchemarde* that he would be using, Jason took it with a nonchalance that belied the foreboding hanging over him. With a determination born of discipline, he began to limber up his muscles by running through several feints and parries until a light film of sweat coated his skin under the fine lawn of his shirt. Pausing to catch his breath, he looked around just in time to see di Ponti and his second arriving.

While Girod met with his opponent's second, Jason studied di Ponti. The count wore black pantaloons and a dark shirt under his coat, ensuring that no part of his body was an obvious target for Jason's sword. Jason had to give di Ponti marks for his knowledge and caution.

When the seconds parted, Jason moved forward to meet his opponent. Having learned to fence from the French school, Jason took the "on guard" position with his torso half-turned to his adversary. He found that this gave him the advantage of more comfort and less fatigue. Also better vision. He noted that di Ponti fought as the Italians dictated, his feet closer together and his stomach and shoulders rotated so that he presented almost no target.

Jason realized that di Ponti might very well be a formidable adversary with his dark clothing and style of fencing. All the better. It would be more convincing for Girod.

At a signal from di Ponti's second, the count lunged toward Jason. Jason went on the defensive, deciding that he had the endurance to play a waiting game since it appeared that di Ponti intended to be the aggressor.

For long minutes, Jason parried each attack, his eye narrowed in concentration on his opponent. Di Ponti was becoming winded, and Jason knew that if the count continued as he'd begun it would soon be over.

Di Ponti must have realized it, too, for he lunged forward, his sword whirling in the air. Jason caught the other weapon on the blade of his, and the two men met chest-to-chest, their hilts locked.

"Cry craven, cripple," Ricci said, his mouth thinned into a sneer; sweat highlighting his upper lip. "And I will spare your life."

Jason stared into the dark eyes challenging him and laughed. The bastard was trying to intimidate him, but it wouldn't work. Jason had accepted his loss of one eye long ago, except where it concerned Genna.

"You'll have to do better than that di Ponti if

you hope to walk away."

Their sword hilts still engaged, Ricci pushed with his arm, making Jason back up. Under his breath, Ricci hissed, "You will be the one who does not leave this field, Viscount Everly."

Di Ponti's knowledge of his true identity didn't surprise Jason. Jason had made no attempt to hide his true persona at the Duchess of Richmond's ball, thinking his incognito days were over. But Jason was interested in the fact that di Ponti took this opportunity to let him know. He let the man disengage his sword.

Before Jason could consider for long, di Ponti was on the attack again. Their blades met and flashed in the pale light from the rising sun.

An instant before it happened, Jason realized that di Ponti was stooping down to grab a handful of dirt, not to position for a new lunge. Jason danced away, barely avoiding a blinding incident.

From a distance, Jason heard Girod call foul, but there was nothing to do for it. Di Ponti continued to advance.

The count moved in closer, his face a mask of hatred. "I should have made sure in Paris that you were dead."

Jason's eye widened, but he managed to maintain his concentration. It explained many things. "You?"

Gloating, Ricci said, "I knifed you and left you for dead. It was a mistake I will not repeat. Today I will finish what I started."

Jason grinned. "Then I owe you a debt of gratitude I can never repay." He began to take the initiative, forcing di Ponti back. "Without you, I would have never met Genna."

Ricci's countenance turned ugly and his step faltered. "You will never have her. I will kill you first."

Jason saw di Ponti gasping for air. Very likely the count was revealing this information in an attempt to throw Jason off his guard.

In a tone that would have been conversational if Jason hadn't felt like he'd been running for an hour, he asked, "Were you the man who followed me to Brussels?"

A lock of black hair falling over his forehead, Ricci countered Jason's thrust. "Of course. When Genna failed to accompany her servants to the rendezvous, I didn't show myself." He took in great gulps of air and dodged the blow Jason aimed at his head. "I laid low and sent one of my men into the house with orders to kill her. Instead, I found him tied up and her gone."

Jason scowled at the bastard's cold statement, but he held himself back from attacking as his fury urged him to do. "Why kill her?"

Taking in great gulps of air, Ricci sneered. "Something was going on, and I could not take the chance that whatever it was would keep her from marrying me. With her dead, the money would be mine anyway."

Wrath twisted Jason's lips until they were drawn tightly up to his teeth. The bastard would pay. Through slitted eye, he studied his opponent. Di Ponti was winded and talking to buy himself some reprieve from attack. But Jason was through playing with the man. With an *appel* that had his lead foot touching ground twice, he engaged di Ponti's sword, sending it flashing into the air.

Ricci's mouth fell open and he cried, "Cur!"

Jason stepped back and made an elaborate bow. "I would run you through for what you planned to do to Genna, but I don't fight unarmed men. I will wait while you fetch your sword."

Genna, crouching behind the shrubbery that flanked Ricci's right side, watched in horror as Jason let Ricci retrieve his sword. Why didn't Jason claim victory?

Next to her, Alphonse grumbled. She cast one warning glance at him and he stopped. They dared not reveal their presence.

She looked back to the field. Before her horrified eyes, the two men squared off again. This time she noticed that Jason's sword arm was lower than it had been initially and that the lines around his mouth were deeper. He was tiring.

Her attention shifted to Ricci, and she realized that he was in worse shape. His shoulders were hunched forward, and his lips were pulled back against his teeth in a rictus as he labored for breath.

Exultation swelled her chest. Jason would win.

She felt Alphonse stir, and her gaze shifted back to him, preparatory to quelling him with another glare. But he wasn't looking at the duelists. He was watching Ricci's second.

Genna immediately focused on the other man. He was taking a pistol out from the concealing folds of his cape.

Instantly, she understood. Ricci's second would shoot Jason. It was dishonorable, but once done. . . .

She had to stop the man. He couldn't kill Jason. She wouldn't let him.

Leaping up from her concealment, her heart beating like a drum, she dodged around Alphonse's outstretched arm, screaming, "Scoundrel!"

Jason's head jerked around toward the shout. Genna! She was racing this way. Before he realized what she was doing, she was grappling with di Ponti's second.

Genna needed him. His guts knotted with dread that she'd be harmed, Jason twisted away from di Ponti's lunge. He lowered his sword to keep from engaging his opponent's, thinking that as soon as the count realized what was happening he would stop.

But a weight pulled Jason's weapon down and he turned to see what it was. "Oh, my God," he murmured.

Di Ponti had run himself through on Jason's lowered sword. Quickly, Jason pulled his weapon back, but it was too late. His adversary had impaled himself through the heart. Even as Jason withdrew the blade, di Ponti sank to the ground.

All Jason could spare di Ponti was a glance as he sped past the fallen man toward Genna and di Ponti's second as they struggled over possession of a pistol.

From behind Jason, Girod yelled, "Gaston, drop."

Reacting by instinct, Jason dropped to his

hands and knees. Simultaneously, two pistol shots rang through the morning air.

Jason saw the man who'd been fighting Genna fall backwards. Relief brought Jason's breath back. But even as he came to his feet, intent on reaching Genna, she whimpered in pain.

The sound was barely above a whisper, but it pierced Jason's heart like an arrow. Everything began to move slowly for him, like the stately performance of a minuet.

Genna's full, coral lips puckered in surprise. Her hand went to her side and came away red with blood. She turned to look at Jason, who cursed his lack of speed. Her eyes were wide with fright in the early morning glow.

Panting with fear, Jason reached her as she folded up and collapsed onto the dew sparkled grass. He caught her in his arms and cradled her to his chest.

"Bloody hell!" He held her tight, his breath coming in raged gasps. Frantic, he searched her face for signs of life. She was pale as the new moon. "Oh, God," he prayed, "don't let her be dead. Please."

She meant everything to him. She was the air he breathed, the food he ate. She was life to him, and she had been willing to give her life for him.

Her bravery humbled him as nothing else ever had. She had intentionally put herself in the way of a bullet to save him. Her love for him was that strong even after what he'd done to her; letting her think him dead after Waterloo because of his own stupid pride.

His heart ravaged with desolation that he might lose her, Jason bent his head over hers. Gently, he pushed the copper tresses from her forehead, feeling the heat radiating from her.

With fingers that shook, he felt along her side where the flow of blood was already beginning to abate. He didn't think anything vital had been damaged, but he was no doctor and she was so still. Taking off his shirt, he wadded it up and pressed it to her side.

"Dear Lord," he asked, "only let her live and I promise to cherish her for the rest of our lives. Only, please, let her live."

Genna, searing pain running the length of her ribs, heard Jason's pleas as though he were in a tunnel and many feet distant from her. But she heard them.

Her eyes fluttered open, and she looked into the haunted anguish of Jason's one eye. A single tear hung from his lashes, like a jewel in a bed of brown fur. She reached up and with the tip of one finger caught the drop and brought it to her lips.

"I'm here, Jason, and I'll never leave you."

He was awed by the strength of her love. Having experienced for only seconds the devastation of thinking her dead, he began to understand a small amount of the horror and desolation he had put her through after Waterloo. And she loved him through it all.

"God, Genna, I don't deserve your love. Not after what I did to you." He paused to swallow the lump in his throat. "When I thought you might be dying. I . . . Life wasn't worth living any more.

Can you ever forgive me for what I put you through?"

She smiled up at him, her heart overflowing with the love she felt for him. "I love you so much, Jason, that just knowing you're alive is all I need to erase the pain."

With a choked sob, he buried his face in the curve of her neck. "I swear I'll never doubt you again."

Girod chose that moment to kneel beside them. "We must be quick, my friends. I've sent your lackey to fetch a carriage and you two must flee. I killed the second and di Ponti is dead. For your own safety, you must leave New Orleans immediately."

Genna struggled to sit up and Jason promptly helped her rise enough to lean back against his chest. Her side hurt, but she knew there was more blood than any true danger.

"What do you mean?" she asked.

Girod sighed in exasperation, but spoke precisely. "When you screamed, ma'am, Gaston's attention was diverted and di Ponti picked that instant to try and run Gaston through. Unfortunately, for di Ponti, Gaston also chose that moment to turn to you and thus lower his sword arm. The count ran himself through on Gaston's weapon." He looked directly into Jason's eyes. "There are many people in New Orleans who will not thank you for this day's work, my friend."

Jason nodded his understanding. Girod was telling him that every Creole involved in the plot to free Napoleon from St. Helena would be bent on challenging him to a duel until one of them killed him in revenge. It wouldn't matter to them that di Ponti had brought his death upon himself.

"You're right," he said to Girod. "As soon as Alphonse returns with the carriage we'll be on our way. I trust that you'll be remiss in reporting this incident."

Girod smiled as he stood. "I must send for a surgeon first. And," he rose and moved to where the horses still stood, "it appears that I must walk to fetch him." He gave the animals a swat on the rump that sent them trotting down the street. With those words, the Creole turned and started on his way.

Jason, confident that there would be time to get Genna bandaged and her household ready to flee for a second time, turned his attention back to his beloved. Scooping her up into his arms, he rose and began walking toward Levee Street.

"Jason, you can't carry me."

He gazed down at her, seeing the pinched look around her eyes. "I can and I will."

They'd barely gone a block when Alphonse rounded the corner at a dangerous clip. Coming to an abrupt halt, the lackey leapt down from the closed carriage and helped Jason settle Genna in as comfortably as possible.

Within minutes they were at the house and Jason was carrying Genna through the door Michaels held open. Mrs. Michaels hovered in the background.

Mounting the stairs two at a time, Jason ordered, "Get some bandages. The contessa is wounded. Then start packing your bags. Take only essentials

We must be gone in half an hour."

Jason reached Genna's room and laid her tenderly on the bed. He was down to her corset and chemise when Mrs. Michaels arrived with bandages and a basin of water.

"Milord," she said, her voice and bearing screaming her opinion on the impropriety of a gentleman undressing a woman who wasn't his wife, "I'll finish taking care of Contessa di Ponti."

Jason winked at Genna, before turning to Mrs. Michaels. His grin was as wide as his face. "Thank you, Mrs. Michaels, but I believe I owe the contessa the value of my expertise in doctoring."

Mrs. Michaels sputtered and her round face turned the color of a cherry, but she handed him the materials and withdrew to the doorway. Jason tried hard not to laugh, knowing it would be unkind to treat the woman thusly, but it was nigh impossible when he could feel Genna shaking with her own amusement.

Genna gasped softly as her laughter caused her side to burn, but she managed to say, "Thank you Mrs. Michaels for your concern, but you'd best be about your packing. The viscount says we must leave immediately. And please notify my aunt."

Knowing a dismissal when she heard it, the housekeeper cast the pair one last disapproving glance and left.

Jason bent to kiss Genna lightly on the lips. "You're incorrigible, my love."

She stroked her hand down his cheek, delighting in the feel of the short hairs that were beginning to roughen his face. "And you need to shave, unless you intend to spirit us away like the brigand I'm beginning to believe you are."

He caught her hand and kissed her palm. "And you need to lie still and let me tend to you. As much as I would like to prolong this, you spoke the truth. We must be gone. There's a ship in the harbor waiting for my word to sail."

"Then you'd best make haste, my love."

A frown pulled Jason's brows into a straight bar as he undid her corset and began to remove the chemise beneath. "This won't be painless."

Genna bit into her lip, but her eyes held trust for the man who cared enough to hurt with her. "I'm not a child."

Jason started sponging the linen that clung to her wound. Gently, he removed the chemise, flinching with every thread that the blood had glued to her body. When the last piece of cloth was removed, Jason released the breath he'd held.

"I'm sorry, Genna. I'd do anything not to cause you further discomfort."

She smiled up at him, comprehending fully what he was going through. The same emotions had assailed her every time she'd cared for his wound. "You do what you must, but I don't believe there is any real damage."

Wiping the dried blood from her milk-white skin, forcing himself to ignore the ripe fullness of her breasts, Jason agreed with her. "No, love, the only damage you're like to endure would come from me if I don't get you bandaged and dressed again." His lips quirked in a rueful grin. "The sight of you is making it very difficult for me to keep my mind on wounds and fleeing New Orleans."

She chuckled, wincing at the pull on her cut.

He was immediately contrite. "Don't move. 'Twill only make it hurt."

"True. Instead of discussing this, tell me what happened."

Seeing the humor in her velvety brown eyes, Jason marveled at the strength of this woman. As he dusted the long cut with basilicum powder, the bullet having only grazed her side, he talked.

"It appears that Ricci was a spy for Napoleon." Her sharp intake of breath made him pause, but her nod for him to continue told him that it was surprise over di Ponti that had caused her action, not pain. "Hard to believe, but he was Napoleon's agent as far back as Paris. He even confessed to being the one who knifed me."

"Not Ricci. He was a sniveling coward." It was almost impossible for her to conceive of Ricci in the light Jason was now painting him.

Jason nodded and propped her up on the pillows to begin wrapping the wound. "He was also the one who followed us from Paris to Brussels. Girod, who was my second, told me just yesterday that di Ponti was here as Napoleon's representative."

"But why did he challenge you to a duel? And why did you provoke him to it?"

He looked thoughtful. "I believe di Ponti wanted me out of the way, but I'm not sure why he didn't tell Girod and the others about me. My theory is that he was afraid they might not believe him, or that finding out that there were problems they would change their minds about freeing Napoleon. As for me, it suited my purpose to duel with di Ponti. Should he have decided to expose me later, there would be the shadow of our duel hanging over his head and the possibility that people would believe he was slandering me over jealousy. It would conceal my true identity."

Jason stopped speaking and took a deep breath, his gaze riveted to Genna's face for her feelings over what he was about to say. "However, I didn't intend to kill him. But I can't deny that it makes things easier and has worked to my good. Girod will never realize that I was a British agent, and my leaving New Orleans is explained as having to leave or face retribution. For me and my mission, this couldn't have worked better."

Genna realized that Jason was worried about her reaction to Ricci's death and she strove to reassure him. She reached up and caressed his cheek, ignoring the twinge of pain in her side.

"I never thought you intended to kill him. And while I'm sorry that he had to end that way, I can see that 'tis best for you. For us."

The words were barely out of her mouth, when the door slammed open. Aunt Hester stood dramatically posed, one hand at her throat. "Genna, I cannot believe what Mrs. Michaels is saying. Surely, we are not to flee New Orleans as we did Paris. There is no threat here."

Genna exchanged a glance with Jason. "Yes, dear, I'm sorry to have to do this to you again, but we must leave here as soon as I'm bandaged."

As though aware for the first time of her niece's compromising position, Hester's face took on a scandalized look. "Really, Genna, must I always find you in this scoundrel's arms? And you not even married to the man!" Then her eyes softened and her lips smiled. "But I assume that will change shortly."

Jason finished tying off the bandage just as Hester finished. He turned and went to her. Taking the older woman's plump hand in his, he raised it to his lips. "Aunt Hester, if I may so presume, we will most assuredly remedy our matrimonial state. However, it can't be done here. I'm afraid that I've gotten in some trouble and must leave without further ado."

Impressed by his gallantry and finally reconciled to accepting this man for Genna's sake, Hester nodded. "I suppose I must pack. 'Tis not as though I have not been wanting to leave this past fortnight and more."

Jason closed the door behind his aunt-to-be and returned to Genna. "Now, my love, we must get you ready."

Several minutes later, Genna's portmanteau in one hand and his arm around her for support, the two descended the stairs. At the foot stood Hester, Mr. and Mrs. Michaels, and Alphonse. They were the only ones who'd come with Genna from Brussels.

"Quickly," Jason ordered, "get the closed carriage. We must go to the docks."

Alphonse, normally suspicious, didn't hesitate. Within minutes, the small party was on its way.

When Jason went to sit up front with Alphonse, Genna clung to him.

He kissed her lightly on the lips, a gesture of reassurance. "Genna, I must show Alphonse where to go."

"I don't want anything to happen to you." The knowledge that things were going too smoothly made her nerves dance with apprehension. They were so close to being united forever, she was afraid that something would keep them from their goal.

Jason understood her anxiety without having to be told. He, too, was leery of the simplicity with which they were escaping. Happiness, so long a tardy friend, was within his grasp and he feared it would elude him once more.

"Trust me, my love," was all he could say to her.

Chapter Nineteen

"Oh dear. Oh dear," Aunt Hester continued to bemoan in a soft tone barely audible above the slapping of water against the pier. Wringing her gloved hands, she complained, "What is keeping the man?"

Genna exchanged a commiserating glance with Mrs. Michaels who sat across from them in the carriage. Everyone was anxious and they were all scared, but only Hester allowed herself to run on.

"Alphonse, Michaels," Genna whispered through the hole in the vehicle designed to communicate with the driver, "do you see anything?" Jason had been gone for what seemed like hours, and the docks of any city were dangerous. Or perhaps the ship had already sailed.

Alphonse answered for both men. "No, milady. But he has not been gone long."

She knew he meant to reassure her, and she allowed him to do so. If only Jason would come back. Her heart's desire was so close, that she couldn't rid herself of the dread that something would happen to keep her and Jason apart.

To pass the time, Genna told the two women the story of this night's adventure. She left out only the part about Jason being a spy for England. It no longer mattered if they knew about Ricci.

The story finished and the questions answered, Genna looked anxiously out the coach window in time to see a shadow detach itself from the side of one of the warehouses. Her breath caught and her palms turned to ice. Then she recognized the set of Jason's shoulders and the proud way he held his head. A sigh of relief escaped her as she jumped from the carriage and ran to him.

He caught her in his arms and gave her a swift kiss. "We must hurry. The captain is waiting to help us aboard and then as soon as the tide allows he will set for the open sea."

She nodded, ignoring the twinge from her side, and left the warmth and security of his embrace to fetch Hester. Genna picked up Hester's portmanteau which Jason promptly took from her. Quickly, making as little noise as possible, the small band made it to the ship.

They were met as they boarded by the captain and several of his crew. Captain Eber was a stout man with gray whiskers and a balding head, but he smiled at them and made them welcome. Alphonse and Mr. and Mrs. Michaels were taken to the quarters they'd occupy.

Captain Eber led Genna, Jason, and Aunt Hester to his quarters.

Entering the small room, Genna was pleasantly

surprised by the amenities. There was a built-in bed, a desk and chair, and plenty of light from several lanterns hanging from the walls.

"Captain Eber," Jason said, taking Genna's hand and pulling her forward, "I would like to introduce you to the Contessa di Ponti and her aunt."

"My pleasure, ladies," the captain said, bowing. "I hope you will find my quarters comfortable during our trip."

Before Genna could reply, Jason said, "The contessa won't be able to share with her aunt, I'm afraid."

Genna's gaze flew to Jason's face where she saw more love and mischief shining from his eyes than she'd ever seen before.

Jason grinned at everyone. Then he immediately sobered and looked at Genna. "I'd like you to marry the contessa and myself before you do anything else. If she'll have me."

With a small cry of happiness, Genna flung herself into her love's arms. Everything would be all right.

And Jason caught her willingly, knowing that only with her would he ever find the kind of joy that made life worth living.

Author's Note

Endless Surrender is first and foremost a romance, but since it is set in the past I've followed historical fact when available and extrapolated from it when necessary to facilitate my plot.

The first case of this occurs in Paris when Jason is trying to find out information about Napoleon. To the best of my knowledge, the British had no reason to think Napoleon would escape Elba. But neither had Napoleon made a secret of the fact that he didn't like the island. Therefore, I took that fact and used it. Thus, Jason is looking for any information to indicate that Napoleon might actually be planning an escape.

The second case of embroidering on historical data occurs in New Orleans. According to Henry C. Castellanos in his book, *New Orleans As It Was*, originally published in 1895, Nicholas Girod actually did build a house for Napoleon at No. 124 Chartres Street, on the same side of Chartres as Mr. Girod's own residence was located. Unfortunately,

Mr. Castellanos doesn't say when the house for Napoleon was started or finished, so I've taken artistic license and have begun the construction in 1816, the year of my story. For any readers who know the exact dates, if they don't match up with my fabrication, please forgive me.

And, yes, there really was a plan by the Creoles to free Napoleon. However, the emperor died before it could be carried out.

If anyone has any details on these incidents, I'd be very interested in hearing from you. Please write to me at:

>Amber Kaye
>c/o Zebra Books
>475 Park Ave. So.
>New York, NY 10016